THE STARS UNBOUND

THE GIFT OF THE STARS BOOK 2

LENA ALISON KNIGHT

ONE

PALHEE, Kerelle mused as she munched her snack, was easily the second-seediest place she had ever been - and if they'd made it here without the detour to Kalnis, it would assuredly top the list.

The streets were narrow and winding, snaking haphazardly between shabby shops and crowded apartments, and seemed perpetually dim. Those same narrow streets were lined by vendors hawking all manner of wares, ranging from probably-not to quite-obviously stolen. Of those people packing said streets, many had the air of those who tried to avoid attention.

But at the same time, Palhee was nothing like Kalnis. The site of their ill-fated repair stop had been a psychic mire of misery and despair. There was misery and despair here as well, of course, but there was also hope and excitement and opportunity. Adventures were planned over spiced coffee, in shops tucked away between larger businesses. Children played in the packed blocks' nooks and crannies. Interspersed within the merchant stalls were food vendors, and a faint, delicious aroma wafted above the open-air market.

It was fascinating.

Sandrel had planted her at the edge of the market, procured her something to eat and instructed her to wait for his return. While she felt a bit like a child being kept out of trouble while her parents were busy, Kerelle really didn't mind much. It gave her an excellent opportunity to simply sit back and observe the world around her - a world that, for the first time in her life, was not reacting to her as a PsiCorp agent. Simply being ignored as part of the throng was a new experience in itself.

Whatever it was she was eating was rather excellent as well. It was some sort of fruit pastry, fried, rolled in sugar, and served on a stick. Nalea had earlier declined to leave the sanctuary of the ship, but Kerelle thought these pastries might be able to lure her out. The only reason Kerelle herself wasn't eating a second one was because she lacked the hard currency to buy it.

She was idly contemplating how many pastries one of her earrings might be worth when Sandrel rematerialized out of the crowd.

"You're still here," he observed with note of teasing. "I think that means this is the longest we've gone without a disaster since I met you."

She raised her now-sadly-empty pastry stick in a salute. "Glad you noticed. I've been trying to improve." She cocked an eyebrow. "I take it your business was successful?"

"That it was. Got us a price I can live with, we bring the ship in tomorrow. Should take about a week to get everything back up to top shape."

"Was there doubt about the price? I thought you and the owner were friends?"

"We are. That's why he's only charging me an arm and a leg instead of two, especially for one week turnaround on that kind of damage." Sandrel shrugged, a half smile on his lips "Really, he's just being generous. Gerunel runs the best repair yard on Palhee. I can pretend to haggle, but we both know I wouldn't trust my baby with anyone else here."

Kerelle couldn't resist. "Particularly since your baby has some non-standard modifications?"

Sandrel threw back his head and laughed. "This is *Palhee*, Fury. If I didn't have some kind of *non-standard modifications* they'd assume I was an undercover marshal."

Kerelle smiled back, a warmth spreading in her chest. Things had been different between her and Sandrel since their talk in the engine room. Their pilot treated her less like a bothersome client and more like, well, an actual friend. He'd even offered to give her a hand going incognito - which was the very reason she was waiting here now.

Sandrel offered her his grip and pulled her up from her seat. "So, you ready to get started?"

She nodded her affirmative and they set out through the throng of people, Kerelle taking care to stick close in the packed, mazelike streets. She could find Sandrel telepathically if she lost him, of course, but she'd prefer not to get lost at all.

"So I'm thinking our first stop is to get you some currency in more usable increments than 'small fortune,'" he murmured in her ear as they passed through the next block. "That jewel collection of yours was a clever idea, but it's not exactly practical now that you've actually made it out."

Kerelle nodded her emphatic agreement. "The only reason I didn't have more of those pastries you bought me is that I didn't think the stall vendor could make change for platinum."

He gave her a surprised grin. "You liked the *ranla*, then?"

"Is that what it's called? It was delicious."

"Glad you think so. They were my favorite thing when we lived on the Station, you don't find a lot of people that make them planetside. Palhee's one of the only places with enough station brats to make a market."

"You're a station kid?" It made sense; many spacer families either lived in their ships or on one of the artificial port stations dotting the galaxy. And many space-born people followed in their parents' footsteps and became spacers themselves.

"Sort of. When we were hauling freight we just lived on the ship, but there were few years we lived part-time on a station in the Olnarr Ring," he answered. "Didn't really appreciate it until I got older. When I was a kid it seemed like planetside always had a better version of everything. Then I started taking my own jobs and actually spending time on solid ground. It's overrated."

She sorted through that. "Was your ship your parents' ship, first?" She'd heard that some ships were passed down through generations of spacer families, a home and a livelihood all in one.

"Nah, I bought her with a lot of hard-earned money. Mom sold theirs after Dad died."

He stopped and waved her towards a nondescript door. "And here we are. Let me do the talking."

Even if they hadn't arrived when they did, Kerelle sensed Sandrel didn't care to say anything else on the subject. She gave a mental shrug and followed him through the door. It was none of her business anyway.

The pawn shop was barely more than a closet; Kerelle could nearly touch both walls of cluttered, overflowing shelves from the center of the room. Kerelle eyed the haphazard stacks of dusty junk with a skepticism she tried to keep off her face. This certainly wasn't anywhere she would have stopped, but she trusted Sandrel to know what he was doing.

The owner looked as ancient and run-down as his goods. He peered over the counter at them with a combination of disdain and suspicion.

Sandrel greeted him loudly in a dialect Kerelle couldn't quite follow. The old man groused back in the same dialect, but his shoulders seemed to relax a bit. After some back and forth Sandrel leaned over to whisper in her ear. "Just the two pendants and the earrings we set aside earlier. We'll unload the rest elsewhere."

Even with just a portion of her collection, Kerelle walked away with an impressive stack of credits. Sandrel thanked the old man enthusiastically in words she couldn't understand, receiving a disinterested grunt in return. He waved and steered her out of the shop.

"So did that go...well?" she asked curiously.

"It went great. Olen was thrilled, he'll be able to sell those at a huge markup. Plus he usually gives you a break in commission if you chat him up in Starna."

Kerelle was learning all kinds of things today. "Starna?"

"It's a dialect from the stations in the Olnarr ring. I picked it up when we lived there." He cocked his head at her. "You didn't go slumming much, did you?"

Kerelle gave him a rueful laugh. "The Olnarr Ring is definitely not a vacation spot that would make it through management approval."

The scene repeated itself throughout the afternoon, as Sandrel led her to a series of out-of-the-way establishments. Most of the proprietors spoke Standard, though a few carried on lively conversation in Starna. By the end, she'd traded away nearly all her jewelry, and in return she'd acquired what even she could recognize was an eyebrow-raising amount of credits. Even after divvying up what she owed Sandrel for the escape from Zharal V - which was an eyebrow-raising amount in itself - she still found herself a wealthy escapee.

Sandrel seemed impressed in spite of himself. "They *did* pay you well, didn't they?"

"They didn't pay me at all," she reminded him. "That's why I stuffed everything of value in my pockets on the way out."

"Well, that will make this next part easier," Sandrel observed cheerfully. "It's time to be someone else."

KERELLE COULDN'T STOP STARING at her hair. It didn't really *look* like "her" hair anymore - that was the point, after all, but she was still fascinated. It was shorter than it had ever been, the longest tips barely brushing her shoulders, with added layers cut shorter still to frame her chin. She was surprised what a difference it made.

Initially she'd thought she should dye it, but Sandrel had said no - her only option was to go lighter, and that would look attention-grabbingly artificial. Instead, he'd half-dragged her into a fashionable salon.

"Don't change your hair, change how you wear it. Agent Evandra is a practical sort who doesn't bother with how she looks," he'd told her bluntly. "Disguise yourself as someone who does."

As counter-intuitive as it had seemed to make herself less noticeable with a trendy haircut, she trusted Sandrel's judgement when it came to lying low. Now that she'd done it, she could see what he meant. The woman staring back at her looked like any number of others she'd passed by on Palhee. She certainly *didn't* look like Senior Agent Kerelle Evandra's file photo.

Besides, the ID in her pocket said Karia Vela Vendrys now. Apparently Karia went to nice salons.

After more staring, and a few experimental shakes of her head to watch the midnight strands move, Kerelle decided she liked the new look. Hopefully Galhen liked it too.

She also hoped he liked the clothes she'd bought him. It was only a few pieces, acquired alongside her own new wardrobe, but it had felt good to pick them out - a statement of intent that she was actually going to rescue him. That his presence would be real, and not just a constant hovering memory.

And for that to happen, she needed to get to work.

THE FIRST STEP to rescuing Galhen was figuring out where he was. The first step to doing *that* was figuring out where the senator was.

A datanet search on Senator Dalanva turned up a surprising amount of information, which could be generally divided into two types: dry parliamentary records, and the society pages. It was the second one that grabbed her attention.

Estia Parie Dalanva was clearly a fixture in Morafer high society. There was a regular cadence of mentions in connection with charity balls, genteel sporting events, and so on, as well as parties hosted in multiple estates on multiple planets. There was also, however, a flurry of coverage of Dalanva's recent acquisition of a Class 3 psionic aide, the first time such a valuable asset had been leased to a private individual. It had, apparently, been something of a social coup.

Some of the society papers were admiring, others professed to be scandalized by what must have been an astronomical expense. None were even slightly interested in how Galhen might be a human being with his own feelings about all this, and referred to him like some sort of prizewinning horse. Kerelle's jaw hurt from clenching by the time she finished the stack.

She also didn't know much more than when she started, except that this Dalanva woman and the whole Morafer system could go straight to the burning void. She supposed if worst came to worst, they could start crashing benefit galas and trust they'd run into her eventually.

With a sigh she turned her attention to the parliamentary records. She wasn't optimistic that Dalanva's voting record on transportation spending was going to be enlightening, but -

Oh stars and blood. She should have come here first.

The news story covered some speech Dalanva had recently

given on the Senate floor, with an embedded clip of video. The senator was an elegant older woman and a charismatic speaker, but Kerelle tuned her out to stare at the entourage standing a few paces behind her. Closest to the Senator's left was Galhen.

Kerelle stopped the video and simply stared, her pulse racing. It was really him.

He'd cut his hair too - it was shorter now and neatly slicked back, not a style she'd seen on him before. It was well matched with the military-inspired uniform he wore, cut to emphasize both his lean build and the collar. Prominent on the jacket was an intricate design Kerelle recognized from the society papers as Dalanva's personal crest.

Overall the effect was impeccable. Standing behind Dalanva, posture perfect and face impassive, he looked like something out of a fashion feature. Cold but beautiful, dangerous but contained.

He did not look at all like the warm and loving partner she'd known half her life.

Dalanva finished her speech and descended the dais to thunderous applause. Smoothly Galhen offered her his arm, and she took it as they headed out of the senate chamber, assistants following in a tight knot. The camera cut closer to Dalanva - close enough she could see Galhen better as well. His face was set in a serene mask, but there was a terrible emptiness in his eyes.

She watched it three more times.

The door of their rented suite opened to admit Sandrel and Nalea, both carrying full armloads of whatever they'd gone to the market for.

"You missed it, Fury," Sandrel called. "There was a line around the block for these dumplings and this guy-" he cut off as he saw her face. "Kerelle, what happened?"

She waved them both over and played the video again. Nalea watched silently, expression inscrutable as she saw her brother for the first time in twenty-five years. Sandrel glanced between the two of them, then back to the video.

"That's your man, isn't it."

Kerelle just nodded. Sandrel was quiet as they watched the rest. When it was over, he looked over at her.

"So I know this is the whole reason we're here," Sandrel said carefully. "But he doesn't seem to be… in distress… exactly. And Dalanva seems to keep her people comfortable. I know you saw those records, but they could have been an error. Are you sure he's going to want to leave to come be an intergalactic fugitive?" His voice was neutral, but the unspoken question was deafening. *Are we staging a kidnapping?*

"I'm sure." She knew she sounded defensive but she couldn't help it. "He looked unhappy. I know him well enough to see it."

She was aware of how weak that argument sounded, even without his response.

"That's what you *want* to see," he told her gently. "But are you sure it's what *he* wants?"

She wanted to snap back that of *course* it was, but Kerelle forced herself to take a deep breath and disengage her storming emotions. She understood his point, even if she didn't like it.

"We know where they are now," she said. "We can head to the area. When we get close enough, I'll be able to contact Galhen with my powers. If he says…" she had to force it out. "If he says he wants to stay, then that will be the end of it."

She stood up then and headed for her temporary room. "It's been a long day. I think I'm going to lie down."

Sandrel watched her go with concern, but he said nothing, and neither did Nalea, who seemed lost in her own thoughts. Kerelle shut the door behind her and slumped down against it, feeling sick at heart.

Galhen would want to leave with her. She knew he would.

What if he didn't?

TWO

KERELLE TOOK her time as she strolled back to the ship, *ranla* in hand, soaking up the experience of Palhee. It was their last morning in port, and she was surprised to realize she would miss it. The chaotic energy of the street markets was exhilarating - or perhaps it was just the novelty of walking those streets as a free woman.

It still hadn't entirely sunk in. In the back of her mind a feeling hovered, an unconscious habitual knowledge that all this was temporary and she was only passing through until her next assignment. Each time realized she felt it, and that it was wrong this time, there would *be* no new assignment, she couldn't help a grin. From now on, she went wherever she damn well pleased.

She still needed to be careful, of course. Palhee was neutral port, beholden to no corporation, but doubtlessly they all had agents there anyway. There were quite possibly SysTech spies in this very same morning crowd. But they had no reason to be looking for Kerelle Evandra, killed in action on Zharal V, and no reason to be interested in Karia Vela Vendrys, freighter crewswoman on Palhee for shore leave. As long as she didn't do anything visibly psionic, the danger of discovery was relatively low.

Her only regret was that Galhen wasn't here beside her to take in the market as well. After they succeeded, she'd ask Sandrel to make a trip back, so she and Galhen could watch the crowds and wander the streets and eat too many *ranla* together.

All the more reason to get underway.

She met Nalea at the dock, her arms stuffed with various small packages and bags. The scientist had initially been reluctant to venture out into Palhee, preferring to stay first with the ship and later in their suite. Nalea claimed it was an aversion to crowds and noise, but all three of them knew she was nervous after the Kalnis pirate incident. Kerelle's idea of luring her out with pastries had proven ineffective, but Sandrel had had a better plan. As it turned out, Palhee had a number of shops that specialized in grey-market lab materials.

Nalea might have been able to resist pastries, but new toys were a whole different matter.

"Good shopping today?" Kerelle asked. She couldn't pronounce most of the things Nalea had been purchasing, but the other woman had certainly seemed excited about it.

"I wanted to stock up on a few things we might need for, um, *next*," Nalea answered deliberately. For rescuing Galhen, then. Kerelle's stomach gave a little leap - this was becoming real for Nalea too. "I also picked up some more equipment you can help me put together later if you're bored."

Kerelle smiled. She was becoming an expert at holding flashlights and screwdrivers. Nalea may not have *entirely* forgiven her for the Kalnis incident, but it was nice to be on mostly good terms again.

Sandrel popped out of the hatch, whistling to himself. Their pilot had been in a good mood since they landed on Palhee, but finishing the ship's repairs had him positively jubilant.

"Good morning ladies! Everything taken care of before we

leave? Pastries eaten? Mysterious chemicals acquired?" At their nods he waved them inside. "Then stow items, strap in, and let's get this little undertaking up in the air."

Kerelle took one last look around at Palhee and started up the ramp. When she returned, she vowed, it would be with Galhen.

MORAFER WAS TOO FAR to reach directly, even through hyperspace. They needed to pass first through one of the jump gates to get to the system itself, then use the hyperdrive to get closer to their destination. Through some sort of technological wizardry Kerelle didn't pretend to understand, the jump gate would let them cut through time and space to Morafer in a matter of minutes, to come out the exit gate on the other side. It wasn't the travel part itself that made her nervous.

Jump gates meant tolls and inspections.

"For the last time, Fury, there is nothing to worry about." Sandrel was the image of relaxation as he watched her pace. "Nobody's got any reason to pay attention to you, and the border guards at the gate won't care anyway. They just want to get their bribe and get us through so they can get on to the next one."

"But what if they *do* recognize me?"

"Kerelle." He put both hands on her shoulders, arresting her movement. "They won't. If anything gets us in trouble, it will be you hopping around like an agitated squirrel, making them wonder what you're so nervous about. Just sit down, look bored, let me handle it."

As it turned out, he was right. She sat quietly and tried to project distraction to the guards, but it wasn't actually necessary. They hardly looked at her as they pocketed Sandrel's money and gave the cargo a once-over so perfunctory it barely qualified as an inspection. In less than fifteen minutes, they were passing through the metal maw of the gate, and then they were in Morafer.

Kerelle stared out the viewport, her heart racing. They were here. Sandrel hit the hyperdrive and realspace melted away from her vision, into the blurred light of hyperspace. She'd gone over the destination and distance with Sandrel before they went through the gate. Assuming Dalanva and her entourage were still at the Morafer Legislature, she would be in dreaming range to communicate with Galhen in a matter of hours.

It was going to be longest few hours of her life.

KERELLE PACED HER TINY CABIN, too keyed up to sleep. This was it, they should be in range, and suddenly anticipation threatened to overwhelm her. She downed a finger of whiskey to try to soothe her nerves, and when that didn't entirely help she forced herself to sit down and go through the focusing meditation exercises drilled in at the academy. She'd never really taken to meditation, but it was helpful now, and at length she managed to slow her breathing and her heart. She reached out, and hoped he would sense her.

She chose the apartment setting again, with its tall windows and bright accents. Here too Kerelle couldn't keep still, bouncing from the couch to the dining table to leaning against the windows, staring at the illusory sea. As time ticked on, a dull ache of disappointment began to form in her chest, accompanied by a growing trickle of anxiety. He hadn't heard her. Or worse, he hadn't answered.

She felt it, suddenly, and gasped. Kerelle whirled around and watched Galhen's form blossom into view in the center of the room.

She'd thought about what she wanted to say, when she

finally had the chance, but the actual sight of him stole all her words. For a moment they both simply stared at each other, her throat too tight to speak. She didn't know who moved first, only that in the next moment they both were in motion, flying toward an embrace that was almost painful in its intensity.

Neither spoke as they held each other tightly, but she felt his love and joy wash over her mind - and beneath it a bitter sorrow that this was only a temporary reprieve from his life sentence. The intensity startled her and she opened her eyes to regard him. The feeling vanished from her senses as he locked it down, leaving only his relief at her presence behind.

Kerelle reached up to brush her fingers against his face.

"Darling I have so much to tell you, I don't even know where to begin."

He kissed her again. "Then start at the beginning. How are you here? Is SysTech expanding into Morafer now?"

"No... That's just it." Stars, how did one find words for the impossible? "I'm... I'm actually not with SysTech any more." Galhen's brow knit in confusion and she drew his hand to her bare throat. His eyes widened as understanding set in.

"How...I... *How*?"

"It's a very long story and I don't know how much time we have, so the short version is that your sister Nalea is helping me. She found a way to remove my collar and I escaped from the PsiCorp. I...I came here for you, to take you with us, if that was what you wanted. It's very risky, and -"

He cut her off with a kiss. "It's worth any risk. Tell me how."

She did. He was quiet after, lips set in a frown. Finally he looked up at her. "You really did that? That was *absurdly* dangerous."

She couldn't help a small smile. "Yes, well. I didn't exactly have a lot of options for pulling off my impossible escape. This was the best your sister could come up with on short notice."

From his expression, Galhen wasn't overly pleased with the

escape method, but she sensed a hardening of resolve through their bond. *Worth any risk.*

"Well, if that's the path we have to walk to escape the PsiCorp then so be it. What happens now?"

"We'll need a plan and a location to extract you. The first was proving difficult without the second."

"Location is simple. We're scheduled for another two weeks at the legislature, then the Morafer Senate breaks for seasonal recess, and we're spending nearly a month at Dalanva's summer manse. There will be considerable security in both locations, but between the headquarters of the system government and Dalanva's private estate, the estate will be a softer target. I haven't been there yet and I don't know much detail about it, but I'll try to find out more."

Galhen's form wavered then, and he hissed in frustration. "I have to go, we'll do this again soon. I love you." A quick kiss on her lips and he faded from the dream, another rapid shift of emotion registering through their bond before he was gone. Regret, frustration, resolve, and the fragile curl of something she hadn't realized he was missing.

Hope.

THREE

"SO I DIDN'T EXACTLY GET to view the schematics, but from what I've gathered it's an extensive estate. There's a main house, a guest house, a servants lodge and multiple small outbuildings. An entire little complex around swimming pools. A sports green. A small forest. A stable and horses, naturally." Galhen's voice took on a shade of sarcastic disgust as he listed them off.

"All in the same estate?" Kerelle couldn't keep the incredulity from her voice. "That sounds more like a palace than a summer home."

"Yes well, only *the best* for the Mistress." This time the sarcasm held an unmistakably bitter tone. Kerelle reached out to stroke his hand, their bond echoing with the now-familiar sensation of empty cold, immediately locked down. His jaw tightened slightly at her questioning glance, and she let it go.

It was the third time they'd been able to meet in the dream. There had been little time for anything but plotting the escape, but even if they weren't on a deadline she suspected it would be the same. Whatever had happened with Dalanva, Galhen wasn't ready to discuss it.

It troubled her, but all she could do was focus on the mission at hand - the sooner to have him away from Dalanva and safe in her arms. That focus was reflected in their surroundings; unlike their usual relaxing dream settings, this time they met in a conference room.

At the top of a high-rise, naturally. Kerelle wasn't prepared to *completely* abandon aesthetics.

"There will be significant security at the mansion, obviously," he went on, "but Dalanva also keeps a large staff, including some people who work onsite at her properties whether she's there or not."

"My goodness, is that a *lot* of people?"

"I doubt she even knows. But that's the point - nobody on staff is going to know everyone else. Once you make it in, you can probably blend in with the servants."

"'Janitor' is becoming my new alter ego," she commented wryly. Galhen's eyebrows went up in question and she sighed. "I'll explain everything later, darling. Anything else we should know?"

"Some good news, actually. I had thought that getting in would be the hard part, but Dalanva is actually presenting us with an excellent opportunity. She's holding a party to celebrate the start of the season, shortly after we arrive." He glanced out the large window of their illusory war room. "I'll know more once we actually arrive at the summer manse, but given the likely scale of the event we can probably use the guests' arrival as cover for you to land."

"That certainly sounds promising for getting *in*," she agreed, swiveling her seat to face him. "But we need to think about getting *out*, too - particularly how we get you away without making it obvious you escaped. We might be able to outrun pursuit in the short term, but having SysTech actively searching for us would definitely be a complication."

Galhen leaned back in his own chair, face thoughtful. "Well, you faked your death to escape. I could do the same."

She raised her eyebrows. "I was in a warzone. The idea seems… rather less plausible at the Senator's social gathering?"

"Accidents happen," he replied with a half shrug. "I'm as mortal as the next mundane, particularly since I don't have your high-powered telekinetics to stave off disaster."

"Accidents happen, yes, but accidents that don't leave a body?"

Galhen was undaunted. "Something involving an explosion would work. I'll keep an eye out for something promising to blow up around Dalanva's mansion." *Preferably with Dalanva in it,* she caught through their bond. A surge of guilt followed before disappearing into lockdown. That wasn't a thought he'd meant to share.

He continued briskly. "With enough witnesses, we won't even *need* a body."

She looked at him. "You want to convince an entire room full of people they saw you die, gruesomely enough that they don't expect a body, *at a party*? That sounds… daunting."

"It wouldn't be a walk in the park," he acknowledged. "But think of it." Galhen leaned forward, green eyes glittering as they held hers. "The two of us, together? With those people seeing the explosion and *expecting* casualties? We can *do* this, Kerelle. We're strong enough.

"And besides," he added, "the resultant uproar will give us cover to escape." His smile faltered a bit as he said it, and he abruptly got up to pace to the window. "We'll just need to avoid Dalanva herself. She has a psiblocker circlet and will quite literally see right through it."

It was quiet for a moment, and the air thickened with tension. Kerelle stayed quiet, letting him work up to whatever he needed to say next.

"There's one more thing," Galhen said finally. He stared resolutely out the false window, not looking at her. "If she does get wind that we're trying to escape, Dalanva won't hesitate to turn my collar on. She won't kill me. Probably. I was very expensive." He still wouldn't look at her. "But you might need to carry me out."

Kerelle got up then and walked over to the window, slipping her arms around him. Galhen was silent, but she felt the tension in his body and her heart ached. She pressed her lips lightly to the back of his neck, sending love and warmth through their bond.

"Dalanva hurt you," she said softly.

He nodded tersely. That tightened jaw again, the sharp cold of emotional lockdown. "That's not important now. We can rehash this whole miserable experience once we're safely away."

He finally turned to face her, returning her embrace. "Just a bit longer," he said softly. Kerelle didn't know if he was speaking to her or himself.

<hr>

"IS THIS A PSICORP THING?" Nalea asked skeptically. "Do you all just assume your powers will solve problems for you, and that's why none of you can plan? Because this sounds insane. Again."

"It's not the worst plan I've heard," Sandrel commented, in what Kerelle had begun to identify as his diplomatic tone. "But I have some concerns. It sounds like a lot of things have to go right."

"They do," Kerelle conceded. "But Galhen is right, this is the best chance we're likely to get. Her estate won't be as heavily guarded as the Senate itself, and the party gives us an opening to slip in. Once we're on the estate, Galhen and I can handle the rest. All you need to do is be ready for a hasty exit."

Sandrel's frown didn't change. "Are you sure the two of you will be enough? I saw you on Kalnis, I know you can handle a lot, but this still sounds pretty damn dangerous."

Well, it was, but she was trying to project confidence here. "We'll be fine," she assured him. "I've gone alone into much more dangerous situations than a rich woman's party."

Sandrel still didn't look wholly convinced, but he only nodded and headed for the cockpit, saying something about entering their course coordinates. Nalea lingered a bit longer, mouth compressed.

"If I end up in restraint cuffs again," she said icily, "I'm telling them you kidnapped me and forced me into this." Nalea swept out of the room, leaving Kerelle alone and hoping she wasn't leading them all into disaster.

FOUR

THE LUSH LITTLE planet sat in the viewport, a green jewel amidst the stark black and white of the space and stars. Kerelle stared at it, fascinated. Somewhere down there was Galhen.

"Let's see, privately-chartered garden world, mostly carved up into estates, two large-ish towns on the opposite side from where we're heading. No craft allowed to land without prior registration, special permit required to land for more than one business day." Sandrel leaned forward, eyes scanning the almanac entry. "Doesn't look like this place has much of a tourism board. You sure your boyfriend worked out the clearance to get us down there?"

"I'm sure." She'd met Galhen the night before to hammer out the final details on how they were getting in. "Galhen pulled this woman's name off the guest list. She declined her invite, but he's convincing the steward she changed her mind. If we tell them we're her ship, we should get clearance to land on Dalanva's estate."

Sandrel cut a glance over to her. "Does he 'convince' people like you do?"

"Not like I do," she answered with a half-smile. "He's much

better at it. If Galhen says he took care of this, it's taken care of."

She meant that, and she meant what she'd said that this was their best chance to rescue Galhen and get away clean. And she was confident they could pull off the entrance and the rescue. It was the get-away-clean part she had concerns about.

"I've found an excellent spot for my untimely demise," Galhen had told her cheerfully. "I spent some time yesterday exploring the estate, and there are a few large, breathtakingly hideous chandeliers in the ballroom."

He shared the memory through their bond and she had to agree with his assessment on all counts. "Where did she even *get* those?"

"Oh, I have no doubt they were handmade by some famous designer for more than most people make in a decade. Pity she probably has them insured, it rather takes the fun out of wanton destruction. Anyway," he'd continued blithely, "You should drop one on my head."

Her guts twisted uncomfortably as she reexamined the image, an intricate heap of jagged metal and glass. "Galhen, are you *sure* about this? That looks... messy."

"Precisely. No one will expect to find more than a puddle of bloody mess once they've pried it up. We can nudge the other guests out of the impact zone, so it will just be me there when it hits."

Even knowing this was part of the ruse, just thinking about it made Kerelle uncomfortable. "We still have to make sure *you* aren't in the impact zone." She tried to summon a smile. "I didn't come all this way just to crush the love of my life under a monstrous chandelier."

He leaned in and kissed her lightly. "You won't. I have faith in you, Kerelle. You would never let me come to harm." He pulled back then, a mischievous glint in his eyes. "We just have to make everyone *believe* you did."

And so here she was ten hours later, watching the green planet grow larger and trying to tamp down the anxious excitement that fizzed in her veins. If all went to plan, the previous night was the last time she and Galhen would share the dream together, the last time they would need it. By that same time tonight, he would *be here*.

If all went to plan.

THE SWAPPED INVITATION worked as promised, and "Ms. Hanacha's private craft" was granted immediate clearance without questions. Dalanva's air-control staff directed Sandrel to the landing pad set up in a meadow a short distance from the main house, noted a coach would be making regular rounds to ferry guests from their craft to the party, and bid him good night. They couldn't have hoped for better cover - many other guests were arriving as well, and they were just one of many small ships landing in the area. Granted, their little freighter was conspicuously less posh than the other ships, but hopefully the deepening twilight would blunt the obvious.

Sandrel's mouth was a tight line. "All set, Fury?" She nodded her assent.

"As ready as I'm going to be. Keep the engines hot for us, we may need to leave in a hurry."

He snorted softly. "When you're involved, I *always* assume we'll leave in a hurry."

His expression sobered, and he gripped her shoulder for a moment. "Get in, get your man, get out in one piece. We'll be ready."

Kerelle gave him a tight nod of acknowledgement and turned to go. Nalea stepped out of the corridor.

The scientist's face was tight with tension, and her closed-off expression didn't change as she pressed a small packet into

Kerelle's hand. Surprised, Kerelle held up the neatly-packaged syringes.

"It's a dosage of the dampener we used in your extraction," Nalea explained without preamble. "If the collar goes active, it might temporarily lessen the effect. I'm not sure it will actually work." She attempted a nonchalant shrug. "Hopefully it's better than nothing though."

Kerelle tucked the packet into her jacket, oddly touched by the gesture despite Nalea's obvious discomfort with the situation. "Thank you, Nalea."

"It's nothing. It might not even help," she answered brusquely, not looking at Kerelle. "Just don't die or anything. Don't get your boyfriend killed either." She turned and strode purposefully away, back down the corridor toward the medbay.

"I won't," Kerelle answered softly to the empty corridor. She turned to go.

SLIPPING into the party itself actually proved quite simple. A shroud of non-interest around herself, a quick dart into the bustling servants' hall, a set of livery borrowed from the uniform closet, and she was invisible. She kept the shield of anonymity up throughout the servants' quarters, but as Galhen predicted they paid her no mind. Everyone was busy rushing about their own tasks, and if anyone noticed her they assumed she was with a different group of servants. In short order she had collected a tray of appetizers, and passed unchallenged into the main house.

It was not all that different from sneaking into the Kalnis pirate base, although the aesthetics were mercifully different. Dalanva's "summer home" looked like something out of a luxury brand's stylebook, a carefully constructed temple to understated opulence. The unseen hand of the interior decorator seemed to hover over each room, its pieces carefully selected for mood, coherence, and the kind of affected, self-important carelessness that indicated great expense.

Well, she'd certainly take pretentious interior design over the casual brutality of the pirates.

Kerelle wandered slowly through the house, pausing to smile and offer her refreshments to groups of guests as she weaved between them. She kept up her shield of deflected attention, but it was hardly necessary - this crowd didn't notice the help. She was simply one of several uniformed, interchangeable sources of artisanal cheese.

All the same, she needed to be careful to *stay* unremarkable, needed to keep her steps measured and her face in a bland smile. It grew harder and harder as she drew deeper into the house, and closer and closer to Galhen.

She felt his presence like a beacon, and her heart rate began to pick up even before she felt his gentle caress on her mind. *Darling.* The single world was overlaid with a range of emotion - hope, relief, excitement, anticipation, love. The telepathic equivalent of a soft kiss, then it was back to business. The hard part was still to come.

Are you inside then? She sent him her affirmation and shared the image of her location. *Ah, that's the west conservatory - through those double doors, down the hallway, ballroom is on the left.*

On my way, she answered, letting herself drift through the guests towards the doors. *Is that where you are?*

No, we're upstairs. Dalanva's having a private chat with some of her inner circle. He shared a brief image - another impeccably-decorated room, this one with Dalanva holding court from a large chair while several distinguished-looking people sat around her. One woman, though sumptuously dressed, was noticeably younger than the rest. All of them ignored Galhen as he quietly observed them from his vantage point at Dalanva's elbow, standing blank-faced with folded hands like some kind of well-dressed mannequin.

A couple of other senators and some captain-of-industry types, Galhen summarized for her. *I didn't give a damn enough to learn names, but I caught something about SysTech for that girl on the end. Maybe if you need to drop another chandelier you can aim for her.*

Kerelle was not entirely sure if he was joking. He gave her a mental shrug. *Let me know when you're in position, darling. In the mean time I'll be standing up here, quietly looking expensive.*

Kerelle paused to collect another tray of cheese on her way out of the conservatory, and followed Galhen's directions down to the ballroom. She stepped into the cavernous space and tried not to stare.

I'm here, she pinged him. *And burning stars, darling, these chandeliers are even more hideous in person.*

Aren't they? I can't decide if I'm appalled or impressed. Hang on just a moment, I'm convincing Senator Mustache that he's terribly sober and should really ask Dalanva to send me down for more wine.

Is he terribly sober?

Heavens no. But he isn't falling off the sofa yet, so there's room for one more at least.

Kerelle remembered to smile and offer her tray of cheese to a group of guests milling past, keeping one eye on her surroundings as Galhen linked with her.

The red-faced man, who really did have a rather impressive mustache, was slouched back in his chair in a way that suggested he had indeed been making a sustained journey away from sobriety. He leaned forward, trying to catch Dalanva's eye.

"Estia, I fear I'm becoming severely parched. Can your man bring up more wine?"

There were a few nods of agreement around the room, even from those whose glasses weren't yet empty.

Casting a wide net, darling? She teased with a mental smirk.

I never like to leave all my eggs in the same gin-soaked basket.

"Of course," Dalanva answered airily, a quarter-full glass held languidly to her side. She glanced over her shoulder, making eye contact with Galhen for the first time.

"Galhen, do go fetch us another round of the Belu red. Make sure it's properly aerated this time, I won't have you waste another good bottle."

"As you wish, mistress," he murmured in answer, bowing his head respectfully. A few strides and Galhen was out of the room. But not quite out of earshot.

"Such a *pearl*, Estia! Did your peerless Class 3 *arrive* this well trained?" It was one of the other women, sounding amused.

"Oh, stars no," Dalanva answered. "He was actually rather headstrong and undisciplined. I was quite disappointed, to be honest, I expected much more from the PsiCorp…"

Her voice faded as Galhen turned a corner and started down the stairs. For a moment the bond stuttered - he wished she hadn't heard that part. For a moment she could sense his churning emotions, anger and shame and embarrassment, shoved aside with a grim determination that *it would be last fucking time -*

Lockdown. Kerelle reached out in a telepathic embrace, trying to send soothing comfort - and suppress her own furious protective instincts. Charging up the stairs and putting a rich sociopath through the wall might *feel* good, but it wouldn't help them escape.

Are you all right?

Yes, he answered curtly. After a moment's silence, *but I'm rather eager to get this next part over with and never see any of these vultures again. Can you start herding people away from the drop radius?*

That she could. Kerelle began to apply soft pushes to the guests around her, guiding them to drift closer to the edges of the ballroom with the vague idea that they wanted to look out the large windows, or that perhaps there was better cheese on offer at the perimeter. Fortunately the party was well enough underway that most people had had a libation or several, and were loosened enough not to examine their sudden impulse.

She'd made good progress in gradually clearing the center of the room, with a noticeable bare patch under the chandelier - noticeable if you were looking for it, that was. Then Galhen passed through those great double doors, and the other party-goers scattered to the walls like a school of sparkling fish.

He'd always been better at telepathic suggestion, but when the room turned as one with low murmurs to watch her lover carry his tray of glasses to the refreshment table, Kerelle realized it was hardly necessary. Even without Galhen's subtle mental prompts, everyone wanted a glimpse of Dalanva's pet psionic. These people were rich enough that they'd seen class-1 secretaries - half the room probably had one themselves - but class-3 was something special.

No wonder Dalanva had been so eager to acquire one.

Galhen outwardly ignored the whispers and stares of the crowd, serenely filling the wine glasses. Inwardly he made a final check of the room, confirming with Kerelle that he had a safe buffer of empty space. Galhen lowered his head slightly to better judge the pour, no hint in his face of the nervous anticipation Kerelle felt fluttering through their bond.

Now, darling.

Kerelle quashed her own nervousness. She had to trust Galhen, and trust herself. She turned to get both the chandelier and Galhen in view and, offering her tray of cheese to a knot of guests with a smile, shattered the top of the chandelier.

Splintered glass rained down, and she hurriedly threw up a shield over the screaming crowd to funnel the debris away from them. These people might be awful, but all they were guilty of tonight was attending a particularly awful woman's party. They didn't deserve to be murdered by chandelier.

The chandelier itself, unfortunately, seemed rather intent on murder. It listed hard to the side, sweeping madly above the crowd on a thin, fragile-looking cord that still connected it to the ceiling. She'd missed that bit earlier. Biting back a curse, Kerelle swung the chandelier back towards the empty spot as though its momentum had jerked the cord. It sailed back over Galhen, who was watching it in apparently frozen horror.

It sailed toward him, and she cut the final cord.

Even without her push to slow it, the heavy chandelier lost momentum almost immediately, and dropped like a stone toward Galhen. Kerelle encased him in the strongest shield she could muster. *Darling,* move!

The chandelier hit the floor with a deafening crash, and Kerelle stumbled as she was hit with double vision. With her eyes, she saw Galhen deftly pivot aside, felt her shields hold as shrapnel bounced harmlessly off him. Superimposed over her sight, her mind saw a scene from her deepest nightmares as the chandelier impaled and crushed its victim.

All her breath left her as the room dissolved into shrieking chaos, her eyes transfixed on the shattered ruin of the chandelier. It had been an illusion, she *knew* it had been an illusion, but it had seemed so very real, what if -

Galhen's hand slipped into hers. He'd found his way to her side in the tumult. *All according to plan, darling, remember?*

She gripped his hand tightly. *You're too good at that.*

Sorry you had to see it. I didn't have much room for precision. He glanced quickly around them. *Speaking of?*

They deepened their link, amplifying each other as they eased through room, pushing hard on the other partygoers to internalize the illusion - and to take no notice of them. *Dalanva's psionic is not walking among you, you watched him die beneath the chandelier. You watched it, it happened, it's real.*

The other guests in the ballroom had graduated from frozen shock to full-fledged panic. Someone shouted that the ceiling was going to come down, and the cry was taken up around the room before Kerelle and Galhen even needed to encourage it.

The screaming throng began to lurch towards the exit in a sea of pushes and shoves. Kerelle tightened her grip on Galhen's hand and threaded them forward, augmenting sharp elbows with a judicious whisper of telekinetic force as she pushed through the chaos. At last they cleared the double doors, spilling into the main hallway with the rest of the escaping room. The ballroom's panic had spread to the rest of the manse, and people ran every which way through the wide hall. Dodging bodies in motion, Galhen pulled her through a small door on the other side.

There's a servants' passage that connects near here, we'll have a clear line to -

One of the adjoining doors burst open before he could finish his thought, and Estia Parie Dalanva stared openmouthed back at them.

FIVE

FOR SEVERAL LONG seconds they all simply stared, frozen in shocked tableau. The senator was smaller and more frail than she had looked in pictures, and her elegant gown and carefully-styled hair were slightly mussed - probably from hurrying downstairs to investigate the crash that had surely shaken her entire house. Still firmly in place, however, was the promised psiblocker circlet. Unlike the Elekar governor's flimsy bauble, this one was top of the line, and wouldn't be out of place on a PsiCorp manager.

She was flanked by two people Kerelle recognized from Galhen's view of the upstairs room - Senator Mustache and the SysTech girl. Kerelle knew she should shove them away, but she felt a flash of hesitation at using force against an old woman -

Her momentary wavering let Dalanva recover first. The senator's eyes dropped to their clasped hands and narrowed, and her own hand darted to something hidden among her costume jewelry.

Pain exploded through their bond. Kerelle heard herself cry out as her every nerve ending seemed to burst into flame, dark spots rushing into her vision. Reflexively she blocked the bond and the pain vanished - for her. As her vision cleared Galhen fell beside her, his screams echoing against the ornately-carved ceilings.

The collar. That bitch had turned his collar on.

All Kerelle's pity vanished. Fueled by her anger, the tele-kinetic wave struck Dalanva and her minions with savage force, and they were flung back like rag dolls towards the other end of the hall. The room's high, graceful windows shattered as one. Kerelle wrenched a decorative column from its socket for good measure, flinging it down to block the passageway before them.

Galhen's harsh sobs of pain echoed behind her. Kerelle's throat closed up at the sound, and the sight of her always-poised lover forced to his hands and knees. She tamped down hard on her storming emotions, willing her stinging eyes to clear. Tears wouldn't help here - she could fall apart after Galhen was safe.

Trusting the fallen masonry to hold their opponents for now, Kerelle frantically withdrew the little packet of syringes Nalea had entrusted to her. The first one came open easily, and after a moment's struggle with his jacket Kerelle cursed and ripped off the sleeve. She quickly selected a vein, gave him the injection - *three cheers for field first aid* - and prayed Nalea was right.

Galhen's shuddering breath sounded more like a groan, but his eyes focused again and he staggered to his feet. Face tight with pain, he gave her a small nod and tugged her hand. *I can move. We need to go.*

They set out at a run - or as close to a run as he could manage. Kerelle tried not to count the long seconds it took them to clear the hall, knowing Galhen was as aware as she of their painfully slow progress, and that their pace was already pushing him.

Outside the manse, the grounds were consumed in chaos. Kerelle's window-breaking wave had been interpreted as a bomb, and now the panicked civilians saw terrorists in every deepened shadow. Kerelle tried to keep up a low-level veil of deflection, cementing them as just two more bodies in the mass of humanity. They made slow but steady progress across the yard, until Galhen stumbled for the second time and nearly fell. She threw his arm over her shoulder and helped him steady himself, grateful they were roughly the same height. *Just a bit further, love. We just have to get to the ship. We can do this.*

He gave her a tight nod and turned to move forward, when a sudden sixth sense prickled at her. Unthinking, she threw up a shield around them - almost in time.

She managed to deflect most of the force behind the psionic blow, but it still shook her footing, and Galhen's piteous moan clawed at her guts. He collapsed in a dead weight against her, nearly knocking her over as well. Kerelle steadied him as best she could and drew her power close, as she sought their attacker *and tried to figure out what in the burning void had just happened-*

The dust cleared, and she made eye contact with the young woman she'd seen at Dalanva's side. The SysTech girl.

The uncollared psionic.

No time to ponder the impossibility - the girl threw another wave of force at them, though this time Kerelle was ready. She absorbed the blow on her shields and pushed back, sending her opponent staggering. Kerelle struck again before she could get steady and the girl flew backwards, vanishing as she landed in a mass of people.

Hoping she'd bought them a few seconds, Kerelle hurriedly gave Galhen a second shot of the dampener. *Stars, I hope you can't overdose on this.* His breathing steadied, but they hadn't gone more than a few steps before he collapsed against her again. Galhen was built lean, but he still outweighed her by quite a bit. If she had to drag him over her shoulder, they wouldn't move nearly fast enough.

As if to underscore her thought, another hard push buffeted her shields. The SysTech girl had recovered quickly.

A split-second consideration, and Kerelle focused nearly all her energy around the shields, with a whisper diverted to gently support Galhen beside her. Dueling the other psionic would only waste time he didn't have. They had to *move*.

It was easier said than done. Kerelle was reasonably certain she was the stronger telekinetic, but the other woman wasn't also trying to run and support an injured man at the same time. Stones and debris flew at them from all directions, most bouncing harmlessly off the shields but occupying enough of Kerelle's attention that she had to struggle to keep Galhen upright as well. She also still didn't have line of sight on her opponent - and unleashing an unfocused wave of force risked injuring civilians. She gritted her teeth and forged onward.

The bulk of the party guests were running this way as well, towards escape in their own ships from whatever unknown danger was assaulting the party. Already she heard the roar of engines taking off with those who had already made it, and distant shouts of what sounded like Dalanva's security team approaching the scene. The outline of Sandrel's ship was visible in the gloom, but they were nearly out of time.

A sharp shove nearly sent her sprawling. Kerelle spun around quickly scanning the crowd for sight of their assailant. She had to be close enough that she could see *them* - and close enough she'd be able to see the ship they got into. Kerelle didn't know if their enemy had the strength to damage a ship in flight, but they couldn't risk finding out.

A flash of movement caught her eye. *There*. Kerelle yanked on the furtive figure, confirming it was their attacker. The girl's eyes met hers in cold challenge and she threw her own shield up, abruptly disengaging Kerelle's hold.

Oh no you don't. Kerelle pushed Galhen behind her and hit the girl hard from the other direction, determined not to let her get back into cover. Her opponent staggered and tried to counterattack, but this time her burst of energy dissipated harmlessly against Kerelle's shield. Before she could regain her footing

Kerelle grabbed her from below and slammed her to the ground with enough force to leave her sprawled on the lawn, stunned. Kerelle flung her prone assailant backwards out of sight, grabbed Galhen's hand, and sprinted.

No time for subtlety. Hoping the general chaos across the darkened field would divert notice, she carried him with her power those last few endless meters toward the ship. The cacophony of shouts and ships faded to a dull roar beneath the rough boom of her pulse pounding in her ears, and the rhythmic force of her footfalls.

Sandrel met her at the hatch. "Complications," she panted as he slammed the door behind her, a quick staccato on the controls engaging the airlock.

"There always are." Sandrel was already jogging down towards the cockpit. "Thirty seconds to takeoff, get to the infirmary and strap in."

Kerelle's feet were already in motion. She'd slung Galhen over her shoulder again, her power helping support his weight as she pushed on to the infirmary.

"We're here, darling, it's almost over." She glanced over sharply as he didn't respond, all the fear and panic she'd suppressed during their flight from the manse beginning to boil up from the mental compartment she'd confined it to. "Galhen? Stay with me, love."

This time he gave her a weak nod, but his eyes lacked focus and his breathing was coming in ragged gasps. Kerelle's choking fear intensified.

Nalea appeared at her side and grabbed his other arm. Together, they hurried him into the infirmary. Galhen slid limp and unresisting into the medbay's narrow bed, his hold on consciousness clearly slipping.

"What's wrong with him?" Nalea asked sharply, fingers flying as she connected their little monitor and turned to her supplies, carefully laid out on the medbay's counter. She yelped and grabbed them up as the ship shot suddenly upward and they were nearly thrown over. The telltale hum of the stealth field buzzed to life.

"Collar's active," Kerelle panted out as they steadied, the exertion of the escape beginning to catch up with her. "Dalanva turned it on before we could escape the manse. I gave him two of your dampener syringes on the way here."

Nalea swore softly and bit her lip, eyes darting quickly from Galhen to the waiting syringes. "If he's already had two, but they might be wearing off..." she trailed off, apparently doing calculations in her head. Kerelle just watched her silently, Galhen's hand locked in hers. There was nothing more she could do except stay out of Nalea's way.

Suddenly Galhen's fingers jerked, and clamped down over hers in a painful grip. His eyes shot open and he threw back his head and screamed, the monitor's warning lights erupting into flashing consternation. Kerelle heard herself scream as well, the sudden flood of panic in her mind crowding out anything except the sickening shock that oh stars and flame, oh burning void, Dalanva had flipped it to kill, she *flipped it to kill, she was trying to kill him* -

Nalea shook her head quickly and grabbed the middle syringe, forcing his arm down to hold steady enough for the injection. Jaw locked in a silent grimace, she gave him the next one. The monitor flashed and he convulsed with a whimper and went still. The readings flatlined, and Kerelle's sobs were the only sound in the room.

Nalea didn't look up, only grabbed her tools and roughly snapped off the collar, sweeping it out of contact with Galhen in a single fluid motion.

Another syringe.

A moment of terrible quiet.

Galhen gasped awake, the monitor lighting up in joyful confirmation that he was alive as giddy relief flooded Kerelle's nerves. His glassy eyes met hers and she felt a slight squeeze on her hand before his eyelids dropped closed again. The monitor didn't change, though - his heart rate was steady.

"Vitals stable," Nalea confirmed, giving the readings a critical scan. "He'll live." She didn't look happy.

"That's a good thing," Kerelle noted cautiously, creeping unease cooling her earlier euphoria. The scientist's troubled expression didn't change.

"Nalea," Kerelle pressed. "What is it?"

"He'll live," Nalea repeated. She kept her eyes fastened on the wall. "But that was a lot rougher than it was with you. Maybe I should have given him a third shot of the dampener, but I wasn't sure how much was too much and I didn't want to risk it, especially since his body was already in distress." She paused, but Kerelle sensed that wasn't all of it. She waited.

"And nobody really understands how psionics work anyway," Nalea said finally. "Hopefully he's fine with no damage to anything, and he just needs to sleep it off. I hope. I have no idea."

Nalea's deep sigh was tinged with exhaustion. "I need a drink. Let me know when he wakes up, but..." She spread her hands helplessly. "Honestly? If there *is* something wrong, I have no idea how to treat it." She raised her eyebrows at Kerelle's expression, though her face held more resignation than annoyance. "You asked."

She had, and none of this was the other woman's fault. Quite the opposite. "Thank you, Nalea," Kerelle said softly. "For everything."

Nalea nodded uncomfortably and squeezed past her to head for the mess. She paused in the doorway and gave Kerelle an awkward pat on the shoulder.

"He's alive, right?" Nalea reminded her, and then she was gone.

The medbay was silent but for the monitor's steady beeps of

reassurance that Galhen's still form was simply sleeping. Kerelle scooted her chair closer and reached out to stroke his hair. It was shorter than she remembered, but still soft and golden and *real.*

He was real.

The adrenaline from their harrowing escape was fading, and Kerelle felt the strain of the day beginning to settle heavily over her bones. But now that the frenetic struggle was over, it began to sink in that they had *done* it. This wasn't a dream, a few stolen hours before they had to part once more. Her Galhen was here with her, *truly* here, and the over-pale stripe that ringed his throat, the empty space where the collar had lain for most of his life, meant they would never be parted again.

Come what may, that was enough.

Galhen's quiet breathing was steady, and the lines of pain that had creased his face were smoothed away in sleep. Kerelle leaned over to kiss his forehead, and settled in to wait.

SIX

THE NEXT DAYS passed in an agonizing blur.

Kerelle kept her vigil by Galhen's bedside, determined to be with him when he woke. *When,* not if, because surely they could not have come so far, and through so much, only for this to be the end. He gave no sign of stirring, but his heartbeat and his breathing were regular and strong. She had to believe that was a good sign.

Nalea came up a few times and confirmed that his vitals looked good, but she didn't say much otherwise and never stayed long. Always her awkward discomfort thrummed loudly at Kerelle's senses, and Kerelle didn't need telepathy to know that Nalea was avoiding her and the infirmary as much as she could. It did nothing to ease Kerelle's growing sense of dread, though she was unsure if it meant that the prognosis was worse than Nalea let on, or if it was simply Nalea's own aversion to uncertainty.

Nalea never stated aloud the possibility that the removal had damaged Galhen in a way their little monitor couldn't detect. She didn't need to. Kerelle read it in her face as she silently scanned the vitals with brows knit together, and in her refusal to meet Kerelle's eyes when she repeated his physical readings looked fine. It was just as well. Kerelle refused to entertain the idea that she was sitting beside a beautiful shell.

Sandrel stopped in eventually, ostensibly to bring her a meal. But he sat with her rather than handing it over and leaving again, and though they ate in silence she was grateful he was there.

"I'm bringing us out of hyper tomorrow," he told her finally. "We have to get back out the jump gate, then I'm bringing us in to Xan Xaldanan. It's one of the bigger ports in its sector, we'll be able to lie low there for a bit."

She nodded her understanding and continued picking at her food. Sandrel's gaze flicked to Galhen and back to her.

"Try to eat and get some rest, Fury," he said softly. "He's got to make it through this part on his own."

Her eyes burned, and suddenly it seemed the last of her reserves were gone. "What if he doesn't," she whispered, blurring vision locked on her cooling plate. "What if he trusted me to save him, and I led him to his death." She hardly got the last word out as her voice broke, and she finally lost the battle against tears. She couldn't even summon up embarrassment for it. What use was her dignity at this point anyway?

Sandrel sighed sadly and set his own plate aside. He scooted in closer and wrapped an arm around her shoulders in an awkward hug.

"He knew the risks, Kerelle. He's a medic, he might have known them better than *you* did. If he's here, it's because he thought it was worth it."

It didn't make her feel better. "But it was my idea. I'm the one that brought this on him."

"Give your boyfriend some credit," he answered gently. "We didn't decide this *for* him, remember? Maybe he did it for you, maybe he did it for himself. Either way it was his choice to make. And besides," he added with a ghost of a smile, "it's a little early to declare defeat. The man you told me all those stories about didn't sound like the type to just roll over."

"He isn't," she responded in a low whisper. "He'd fight to the end."

"Well, it's not the end yet, so let's give him some time." Sandrel squeezed her shoulders and got up. "I'll be at the nav if you need me. We'll be coming out of hyper in around 12 hours."

He paused at the doorway. "*Rest,* Kerelle," he reminded her firmly, and was gone.

KERELLE COULDN'T BRING herself to leave the infirmary, but she dragged in a few pillows to lean against as she kept watch. Sandrel wasn't wrong; she had to sleep sometime. Slouching upright in a small folding chair wasn't exactly rejuvenating, but it was the most she was willing to compromise.

She was half-dozing in her chair, absent-mindedly stroking Galhen's fingers, when a sudden answering touch jolted her awake. Her suddenly-racing pulse roared in her ears as she leaned in closer, afraid that she had simply imagined it.

But no - his breathing had changed, and she felt his fingers run across hers in a soft caress. Galhen stirred softly, and his vibrant eyes blinked open.

They focused on her, and he smiled. Kerelle burst into tears.

"Darling?" His voice was rough, but any disorientation was rapidly clearing from his face, and those green eyes were as sharp as they'd ever been. Kerelle gave him a watery smile back and tried to get ahold of herself.

"It's nothing, love, I'm just..." her voice shook. "I'm just so very happy to see you." She reached out to stroke his cheek, prickly with unaccustomed stubble. "How are you feeling?"

He stretched as he considered the question. "Terrible, honestly. Everything hurts. But..."

He stopped then, and lifted a hand to where his collar had been, the snow-pale ring against the otherwise healthy pink skin. Kerelle felt the rapid series of emotions that flitted across his face, ending in wonder.

"It's really gone," he breathed. "We actually did it." His face lit with a joy that warmed her bones, and he pulled her into his arms. She embraced him tightly as it sunk in for both of them, and this time the tears were not grief, but happiness too great to contain.

Galhen's stab of alarm came out of nowhere, and struck her like a physical blow. He froze in her arms and Kerelle drew back suddenly, to see his face drained of all color. *Darling?*

He only stared back at her, eyes wide and frightened. Her own fear began to spread its icy tendrils through her gut. "Galhen?"

"I can't feel you," he whispered.

Her stomach lurched and she glanced sharply down at their entwined hands in alarm.

"No," he clarified. His voice sounded strained. "My body is fine. I can't...I can't feel your mind."

Kerelle stared apprehensively back at him. She hadn't examined how strongly she was experiencing his emotions - she assumed he had opened himself fully to their bond. With rising dread, she closed her eyes and deliberately reached out to his mind with hers.

She hadn't read his feelings so deeply because he was sharing them. She'd read them because his defenses were gone. There was no answering touch of his own power, either to keep her out or welcome her in.

His mind felt like a mundane.

She sat back on her heels, the dizzy numb of shock enveloping her. Kerelle forced herself to meet his eyes. Tears streamed silently down her face as she fought to get the words out.

She didn't need to. He read it in her expression.

Galhen closed his eyes and held himself still. Kerelle felt his struggle not to panic, to focus instead on assessment. She realized that she would need to start shielding against his emotions, if he could no longer control and consent to sharing them. The thought sent another sob shuddering through her.

"It's probably burnout," he said carefully, "and temporary." His fear that it was not either of those things bubbled fiercely at her senses, though he kept his tone calm and detached. "I've treated it before, and the symptoms line up. The collar activation and removal put substantial stress on my system. I thought the headache and muscle pain were an aftereffect of the drugs, but those are symptoms of burnout as well. We'll know..." he swallowed, his clinical facade beginning to crack. "We'll know in the coming weeks."

Kerelle opened her mouth and closed it again, unsure of what to say. Instinctively she started to send him warmth and love, and realized abruptly that that wouldn't work for now. Might not work ever again.

No, she couldn't think like that. It was burnout. That was all.

Feeling self-conscious, Kerelle leaned in and embraced him tightly. She would have to get used to showing outwardly how she felt. After a moment he returned the embrace, and she suspected he was thinking the same.

They held each other, each locked in their own thoughts. Finally Galhen chuckled, the sound uncharacteristically brittle.

"Darling, even I can tell that I desperately need a shower."

She released him and stood up, offering a stabilizing hand as he painfully levered himself off the bed. His own numb shock was buffeting against her, and her heart hurt as she raised her shields.

She helped him to the ship's small lavatory, encouraged that he was already steadier on his feet by the time they reached it. She'd intended to join him in the shower, but he hesitated at the door, and she realized with a twist of hurt that he wanted to be alone.

Kerelle forced herself to smile. "Take as much time as you need, love. I'll be around if you need me." She kissed him quickly on the cheek and turned before her expression could betray her, leaving him to the thoughts she was determinedly shielding against. The lavatory door *snicked* softly shut behind her.

She understood, but it still stung - she and Galhen had always been each other's emotional support. But this wasn't about her. Galhen needed time to process, and if part of that processing was solitude then she wanted to give him as much space as he needed. This was his loss to bear much more than it was hers - a loss she couldn't imagine facing. Whatever support he needed from her, she would provide it as best she could.

Still that cold feeling settled in her stomach as she headed toward the mess. This was not at all the reunion she imagined, and that shamefully selfish part of Kerelle's heart felt hollow with disappointment and hurt.

Kerelle ruthlessly squashed the thought, but all the same she was relieved to find the mess empty, and hurried back to her cabin with tea and food as quickly as she could. The strain of the last few days was catching up, and she felt utterly drained. If she met Nalea or Sandrel, they would ask about Galhen, and at this moment she had no idea what she would say.

Perhaps some time alone to process would be good for her too.

KERELLE WAS half asleep when the door to her cabin opened quietly. She blinked heavy eyelids and identified Galhen's presence at the threshold. More than anything, it was his oddly noisy emotions that brought her back to full consciousness.

Galhen had let himself in, but now he hovered just inside the door, radiating uncharacteristic uncertainty.

Kerelle shifted to offer him a place beside her. The bunk was not large and creaked beneath his added weight, but they both could fit. Galhen slipped his arms around her, and they lay holding each other in silence. His hair was still damp, but he was clean and shaven and more himself again, at least in appearance. When she nestled herself into her favorite spot in the crook between his chest and shoulder, his heart beat the same as it always had.

Again though he felt hesitant, as if he thought she might send him away. She didn't know how to ask him with words what was wrong.

Instead Kerelle simply reached for him, keeping her touch light so that he could easily pull away if he didn't want this. But it seemed she'd misread his hesitation - he responded immediately, leaning eagerly into her caresses and bringing down his lips to cover hers.

Galhen had been her first and only lover. In the dream and in waking life, he'd shared her bed for over a decade. And yet it felt strange and unfamiliar to make love like this, with only their bodies entwined. Opening fully to each other through their bond was the deepest intimacy Kerelle could imagine, and it had always been the natural precursor to any physical joining. She had always simply *known* what he wanted her to do, had sensed the pleasure that arced through his body when she did it. How did mundanes do it, unable to *feel* their lovers' desires?

She'd figure it out, she resolved, and determinedly shoved such thoughts away. *Her Galhen* was still here in her arms, the same person he'd always been. And surely she didn't need telepathy to remind her how her lover liked to be touched.

He didn't need it either.

Afterwards he lay panting beside her in a tangled embrace, his sated contentment wrapping her unguarded senses in a warm and welcome glow. He gazed up at the ceiling, one hand absentmindedly caressing her hair.

"I thought we would never be like this again," he said finally. "Even now it feels like some kind of dream."

Hopefully not a nightmare, the back of Kerelle's mind supplied unhelpfully. She ignored it, instead reaching up to stroke his cheek.

"But it's not a dream," she responded with a soft smile. "We don't have to wake up this time."

A pensive nod. "You're here. I'm here. What else do we really need?" His eyes stayed on the ceiling, and Kerelle felt like he might be speaking as much to himself as to her.

His stomach growled loudly then, rather ruining the moment. Kerelle couldn't help the laugh that bubbled up through her lips, or the grin on her face as she leaned in for another kiss.

"We need *food*, maybe?"

She led him down to the mess, hands clasped. It was not really much substitute for their psionic bond, but the physical contact made her feel connected to him anyway, and she treasured the feeling. Given his grip on her hand, he might feel the same.

They rounded a corner into the mess, and came face to face with Nalea. Two pairs of vibrant green eyes locked across the small room.

The scientist froze, the steaming tea kettle still raised in her hand, as Galhen stopped short behind Kerelle. Long seconds passed in silence as they both simply stared at each other.

Galhen rallied first, though his uncertainty radiated like a furnace - her always self-possessed lover was, for once, at a loss for words. "Nalea. It's....good to see you." A flash of mortification, *burning stars I sound stupid, who even* says *something like that*. Kerelle suppressed a wince as she belatedly shielded again.

Nalea wrenched her gaze away, and suddenly found the tea kettle utterly fascinating.

"Uhm...yeah. Same. Good to see that you're... alive and everything." Her fair skin flushed nearly as red as the kettle and awkward silence descended.

In their years together, Galhen had regularly rescued Kerelle from conversational breakdown, but she'd never before had to reciprocate. Today was filled to the brim with new experiences.

"Nalea, we were just about to fix something to eat," she said encouragingly. "Would you like to join us?"

"Um...no thanks." Nalea hastily poured her tea and snatched it up, hissing slightly at the heat of the mug. "I've got some notes I have to compile. And I have to get ready to leave." She darted a glance at Galhen, then back to her tea. "Now that things are...done, I can go back to real life."

She scooted hurriedly past them, not looking at Galhen. He turned slightly to watch her go, expression unreadable. Even through her shields, though, Kerelle sensed hurt and disappointment. She sighed and squeezed his hand.

"You might need to give her some time. Whatever it is, I think it's her, not you." Galhen said nothing, but he didn't look much encouraged. Kerelle tried again. "I don't know what she was like as a child, but I've known her to be somewhat prickly. Where it counted, though, she very much came through for us."

Kerelle picked up the kettle Nalea had left behind and shook it - at least enough water left for another cup. She poured one and handed it to him with a smile.

"Ready to hear the long version of how we got here?"

"THE LONG VERSION" was an apt description, lasting steadily through their meal and several cups of tea afterward. Kerelle was a mostly-useless cook - another life skill she'd need to pick up, now that the PsiCorp wasn't feeding her - but the directions on the instant noodle packages were simple enough to follow. The result wasn't exactly gourmet, but nonetheless Galhen seemed more enthused than anyone had a right to be when presented with a steaming bowl of chewy noodles, rehydrated vegetables and textured protein.

It was, Kerelle remembered abruptly, at least two days since he'd last eaten. That probably helped.

He mostly listened while she talked, occasionally interjecting a question between slow and deliberative bites. He said nothing when she got to the part about discovering the disciplinary records, but his jaw tightened slightly and his eyes cut away. Kerelle was determinedly staying out of his thoughts, but she didn't need telepathy to read from his body language that he didn't want to discuss it. She moved on quickly, through Zharal V and meeting Nalea, through the escape with Sandrel and their misadventures on Kalnis, to Palhee and tracking down Dalanva.

"Then I ran across a news video of Dalanva at some senate hearing, and you were there with her. Since we knew where you were, we could get close enough that I could reach you in the dream and see if you even *wanted* to escape - "

"What?" Galhen set down his mug and stared at her. "You thought I might *stay* with that woman? Willingly?"

"I didn't think you would," she responded. "But escape meant leaving any semblance of safety and comfort, and there was...*risk*." Her gaze dropped at the weak euphemism, inadequately encompassing all the venture had cost him.

"Are you *mad*?"

Kerelle blinked back at him. Galhen shook his head in disgust.

"There is no safety, or comfort, in being some narcissist's property," he said deliberately. "And that is precisely what I was. I was an expensive bauble to impress her peers, to dress and speak and smile exactly as she instructed."

His face flushed and he looked away. "You already know she used my collar. I learned *damn* quick not to answer her with anything but 'yes mistress,' and I hated myself for giving in." Even through the shields, Kerelle felt his emotions roil, through anger and shame and remembered fear.

All she could do was reach across the table to take his hand. He closed his fingers over hers in acknowledgement, gaze distant.

"Every day for months," he confessed quietly, "I've thought about throwing myself off the Senate Tower. I woke up in the morning, considered the option, and decided that that day was not the day. If you hadn't come for me, I might have done it within the year."

Even hearing it sent jagged shards of ice down her spine. She tightened her grip on his hand.

"I'm so very glad you didn't." Her voice sounded small. Galhen leaned in to rest his forehead against hers.

"I am too," he said softly. "But darling, don't ever think you took me away from anything but despair and death. Even if I... don't recover, I would rather spend a mundane lifetime on the run with you than another five minutes as Dalanva's class-3 trophy."

She wasn't sure whose lips moved first, but the kiss was long and slow and tender, and for the first time it felt like they were truly reunited. *Come what may,* she promised him in her mind, *I will not let go again.*

They broke apart and she met his eyes. But before she could say anything else, the intercom crackled to life.

"I need everyone up in nav," Sandrel's voice echoed tersely. "We've got a problem."

SEVEN

THEY MADE a crowded party in the cockpit, particularly with Nalea still looking everywhere but at Galhen. The reason for Sandrel's concern was clearly visible through the viewport: the jump gate was under heavy blockade, with a long line of ships waiting to cross.

"So that's where we're going," Sandrel confirmed. "And three guesses what has the border patrol in a tizzy." He pulled up a datanet news feed without waiting for anyone to actually guess. The headlines told the story.

Terrorists Strike at Senate Leader. Morafer Reeling After Vicious Attack. Senator Hospitalized in Assault by Unknown Terror Group. Dalanva Attackers Still at Large.

Kerelle felt like she *ought* to feel remorse for injuring Dalanva, badly enough to send her to the hospital. She'd hoped to rescue Galhen without hurting *anyone.* But then she remembered how the senator had coldly flicked on the collar and watched as agony drove Galhen to his knees, and any guilt she *ought* to feel evaporated like a fine mist.

"I'll admit, I was expecting extra security," Sandrel noted tightly. "I didn't expect them to practically seal the borders."

"We probably *should* have foreseen this," Galhen responded, his eyes trained on the jump gate. "Dalanva is the the richest woman in the system, one of the most powerful members of the Senate, has a niece on the board of Morafer's biggest manufacturer and several relatives in prominent military positions. If anyone could inspire a border-sealing level of blowback, it's her."

Sandrel glanced over, noticing him for the first time. "Glad to see you up and about, and sorry there's not time for a proper welcome. Unfortunately where things stand right now, time is one thing we *don't* have."

Sandrel spun his chair around to face the three of them. "So here's the thing. I've been taking it slow, but we're probably on somebody's scanners by now, and it's going to look suspicious if we suddenly turn tail in the other direction." He glanced back over his shoulder at the blockade. "We also have to leave the system sometime, and the longer we wait the longer they have to figure out who they're actually looking for."

The silence hung for a beat. Kerelle suspected they were all thinking the same thing. She voiced it softly.

"They probably already *know* who they're looking for."

Sandrel gave her something between a grimace and a shrug. "That's definitely a possibility. I gave the news chatter a quick read, and they're not saying anything about Dalanva misplacing her top-ranked psionic, but..."

"But they wouldn't," Galhen finished for him. His eyes hadn't left the viewport. "If SysTech believes I was killed in the attack - or that Dalanva finished me with the collar - they wouldn't want the mortality of their vaunted double-class-3s to be morning news chatter." His smile was humorless. "Bad for brand image."

"And if they know we escaped, they won't publicly admit it can be done," Kerelle added. "But..."

"But we have to assume they've quietly told the authorities," Sandrel finished for her.

He sighed heavily and gave the viewport a baleful glance. "Crazy as it sounds, I think our best choice is just to keep on course for the gate. I've got an ident-switcher"- *of course he did -* "so if they're checking clearance records, this ship won't scan as the same one that landed at Dalanva's party. We head in, stick to our honest-freighter cover story, get cleared and get through."

"It's that getting-cleared part that worries me," Kerelle answered with an involuntary glance at the Ambrel siblings. Galhen had no identification, obviously, and creating a record of Nalea's presence here would only put her in further danger. From the scientist's expression, that had occurred to her as well.

"There's still considerable risk," Sandrel admitted. "Especially if Dalanva got any good shots of you on her security feeds. But your man's right, she isn't just going to let this go, and obviously this whole system hops when she snaps her fingers. The longer we stay in Morafer the better her odds of finding us. We just have to avoid undue attention at the checkpoint."

Sandrel leaned back in a stretch, his casual pose belying the tight-strung tension that jangled at her senses. "So if you have any more of that creepy mind stuff, Fury, this is a great time to break it out." He glanced quickly at Galhen. "From what Kerelle says, creepy mind stuff is one of your specialties. Any help you can give us here would be great."

Galhen's jaw tightened slightly. Kerelle answered for them both.

"I'll handle it myself - Galhen is injured." She attempted a reassuring smile. "It'll be fine," she lied.

Sandrel's eyebrows raised just a fraction, and Kerelle didn't need her psionics to tell her he'd picked up on some tension. But all he did was nod.

"If you're sure, then I'll take us in. Cover story is we delivered some cargo in-system, picked up another shipment bound for Fenride, standard courier work. We're just passing through."

"Fenride. Got it."

"This isn't totally on you," Sandrel told her seriously. "I've got a few tricks to help out."

"That's good to know. How long do we have?"

"Judging by the size of that queue? Probably a few hours. We'll want to be ready earlier though, just in case."

"Just in case," she echoed. "We'll make some preparations before then. Call if you need us." She motioned Galhen out with a sharp nod toward the corridor. She put a bit of distance between them and the cockpit before she turned to meet his gaze.

"If they're looking for *you specifically*, this is going to be really difficult," she said bluntly.

"Agreed." Galhen sighed and ran an agitated hand through his hair. Frustration radiated off him so strongly it was practically visible. "A voids-damned time to burn out. Both of us combined could handle it without breaking a sweat."

She didn't disagree. "If they walk in and see the man they're looking for, I don't know that I'll be able to convince them they don't. Not without pushing hard enough it tips them off anyway."

He gazed back at her bleakly. "Then let's make sure that's not who they see."

The ship wasn't exactly a treasure trove of disguise options, but they did the best they could. It didn't need to be perfect - just enough that he wouldn't be immediately recognized on sight as Galhen Tarau Ambrel, escaped SysTech PsiCorp agent.

Fortunately Galhen and Sandrel were roughly the same size, and the smuggler was able to outfit him with a battered set of clothing usually reserved for when the engines needed attention. Galhen also regretfully agreed that his golden hair was too distinctive, and lacking any dye options they ended up simply shaving his head. There wasn't enough time for facial hair, obviously, but a few dirt smudges lent his cheekbones a bit of concealment.

All in all, she determined with a critical once-over, it wasn't bad. There was nothing to be done for those striking eyes, but he looked different enough from his file photos that Kerelle could at least introduce reasonable doubt in their pursuers' minds. Hopefully.

From his tight expression, Galhen wasn't entirely confident either - or maybe it was just his unhappiness at the whole situation. Either way there wasn't much else they could do about it.

Kerelle took his hand and squeezed it. "Just stand to the side and look surly," she told him. "I'll keep them off you."

She hoped she could keep that promise when the time came.

Sandrel met them outside the cockpit with a small stack of documents. He pressed one into Galhen's hand - a set of identification with Sandrel's picture for "Perlen Skendaset Miraas." At Galhen's questioning glance, Sandrel cocked his head back at Kerelle.

"I remember she did better with props," he explained, and she could have hugged him. "I gave one to Doc, too."

She opened her mouth to thank him and he raised a finger to silence her. "Thank me by getting us out of this in one piece, Fury. Preferably with my ship *also* in one piece."

The intercom crackled then, and a terse voice echoed through the ship.

"Freight Vessel *Moondust*, this is Morafer Republic Military Police. Dock with the inspection vessel and prepare for boarding."

THEY ASSEMBLED TENSELY at the hatch to greet their visitors, Sandrel in front as the captain and the others hovering a few paces back. Kerelle tried to clear her mind and focus on steadying her breathing. She couldn't think about how Galhen was standing behind her defenseless but for the thin veil of their last-minute disguise efforts, or how Sandrel and Nalea were once again trusting their lives and safety to her skill at telepathic misdirection. A skill she was far less confident in than her ability to simply blast their enemies into oblivion.

The door opened, and there was no longer any time for doubt.

The hatch admitted a hard-faced man who was clearly the one in charge, along with several others who appeared to be the muscle. Kerelle read them quickly, careful to keep the frown off her face. They were stressed from several days of high alert and uncertainty, and bored from the monotony of searching every single ship. They hoped to find something, anything that would give them an excuse to act.

It was not a good combination.

This ship is dull, she pushed. *It's just yet another freighter, with yet another unremarkable crew. You want to finish with it quickly and move on to the next ship. Maybe the* next *ship will be hiding terrorists.*

Sandrel greeted the newcomers with a congenial smile, his body language admirably relaxed - though Kerelle could sense his inner tension. He made an attempt at small talk with the head inspector, whose curt responses made it clear that he was not interested in socializing.

"Your business in Morafer please, Captain Halas." The inspector's tone held a shade of belligerent sneer, conveying the reminder that he could have "Captain Halas" and crew arrested at his discretion. Kerelle skimmed his thoughts and determined it was more a reflection of the man's current mood than a concrete intention - but she leaned a bit harder on him anyway. *Boring ship. Stupid spacers on a stupid freighter. Move on quickly to the next one.*

Sandrel nodded eagerly back at him, all helpful earnestness.

"Of course, sir. See, my business is hauling freight, was my dad's business first but I took it over a few years back, anyway we haul all over the galaxy - merchandise, dry goods, a little bit of industrial but it's hard to get those contracts, usually they go to the big shippers, but it's good money so I always try to get them anyway, really we haul everything but livestock, animals are the one place I draw the line. Fella wanted me to haul his chickens once and I said-"

"Your business in *Morafer*, Captain Halas." The inspector didn't hide his contempt, and Kerelle caught a flash of wanting to be done with this simpleton captain who couldn't get to the point. She carefully fed that feeling as Sandrel launched into an eager, overly detailed recounting of their imaginary job hauling canned food to a planet in Morafer, and their return trip to Fenride, with numerous meandering asides. Kerelle sensed that even without her psychic urging, the inspector wanted to just extract himself from this interminable conversation, finish up, and move on.

Sandrel, Kerelle was abruptly reminded, essentially did this sort of thing for a living.

The inspector finally cut in again, his annoyance plain. "Manifest please, Captain Halas, then we can send you about your business."

Sandrel produced an impressively legitimate-looking manifest - he must have been working on that while Kerelle and Galhen were busy with disguises. Kerelle leaned on the inspector anyway to accept it. It wasn't too difficult - the man was bored and ready to be done with them. Things were, on the whole, going quite well.

And then the door opened again, and in walked a young man in a SysTech PsiCorp uniform.

EIGHT

SHIT.

Okay. Don't panic. Don't let them see *you panic.* She slammed shields up around the rest of the group to keep any stray thoughts from projecting, but then that introduced a new problem. If he was a telepath and not picking *anything* up, that was suspicious too. Delicately - *so delicately* - she pressed on him not to notice. *These people are all nervous and uncomfortable. You expect them to be nervous and uncomfortable at the sight of you. Nothing here is odd.*

From the ranking on his uniform he was only a C1 - certainly not strong enough to break through a C3's telepathic shield, and probably not strong enough to detect a C3 feeding him suggestion. Except that she had to keep telepathic shields up around four people, while also leaning on the inspectors not to get too interested in their group, and subtly pushing on the C1 to not realize why he wasn't picking anything up.

At least, stars be praised, he wasn't anyone she recognized from Tallimau.

The head inspector only nodded at the psionic as if this was routine. The young agent took up a place beside him.

"Is this...a corporate inspection also?" Sandrel asked, his tone infused with nervousness. It was an entirely appropriate response for a humble freighter captain suddenly confronted with PsiCorp. She wondered how much of it was genuine.

"Not corporate, just some extra security in these circumstances." The inspector sounded more bored now than hostile. Kerelle could work with that. She *had* to work with that, because now for the hard part. "We'll just need to see some identification for all those aboard."

"Of course, of course," Sandrel agreed quickly "Terrible business, that. Stars guide you in finding those responsible." He handed the man a set of ID, presumably for Captain Halas.

Accept it. It's real. She didn't need to push, however - Captain Halas's identification looked quite genuine, and the inspector looked it over and handed it back with no comment. Thank the stars for that - Kerelle felt like she was juggling a dozen grenades. Keep shields on their thoughts. Push the guards to accept them at face value, but not so hard they realized they were being pushed. Project mundanity to the C1, but not so hard he detected that it was *anything* but mundane. Don't let anything drop, or the whole thing explodes.

She knew she was starting to sweat, and she had to push them not to notice *that* either.

The inspector took her ID next, and she fought the urge to hold her breath. But Karia Vela Vendrys also had a very convincing-looking set of identification, and once again the man handed it back without issue. He moved on to Galhen, and the moment of truth.

It's his ID. It's his picture. You see this man and you see that he is the man on the ID. He's not who you're looking for. He's not anyone you notice.

The inspector's brow furrowed a moment and he looked back up from the document in his hand to Galhen. Kerelle pushed harder.

It's his ID. He's nobody. Nondescript. Nondescript. Nondescript.

Suddenly the C1's head snapped around, his eyes wide.

Shit. Too hard.

She should kill him, before he had a chance to act. If he were an enemy psionic and this were a combat engagement, she would. But he was just a C1 kid probably fresh out of the academy, who didn't choose this any more than she did. Who just had the bad luck to be assigned here when they were trying to escape. She hesitated.

All hell broke loose.

The proximity alarm leapt to life, chiming urgently at the sudden appearance of many smaller craft, all heading towards them. Through the viewport, alarm lights flared on the jump gate station. The inspection team startled but recovered quickly, reaching for their weapons. Kerelle dropped her now-useless telepathic shields, and readied herself to unleash her telekinetics.

Somehow, it always seemed to come to that in the end.

The C1 yelled something to the guards and ducked away, looking more terrified than threatening. Kerelle ignored him; he'd passed on his message, the damage he could do was done. Instead she threw up quick shields around the rest of the party and shoved the guards over before they could fire. She'd have to be careful here - too much uncontrolled force could damage the ship.

Galhen and Nalea made it safely behind cover, but Sandrel got off a shot from beside her, scarring the head guard's body armor. The increasingly agitated proximity alarm, however, meant they had bigger problems than the guards.

"Sandrel, get us out of here!" She met his eyes. "I can handle these, we have to go before the rest of them get here!"

He hesitated for an instant, then grimly nodded and spun towards the cockpit. Kerelle turned back to their attackers.

They were on their feet again, and a volley of shots absorbed harmlessly into her shield. She flung them over again, a bit harder this time, and tried to think quickly. These men might be unpleasant, but they too were just doing their jobs, and she didn't particularly want to kill them either. But - she absorbed another shot and hit him back hard in the ribs - there weren't a lot of other options presenting themselves.

Suddenly the hatch cycled open again, and several dark figures darted into the room.

She threw up her shields instinctively, before she could even really register what was happening. A scream rang out - the C1. They'd shot him where he cowered against the wall. Footsteps rang rapidly out the hatch - the other guards were fleeing.

Kerelle threw a wave of force to knock the newcomers over as she had the inspection guards. But instead of flying backwards, the strangers merely slid back a short ways, retaining their footing. She got a good look at them for the first time.

There were four of them in dark uniforms bearing the SysTech logo, of a type she'd never seen before. One was collared - a psionic. The other three wore quality psiblockers.

All were heavily armed.

As one they brought their weapons up to fire on her, some kind of light projectiles bouncing harmlessly off her shields. She reinforced the shields anyway and squared off against her opponents. At least they were focused on fighting *her*.

The psiblockers were a complication. Telepathy was out, direct telekinetic force would be weakened, and she wasn't comfortable throwing enough force to overcome their resistance within the confines of the ship. That meant she had to get creative.

One of them ran at her, slowing as he hit her shield as if he waded through molasses. She danced backward and grabbed the first thing her eyes settled on - a metal toolbox settled against the wall.

Another failed volley, another attempted grab. She dodged

again, broke the toolbox open and flung its contents into the air, whirling them around her like some sort of screwdriver tornado. The part of her mind that apparently found mortal peril hilarious noted that she must look ridiculous.

Ridiculous or not, the screwdrivers were currently her best weapon.

She chose one, straightened it out and hurtled it toward one of her foes like she was firing from a slingshot. Momentum, not telekinetics, carried it through the psiblocker's protections to lodge in his body armor. Score one for physics.

The man grimaced but didn't drop - the armor had absorbed most of the force. She had to duck away as his comrades tried to rush her from either side. They were trying to box her in, and she needed to not let them do it.

All maneuvers abruptly ended, however, as the ship lurched violently forward, throwing them all to the ground. The sick whine of tearing, scraping metal blotted out all sound - they were shearing away from the inspection ship's docking arm.

That inappropriate part of her mind chimed in again. *Maybe we can convince Sandrel's repair shop friend to give us a twice-in-a-month discount.*

The room rocketed forward, tossing them all back like rag dolls. The ship had broken free.

Her attackers tried to capitalize on their sudden proximity by tackling her, and she barely rolled away as the closer one stabbed a syringe at where she'd been. Kerelle lunged backwards and used a gentle telekinetic push to move herself out of reach. A frisson of cold skittered down her spine as she regained her feet.

They'd shot the C1 with a standard blaster, but they were using those light projectiles on her. And syringes. They wanted her alive.

It was significantly more frightening than being wanted dead.

They regained their feet as well. She took out the slowest one with a well-aimed screwdriver between the gaps in his armor, and the other two charged. It was closely fought then, with Kerelle keeping up a barrage of projectiles and the two remaining assailants keeping her at bay - and keeping up their own attacks.

One of them maneuvered too close, and got a shot off inside her shields. Kerelle wrenched sideways to dodge it but wasn't quite fast enough. Bright pain lit her shoulder as it grazed her.

The shock to her system was immediate, like being thrown into an icy pool. The screwdrivers clattered noisily around her as she staggered to her knees. Her psionics were quite simply *extinguished*, leaving a horribly numb void, unlike anything she'd ever felt - except when Nalea removed her collar.

Suppressant. They were coated in suppressant.

Kerelle struggled for her feet but knew she wouldn't be fast enough, they were going to overwhelm her -

A short scream pierced through her pounding ears, abruptly cut off. Her eyes jerked up to see the further of her two assailants drop like a rag doll, one of the SysTech psionic's knives embedded in his throat. The attacker closer to her swore loudly and scrabbled for something in his pocket.

He never made it. Before Kerelle could even react, the psionic appeared behind him, hands already moving in a vicious thrust of his other knife. The final commando went limp in his grasp.

Oh holy stars. Teleporter. The rarest of the psionic gifts. Supposedly, no teleporters had been born in decades.

The dark-haired young man nonchalantly wiping his blade on the dead man's jacket indicated that she had been misinformed.

"You escaped your collars and broke your contracts," he said abruptly. "I want in."

"What?" Kerelle sounded inane even to her own ears, but it

was the only response she had as she climbed painfully to her feet. The suppressant's effect was already starting to fade - thank the stars it only grazed her - and her psionics were reassuringly blossoming back to life, but she still felt a bit unsteady. Hopefully that would pass just as quickly.

The teleporter gestured impatiently. "You are Kerelle Evandra and Galhen Tarau Ambrel, yes? The two escaped PsiCorp?"

"We are," she started cautiously, "but - "

The ship banked hard and they were nearly bowled over. Kerelle was abruptly reminded that the dead guards were the least of their worries.

Galhen apparently shared her thoughts. He addressed the newcomer briskly. "None of us are escaping much of anywhere if we don't survive *this* first. If you can help, wonderful, if not stay out of the way." He lifted the fallen C1 over his shoulder with a grunt, and Kerelle belatedly realized he'd dragged the boy to cover at some point during the fight.

Galhen met her eyes. "I'll do what I can for him. The rest of us are in your and Sandrel's hands."

She nodded briskly back, and the ship rocked precariously as something hard struck them. Unbalanced as he was with the C1's weight, Galhen was nearly thrown off his feet. Nalea swooped in to his side and took the C1's other arm over her shoulder to steady him. Galhen gave her a quick nod and they sped together towards the medbay.

Kerelle was already running toward the cockpit, the teleporter close on her heels. The back of her mind appreciated that he could be lying, and luring her into a trap. After watching him effortlessly drop the rest of his squad, however, she had to acknowledge with bleak honesty that if it were a trap he could have sprung it at any time.

Sandrel was tight-faced in the cockpit, sitting silent and still except to lead the ship in its twists and dives. The vidport and the proximity sensors both showed a distressing number of pursuers.

Kerelle braced herself against the wall as he took them into a tight corkscrew, weaving through a narrow gap between two ships docked for inspection. Kerelle's stomach dropped as they squeezed past with no visible clearance, but Sandrel knew his ship, and they burst out the other side with all pieces attached.

A knot of pursuit craft re-formed behind them. Sandrel pulled up from the other ships and shot towards the jump gate. It loomed ahead, tantalizingly close and impossibly far.

Suddenly the gates' steady green lights began to blink amber. Sandrel swore violently, and beside her the teleporter leaned forward in alarm. "They're closing the gate!"

"Well aware of that," Sandrel answered through gritted teeth. His eyes darted quickly over to them, taking in the teleporter, but there was no time for explanations. He gave them both a quick nod.

"Keep them off me, Fury. If this doesn't work, it was a hell of a ride."

He pulled hard on the controls and the ship straightened suddenly, then shot forward straight for the gate.

Kerelle powered up. The aftereffects of the suppressant lingered like a low-grade hangover and her psionics lurched to life a bit reluctantly, as if grumpy to be roused. But roused they were, and when she reached out to wrap the ship in a shield she could draw on her full strength. It'd probably hurt later, but first there had to be a *later* to get to.

The ship was large and unwieldy, and her shield strained and thinned as she struggled to enclose it. A cannon burst hit them hard, and she gasped in pain as the whole shield snapped. This wasn't going to work - the ship was too big. Bracing herself against the wall, she dug deep and reformed the telekinetic shield, this time covering the back side of the ship - uniquely vulnerable, since Sandrel had abandoned maneuvers for pure velocity. Another blast, and this time it held, though the strain of it began to throb behind her temples. Beside her, the engine alarm began to sound.

An explosion startled her eyes open, and the shield stuttered as her concentration skipped. She doubled down on it and opened her eyes again, more deliberately this time.

The teleporter was leaned forward over the copilot's seat with undisguised glee, eyes focused out the vidport on the handful of small fighter craft that were circling in from closer to the gate. Another explosion sounded, and fire blossomed around one of the craft as a crucial piece of it sheared off beneath a telekinetic blow.

A small part of her mind filed that away for that precarious-feeling *later*. He was at least a dual-gift.

The engine alarm rose in timbre and cadence, its nagging bleat crescendoing to a piercing scream. The cockpit was a sea of flashing red lights, and Kerelle was forced to grab on to a seat as they began to violently shake. Sandrel didn't react, kept his eyes on the gate as if mesmerized. They were close now, so very close, but the ring of light was shrinking as the gate closed, smaller, smaller -

Sandrel thrust forward and the world exploded in brightness as they slipped through. The ship shuddered and panic rose in her, they hadn't made it after all, they were going to disintegrate and Galhen would die here with her, impossibly far away, and they didn't say goodbye -

The light abruptly vanished, leaving a painful afterimage seared into her eyes. When her vision cleared, they were in one piece, and the viewport showed only a vast, empty sea of glittering stars.

NINE

FOR A MOMENT THEY ONLY STARED. The warning lights flashed and the alarm retreated to a plaintive beep, but around them all was utterly still. Still and empty.

Kerelle found her voice. "I...don't remember the other side of the jump gate looking like this."

"It doesn't," Sandrel replied grimly. "The gate was nearly closed when we went through. It must have distorted the exit path."

She waited for him to elaborate, but he just stared impassively out at the empty expanse. She finally tried again.

"So where are we, then?"

"I have no idea."

Sandrel's face was calm, but it was the cool facade she had begun to recognize as his response to stress, and beneath it she could clearly sense his rising fear. *We're nowhere, we're nowhere and what if we're too far to get back, what if we're off the map and we can't get back and we just float hopelessly in the empty black, watching the food and the air run out and knowing from the long-range scans that we won't make it to safety before the ship becomes our tomb -*

Kerelle stepped back involuntarily as she forced up a

stronger shield. Sandrel looked sharply up at her. She lifted her hands in apology.

"I'm sorry, I didn't mean to eavesdrop. You're...projecting loudly."

He waved off her apology, suddenly seeming more tired than anything. "It's not for sure." He knew exactly what she'd overheard. "I'll see what I can do to get our bearings. If the hyperdrive isn't too banged up we'll be fine." He turned back to the vidport, his eyes far away. "You should go check on your boyfriend."

He was prevaricating and she knew it - even if the hyperdrive was functional, if they had been thrown far enough off course it wouldn't be enough. There was a reason that you had to use the jump gates to get to Morafer instead of hyper. But whatever could or could not be done was up to Sandrel. She would accomplish nothing by hovering around him, and he very obviously wanted some time alone.

The teleporter followed at her heels as she headed briskly to the medbay. The situation there was not an improvement.

The smell of blood and antiseptic hit her immediately. Inside, Galhen bent over the C1, surgical instruments glinting as he tried to mend something Kerelle didn't want to see too closely. The medbay was silent but for the slow beeping of the monitor, and Galhen's terse requests for Nalea to hand him items. In this moment there was no tension between the two siblings - two furrowed brows bent over their patient in concentration, united by their work. The resemblance between them had never been stronger.

She lingered a moment in the doorway before turning to leave, loathe to interrupt them. Through her shields she could sense Galhen's rising despair, ruthlessly shoved beneath a defiant determination. He was fighting for the C1's life, and afraid he was going to lose.

With a pang, she realized they didn't even know the C1's name.

Wordlessly she shut the medbay door behind her and started back up the corridor. The teleporter followed her in silence. Apparently they were friends now. Or something.

A sense of uselessness settled over her as she retreated from the medbay and its crisis, as she had from the cockpit and *its* crisis. With nothing that needed to be exploded, there wasn't much she could really do to help.

Metaphor for her life, really.

Absent any other productive task, she headed back to the hatch where they'd fought the mysterious SysTech squad. She might as well clean up the mess they'd made - and, she admitted, it was far past time to get some answers out of their strange new acquaintance.

The bodies were still sprawled by the hatch where they'd fought, blood pooled and smeared where they'd been thrown by the ship's maneuvers. A quick search of the ship turned up a small cabinet stocked with cleaning chemicals and disposable gloves. The teleporter joined her as she settled into the macabre task of cleaning up bodies and blood alike.

For his part, he seemed unbothered. "We're tossing these out the airlock, right?"

"Yes," she agreed cautiously. She wouldn't have put it quite so baldly, but he simply shrugged and made to grab the closest body by the ankles.

It was an absurd time to get to know someone, and as good a time as any.

"So," she started.

He paused and looked up at her expectantly. It was the first good look she'd gotten at his face - he was younger than she'd first thought, probably late twenties, his smooth hair raven-dark and his pale golden skin unlined. Ice-blue eyes, framed by thick soot-black lashes, watched her with a trace of amusement.

"So I appreciate that you've helped us thus far," she continued, "But there are still a lot of open questions about what you're doing here and why. Let's start this over. You already know I'm Kerelle Evandra, C3 telepath C3 telekinetic, lately of the SysTech PsiCorp. Who are you?"

"Ilyen Kirana Vanadariel. C2 teleporter, C2 telekinetic. Assassin, infiltrator, totally done with SysTech and their bullshit. You should appreciate that - from what I hear you were done with it too."

Well, he wasn't wrong. "All right Ilyen. Forgive me for being blunt, but it's been a hell of a day and I doubt either of us have the patience at this point to dance around things. What is it you want from us, why did you just kill your team, why should we trust you, and who the hell *were* these people?"

"I've already told you what I want. I want this damn collar off, and if you're throwing bricks through SysTech's window I want in on that too."

He made a little noise of disgust and gestured at the bodies. "And to answer two questions at once, these people were a psionic suppression black-ops squad. They're specially trained to fight psionics, hence the fancy toys, and hence why I ended them before trying to escape." He snorted at her raised eyebrows. "Oh, don't give me that look. They weren't 'my team,' and I didn't owe them shit. I was a tool to them, not a comrade, same as any PsiCorp to the SysTech machine." His voice was shaded with contempt, as if challenging any delusions she might hold to the contrary.

She might not like his tone, but once again, he wasn't wrong.

"I've never heard of psionic suppression soldiers," she commented slowly. Her eyes raked over the black-clad bodies, and a chill went down her back. These people were specially trained, and specially armed, to kill people like her. Either SysTech was paranoid...or they weren't the first to escape.

Ilyen only shrugged nonchalantly. "Yeah well, you wouldn't.

The whole program's highly classified, regular PsiCorp never encounter them. Well," he amended, "never encounter them and live, anyway."

"And you aren't 'regular PsiCorp?'"

He rolled his eyes. "Hardly. I was fast-tracked for a shitty childhood in a military facility as soon as they found out I could port *and* blow things up. But that's enough about that," he said abruptly, crossing his arms. "There's your answers on why I'm here and why I dropped the squad. As for trust, you're a telepath. Go ahead and look."

She did, resting a light hand on his temple - as much to communicate what she was doing as anything. His resentment for SysTech burned hot at the surface of his mind, and she could sense that it ran wide and deep. Confidence in his abilities, a fierce yearning for freedom, a buried whisper of vulnerable uncertainty. No hint of duplicity. He was telling the truth.

She pulled back, lost in thought. She sensed a volatility in him that gave her pause, but unless he was *also* a C3 telepath with amazingly strong defenses - and she had no indication he was a telepath at all - he was sincere about wanting his freedom. She and Galhen had won *their* freedom - in good conscience, could they deny it to anyone else?

Ilyen's impatience grew visible. "Here. I'll even make a show of good faith." He reached blithely into the dead squad leader's pocket and withdrew something small. He handed it to her - a control card.

"The card for my collar. There's your insurance on me. I don't have *any* insurance on you, so don't screw me on this." He met her eyes, expression fierce. "Promise you'll take it off."

Her question to herself was answered. She couldn't look into his eyes and tell him to remain a SysTech slave.

"We'll take it off," she said slowly. "But there are some things you should know about how that works."

Kerelle filled him in as they worked then, cycling the remains out the airlock and scrubbing any evidence off the floors. It was a gruesome task, and the explanation was a welcome distraction from the reality of what they were doing. She knew, intellectually, there hadn't been much choice about how the fight had gone. These people had come here specifically to either murder or capture them - she still wasn't quite sure which - and they had already demonstrated no qualms in shooting bystanders. And if it meant protecting her friends, Kerelle admitted to herself that she'd send a thousand commandos straight to the void. But it still felt like a failure to be cycling fallen enemies out the airlock to the eternal black, a vivid statement that her days as a weapon were not quite behind her after all.

Ilyen might be an odd companion, but when the last of it was done, she was grateful not to be alone.

For his part, he listened quietly as she went through the process of the removal, and if he was nervous he didn't show it. Ilyen simply nodded as if temporarily dying were a perfectly reasonable thing.

"If that's what it is, then that's what it is. I want to get this thing off before SysTech realizes what happened and flips it on."

Understandable, but also not currently an option. "I don't know how to do it - you'll need Nalea or maybe Galhen, and they're busy in the infirmary." Then, less because she was a good hostess than because she desperately needed a cup herself, "Would you like to wait with tea?"

They were in the mess a short time later when Galhen and Nalea joined them, looking worn. They both accepted tea, and sat heavily down.

"We got him stabilized," Galhen explained unprompted. He didn't sound happy, and his eyes fixed on his teacup with a bleak stare.

It was quiet a moment before he spoke again. "He'll live for now, but that shot did a lot of damage, and the ship's medbay isn't set up for that kind of trauma. He needs a real hospital, or else a good psionic healer. As it is there will likely be permanent damage."

Kerelle didn't ask if Galhen believed he could have prevented that permanent damage with his psionics - from the look on his face, he did. She reached out and silently took his hand. She knew her Galhen - telling him he'd done his best would only make him feel worse, driving home that his best hadn't been good enough. He squeezed her hand softly in acknowledgement but didn't look up.

Kerelle sighed softly. As much as she wanted to give him time and space, there was the matter of Ilyen to deal with - whose eyebrows had climbed quite high during their exchange.

The teleporter leaned forward, elbows firmly planted on the small table. "Aren't *you* a psionic healer? Aren't you a *Class-3* psionic healer?"

Galhen's jaw clenched. "That resource is currently unavailable," he answered tersely. He looked up for the first time, eyes narrowing at Ilyen. "And who in the burning void *are* you?"

Kerelle caught them up as they sipped their tea. Galhen listened, his eyes on Ilyen. Frustration vibrated down his hand, now clenched around hers. She could guess the source. This would be an excellent time for a now-impossible silent telepathic discussion.

The first flicker of doubt crossed Ilyen's face when she disclosed the removal had affected Galhen's powers. She referred to it as burnout, but he clearly picked up that it might be more than that. His forehead creased slightly, though he said nothing.

"If you still want to go ahead," she said finally, "And Nalea or Galhen is able to perform the procedure, we can remove your collar. But keep in mind that this is a very serious choice." She met his icy eyes. "It's not too late to pretend we killed those agents and overpowered you. Getting the collar off means a lifetime on the run, with people like you trying to kill us."

He drained his tea and loudly set down the empty cup. "Evandra, if I was trying to kill you, you'd be dead. But yes. It's worth it. Fuck SysTech, and fuck following their orders." His voice took on a faint singsong quality. "I understand the procedure, I understand the risks, I understand the consequences. That good enough, or do I need to sign a waiver?"

From Galhen's expression he had considerable reservations still, but he nodded his acquiescence. Perhaps he'd had the same thought Kerelle did, that they could not deny another psionic the freedom they'd taken for themselves. He turned to Nalea where she sat silently at the edge of the group, sipping her tea and listening.

"You're the only one of us with experience on this. Are you comfortable performing the removal procedure in less than ideal circumstances? Our injured patient is in the only bed in the medbay, and he'll need to improve substantially before I'm willing to entertain moving him."

"Considering SysTech could figure things out and start trying to kill me at any time here," Ilyen cut in, "*I'm* comfortable with it."

Nalea spoke up for the first time.

"I took Kerelle's off in a half-collapsed ruin on Zharal V, and yours had complications from the collar's activation. Arguably he'll get the most ideal circumstances we've ever had." She cut Galhen a quick glance then. "You should be there though. I'm not a medical doctor and it's kind of a miracle neither of you died."

Rather than looking nonplussed by that statement, Ilyen leaned back and broke into a grin. "There you go, we already know it's crazy enough to work. When can we start?"

TEN

"ALL THINGS CONSIDERED," Nalea noted as Ilyen's eyes began to flutter, "that was the least terrifying removal I've done." It had indeed gone quite smoothly. Nalea and Galhen had swapped roles from earlier, with the scientist taking the lead while he acted as her assistant. Whatever awkwardness there might be between them in regular interaction, they worked well together in the lab.

Ilyen blinked fully awake then, his gaze sweeping across them in momentary confusion. Understanding dawned, and the teleporter broke into a pained but triumphant grin.

"See? I knew you wouldn't kill me."

"Yes, I'm getting to be an expert at this," she answered evenly. "How do you feel?"

His brow furrowed in concentration for a moment, and suddenly he vanished and appeared unsteadily in the corridor behind them.

"Shit, that was a bad idea," he laughed with a wince, leaning heavily against the wall for support. "But I think it means I'm fine."

Nalea raised her eyebrows at him. "Yes, I would have advised *not* doing anything like that for several hours afterwards. But it looks like your psionics came through unaffected." She carefully did not look at Galhen. "I would now strongly advise that you get some rest to sleep off the aftereffects."

He didn't argue, just gave her an amused salute and staggered off towards the bunks. Nalea watched him go, then let her gaze drift back towards the discarded collar.

"Kerelle, do you still have that control card he gave you?"

She fished it out of the pocket she'd shoved it in after Ilyen had handed it to her. He'd called it "insurance," but she didn't think she'd be able to deliberately activate a collar even if the person wearing it *was* trying to kill her.

Nalea turned the little piece of metal over in her hand and glanced back to the collar again. "I'll take it off your hands, if you don't mind. There's some tests I'd like to run on how it interacts with the collars." Nalea scooped up the card and collar both. "After some rest myself, maybe. It's been a hell of a day." She paused on her way out. "If we run into any more life-threatening crises in the next few hours, just let me sleep through it."

Kerelle could relate.

KERELLE HAD HOPED a solid night's rest might do all of them good, but apparently even floating aimlessly in deep space, rest was too much to ask for. They had scarcely settled into bed when the little medbay's monitor trilled in alarm, and then they were rushing down the corridor. Galhen took quick stock of the readings and swore softly.

"Is there anything I can do to help?" She asked quietly. He shook his head, attention on what he was doing.

"Go to bed, darling. I'll be along when I can." She hesitated a moment longer, watching the worry lines settle into his face, and left him to work without distraction. There was nothing she could do for their C1 except stay out of Galhen's way.

Very late, or very early, the sound of her cabin's door dragged her partway to wakefulness. Even after Galhen's weight settled on the bed, his restless tossing kept her from drifting back into sleep. Finally she sleepily gathered him into her arms, pressing her lips to the nape of his neck. He stilled then and she felt his muscles relax somewhat against her, but judging by the dark blotches beneath his eyes the next morning sleep had still proved elusive.

Kerelle watched him surreptitiously over the top of her mug, as they drank their coffee in silence. Galhen had been withdrawn since they woke up, and though he'd accepted the cup she offered with a muttered thanks, he now seemed content to stare broodingly into its contents. He'd managed to get the boy stable again, but judging from his mood "stable" wasn't enough. Her senses twanged plaintively at the maelstrom of self-loathing and despair emanating from across the table. She didn't bother to raise shields. His projections were proving difficult to block.

Kerelle had no idea how to comfort him. Normally she would offer her feelings of warmth and affection, enfold his thoughts with hers in a psychic embrace. Feel his grief alongside him, and offer him hope and love to hold on to and pull himself forward. None of that was an option now, and a clasped hand seemed woefully inadequate. And what could she say? How did you put these feelings into words? How could words ever be enough?

And...to be horribly honest with herself, her own emotional reserves were running thin as well. Whatever she could do for him, she wanted to do, but Kerelle was beginning to feel stretched thin enough to be translucent.

This really wasn't going at all like she'd imagined it.

The thought was so patently absurd, her tired mind found it hilarious, and a helpless, hopeless giggle bubbled up through her lips. Galhen lifted his shadowed eyes to hers in question.

Kerelle spread her hands helplessly. "Being an intergalactic fugitive is proving much less appealing than it looked in the movies."

Galhen blinked at her for a moment before he was startled into laughter as well. The sound of it unclenched something in her gut.

"It certainly isn't at all like the brochure," he answered, the side of his mouth quirking up. She could sense clearly that he was tired and feeling beaten down, but the smile he gave her was genuine - albeit a bit sad. He leaned forward, setting his neglected coffee aside.

"I'm sorry," he told her softly. "This is at least as difficult for you as it is for me, perhaps more so because the burden of protecting us falls on you alone. And I haven't been much of a shoulder to lean on." This time he was the one to take her hands. "We'll get through this together, darling, however it ends."

"I love you too," she answered him with a small smile. "And you have nothing to apologize for. I only wish I could do more." She lifted his hands briefly to her lips. "And if this *is* how it's all going to end, there's no one I'd rather starve to death with in the dark reaches of space."

"Nobody's starving to death in space, at least not this week," Sandrel announced as he ducked into the mess. He glanced quickly at their joined hands, gave a small shrug and seated himself. "I found us, and it could be a lot worse. The bad news is we're lightyears away from civilization and the hyperdrive is sputtering more than I'm comfortable with for a long-haul jump."

He poured himself some coffee. "The good news is I can fix it, though not while we're actually in space, and once it's fixed we're still in range to hyper back to humanity. The even *better* news is, there's a small moon nearby that the charts mark as habitable, and the hyperdrive has enough juice left to get us there." He toasted them with his coffee and leaned back to rest his feet on the table. "We're saved."

Kerelle couldn't quite relax at that pronouncement. If Nalea's defense mechanism was a porcupine, keeping others at bay with sharp words, then she'd realized that Sandrel's was a turtle. When things got rough, he retreated into his cool, sardonic persona like a shell. His aggressively laid-back posture as he downed his coffee rather informed her that they weren't out of danger just yet.

Still, it was a vast improvement over yesterday, and she said so.

"Mm, definitely." Sandrel gave her a meaningful glance. "Speaking of yesterday, I can't help but notice we have more people than when we started. Why don't you fill me in on what happened back here?"

She did. Sandrel's eyebrows went up when she got to the part about the C1 and Ilyen, and he sipped his coffee pointedly.

"We couldn't just abandon them," she finished, aware that she sounded rather defensive. "The kid would have died - might still die - and morally we...we couldn't refuse to help another person escape."

Sandrel continued to watch her silently, eyebrows still up.

"And there wasn't time to discuss it with you, because you were busy with..." *saving all our lives, again,* was the proper end to that sentence. A rush of guilt swept up on her then - both that Sandrel had once again had to pull them out of the fire, and that she'd essentially commandeered his ship while he was doing it. Her face went hot.

From Sandrel's growing smirk, he was aware of what she'd meant to say, and he was enjoying watching her squirm a bit. He finally set his cup down with a chuckle.

"All right, and I would have done the same, but I'm not running a mobile hotel here. Let's check in before we add any more guests, hm?" He leaned forward again, dark eyes glinting.

"Or at least let me know before I run into a stranger on my way to the lav."

Oops. Sounded like Ilyen might be joining them soon for coffee.

She blushed again. "Yes. Sorry. And....thank you, Sandrel. We owe you everything."

"Yeah, Fury," he agreed good-naturedly, "you pretty much do. But I didn't want to die in space either, so I'm really helping myself here." He poured himself another cup, looking more genuinely relaxed than he had earlier.

Galhen had been quiet through the exchange, but now he cocked his head. "Why do you call her *Fury*, anyway?"

Sandrel laughed. "You ever been on a military cruiser with Fury-class guns? The big kind, that blow smaller ships out of the sky? That's what your girlfriend hit them like when we got attacked by pirates over Kalnis and she insisted on manning the gunnery. Took me *completely* by surprise, I'd had her pegged as some executive's daughter who had a falling out with Mommy, probably related to whatever she was doing on Zharal V to start with. And since she was a little cagey with names at that point..."

Kerelle gave up trying not to laugh. "*Executive's daughter? Really?*"

"Well what was I *supposed* to think?" He got up to pour another cup, calling back over his shoulder with a teasing glint in his eye. "I was minding my own business getting drunk on Zharal V, when this one comes in, asks for some illegal shit with no subtlety *at all*, offers to pay me in fine jewelry. If she were a decade younger I'd have thought she ran away from boarding school."

"I didn't do *that* badly," she replied archly. "You *did* agree to do it."

"Yes, my judgement is terrible sometimes." He said it with a grin and leaned back against the countertop. "Besides, wouldn't be the first time I'd met a higher-up's kid who was out *finding themselves* by embarrassing their parents, though you're a little old for it. By this age most of them have gotten it out of their systems and taken corporate jobs themselves."

"Is that common?" She asked curiously. Despite growing up in SysTech custody, she'd really never had much contact with its employees outside the PsiCorp. The mysterious psionic girl at Dalanva's party, she realized with a start, was the first member of an executive's family she'd ever encountered.

Who knew, maybe they were *all* secretly uncollared psionics.

Sandrel chuckled, though there was a rueful note in the sound. "I think it depends on the kid. I'm sure some of them go straight to business programs like good little scions. The more rebellious types tend to be more like my ex - dropped out of university to 'reject the fruits of the corrupt corporate machine,' spent a year slumming around with me, went back when he realized the fruits of the corrupt corporate machine were a hell of a lot more comfortable than sleeping in cargo holds and running small-time contraband."

"I'm sorry," Kerelle replied automatically. Sandrel laughed.

"Don't be, by that point I was mostly relieved. Jadren wasn't the *worst* decision I made in my early twenties, but he's probably in the top five." He gave her a wink. "But you can see how I was pleasantly surprised that you could tie your own shoes."

Sandrel downed the rest of his second cup and plunked the mug in the dish sanitizer, then pushed himself off the counter towards the cockpit.

"Anyway, if there are any other mysterious new guests aboard the ship, let them know that we should be coming up on the moon in a few hours. With any luck, we'll be repaired and back on our way to civilization in no time."

THE LITTLE MOON was encouragingly green. Once again everyone was crowded into the cockpit, this time to get a look at their lifeline. Sandrel leaned back in the pilot's chair with an air of satisfaction.

"Here we are, ladies and gentlemen. B-7104 in all its glory."

"That's really what it's called?" Ilyen deftly pushed past Kerelle to get a better look. She bit back an irritated response at the jostling.

"That's really what it's called. From the notes, it doesn't seem like anyone's been here since the initial survey. I guess they didn't bother to name it." Sandrel scanned the notes on the chart. "Looks like a fairly standard garden world - we can breathe down there, gravity's light but reasonable, some flora and fauna safely edible by humans. Not bad."

Galhen frowned. "If this moon is such a picnic, why isn't it colonized?"

Sandrel's brow creased as his dark eyes flicked across the text. "Sounds like the survey team didn't think it was worth it. It's in the ass-end of space with no significant resource deposits, making the remote location economically impractical, and...oh." He looked up at them. "Apparently there are giant predator reptiles in the jungles that would have to be dealt with before any permanent settlements became viable." He stretched. "Well, didn't see *that* coming."

"Giant predator reptiles," Nalea repeated flatly. Her expression spoke volumes.

Kerelle wasn't thrilled about that either, but it was still better than starving to death in the void. "Should we plan to avoid jungles, then?"

"Looks like most of the moon is jungle, but sure, we can start with that. We won't be here long, just enough to do some repairs and stock up on supplies." Sandrel had his aggressively-unconcerned shell up again. Apparently the reptile prospect unnerved him as well. "Besides," he continued a bit more forcefully. "We've got guns and you, Fury. We haven't met an obstacle yet that you couldn't blow up for us."

"You have me now too," Ilyen cut in eagerly. "We'll be more than a match for giant reptiles." The teleporter's icy eyes glittered, and he seemed problematically excited about the possibility of proving that out.

"Hopefully it won't be necessary," she commented firmly. He gave her a half-shrug and turned back to the vidport.

"Here's hoping," Sandrel agreed. "Strap in, kids. Sooner we get ourselves landed and repaired, the sooner we get on our way out of here."

THE DESCENT to the moon's surface was smooth, and refreshingly uneventful.

"I'd forgotten what it was like to land without being shot at," Kerelle murmured to Sandrel as he gently deposited them on a wide clearing. He gave her a smirk back.

"Feels weird, doesn't it? I'm hoping we can make it a regular thing."

The scans confirmed viable air and gravity, and showed no large life forms in the vicinity. Armed with the best assurance of safety they were likely to get, they opened the hatch and stepped out into their unlikely refuge.

The air was warm but not unpleasant, and the breeze carried with it a faint scent of flowers from deeper in the forest. Their makeshift landing pad was a large grassy plain, bounded by trees whose gnarled trunks and spreading branches somehow conveyed a primal timelessness. Kerelle had visited rural worlds, sometimes with wide swathes of undeveloped land, but none with such a pure sense of *wilderness*. They were, she realized with a start of wonder, perhaps only the second group of humans to ever set foot in it.

For a moment they all simply stood and looked around them. It was Sandrel who finally broke the quiet.

"All right, nobody wander off alone. We should be the only people for lightyears in any direction, but the wildlife might get feisty." He indicated a hand back up the ramp. "I'm going to get started on the hyperdrive. The scans showed a freshwater river a kilometer or two south, why don't you lot get the auxiliary water tanks filled and the purifiers started up in the meantime? Also, you can take the list of edible plants, see if you spot anything we can make for dinner."

Kerelle hid a smile. Sandrel rather transparently wanted to get them out from underfoot for the repairs.

"I think we can manage that," she answered. "We'll have our comms up if you need anything." Sandrel gave her a wave as he vanished towards the engine room.

"I'll stay behind as well," Galhen told her. "Our C1 is still fragile, and I don't want to leave him unattended for too long." Kerelle couldn't disagree, and so a short time later she set out for the river with Ilyen and Nalea.

Despite their source's note that the predator reptiles were mostly nocturnal, Kerelle felt a nervous thrill down her spine as they passed out of their clearing and into the trees. But nothing leapt out from the underbrush to snatch them in its jaws, and anyway this part of the forest was hardly thick enough to count as a jungle. Hopefully that meant all the reptiles were further in.

In a way, the isolation was comforting. The water tanks were large and unwieldy, but with no other human eyes to hide from Kerelle could simply float them along with her power. It felt oddly brazen - and oddly exhilarating.

Ilyen seemed to feel the same. Not content to walk alongside Kerelle and Nalea, he kept popping out of thin air a few meters in front of them, sometimes on the ground and sometimes amidst the gnarled branches of the trees. At first his sudden vanishings and reappearances were unsettling, but Kerelle found she got used to it surprisingly quickly. What was one more impossible thing?

"Do you have any idea how he *does* that?" Nalea asked her in a low undertone. She was watching Ilyen with considerable interest. "He reappears with all his clothes and weapons, so obviously it's a power he can exert on matter besides just his own body. Do you think he has to bring things along consciously, or if it's a set field of influence around him? I wonder if there's a mass limit to what he can teleport with?"

"I have no idea," Kerelle told her honestly. "I was taught that teleportation is once-in-a-generation rare, and that nobody knows much about it." Of course, she'd also been taught that there *weren't* any currently-living teleporters, and that was clearly not the case. She wondered what proportion of her education had been complete bullshit. "You'd probably need to direct those kinds of questions to Ilyen himself."

"I might," Nalea answered thoughtfully. Her gaze followed Ilyen's lithe form as he swung down from one of the trees, popping away again a few centimeters away from the ground. "Something to add to my growing body of unpublishable research."

Kerelle wasn't sure how to respond to that, so she just nodded and checked their position relative to their destination. Mechanics of teleportation aside, Ilyen *was* a bit of a puzzle. Sometimes he was all sarcasm and hard edges, and sometimes - like now - alight with joyful enthusiasm. If he was going to be staying with their little group for any length of time, she really ought to try to get to know him better.

She'd never been great at small talk, admittedly, but no time like the present to improve.

They reached the river after roughly twenty minutes of walking. It was wider than she'd been expecting, a broad expanse of clear waters rushing before them as low plants crowded the banks. The water sparkled invitingly, but there was no way

Kerelle would consider a swim - if this world supported giant predator reptiles, then stars only knew what lurked beneath the surface.

There were small pumping mechanisms built into the tanks, thankfully, so they were able to start the water collection without getting their hands dirty. Soon the tanks were humming along at their task, which left their little group at loose ends until they were filled. Ilyen had settled himself on the grass, cheerfully munching something appropriated from Sandrel's pantry. Kerelle sat herself down next to him.

"How are you feeling?" She asked. It seemed like a reasonably good conversation opener.

"Pretty damn good," he answered. "Dr. Ambrel knows her shit." He gave Nalea a blinding smile, and a faint flush crept up the scientist's cheeks. Kerelle kept her face neutral, suspecting as he leaned back in a subtle flex that Ilyen was well aware of the effect his sculpted features and gymnast's physique could have on others.

She was forced to admit, personality quirks aside, he *was* rather stunning. And certainly in no need of encouragement.

"Nalea's at the top of her field," Kerelle agreed instead. "I'm glad we were able to help." It was quiet for a beat as she cast around for something else to say. How did Galhen chat with strangers so easily?

"It's really amazing that you can teleport," she offered, wincing internally. There was probably *something* sillier she could have said. Probably.

"Sure, I guess?" He cocked his head at her and smirked. "You're not much of a conversationalist, are you, Evandra."

Nalea's cough sounded suspiciously like it was covering a giggle.

Well, screw it then. "It's not the top line on my dossier," she replied archly. He shrugged, looking more amused than anything.

"It's not on mine either. I'm gonna guess both of us are better at blowing people up than talking to them."

Again a wince, again he wasn't wrong.

"Still," she rallied. "It must have been interesting, growing up so unique. I imagine you won all the playground games."

He laughed again, but this time it sounded bitter. "Yeah see, you would need a playground for that. And other kids. The black ops intake facility was pretty short on both."

He rolled his eyes at her expression. "What, you think they just set up at some kind of career fair at the Academy and interview people?" He pitched his voice in a mocking imitation of the imagined interviewer. "'Hey there youngsters, ever thought about signing up to play top secret commando? Live in a cell on a secret base, eat shitty rations, get pushed around by a corporate asshole who thinks he's hot shit, but at least the money's good! Ha, just kidding, you don't get paid!'"

He flopped back and gave her an almost challenging look. "If you're going to be a psionic in the the black ops program, you grow up in it, and management doesn't fuck around. All that company-funded high life is *your* PsiCorp, not mine."

She sensed the edge of resentment there, even without his projected feeling. "It wasn't worth it," she answered softly. "None of it was."

He looked unconvinced. "Maybe not. But at least you got to wade through all their bullshit in designer boots. But eh." He stretched again, grinning broadly in another of those lightning mood shifts. "It's alright! I'm out of that shit now, and all lined up with an exciting life of foraging for weird vegetables and fighting off dangerous wildlife."

He still, she thought, sounded unreasonably excited about that.

ELEVEN

THEY TOOK precautions to raise the shields before calling it a night, but it proved unnecessary. The ship slept undisturbed by ferocious wildlife, and when the bright sun crested the treeline it brought a new day in more ways than one.

"Take your time," Galhen told their C1 soothingly. "Your body has been through a great deal. Just try to take sips as you can, you'll feel better when you've had a bit to drink."

The boy clutched his tea like it was all that kept him from drowning. He was groggy and clearly in pain, but also awake and alive. Neither of those things, Galhen had shared privately, seemed guaranteed the day before.

Kerelle was in her increasingly familiar post at the door of the medbay, hovering awkwardly as their patient gingerly lifted his mug. Galhen simply waited at his side with enviable serenity. She knew he must be eager to get more information about their mysterious patient, but his manner offered only calm patience, as if he had all the time in the world to wait until the C1 was recovered enough to talk. She met his eyes and he offered her a half-smile that seemed to convey a reminder, that this was hardly his first time in this position.

At length the C1 had worked through most of his mug. Under the revivifying effects of the tea, his eyes were sharper and more aware than they had been when he first awoke - for better and for worse. The boy stayed quiet with his eyes down, but his knuckles whitened around the mug, and Kerelle felt icy bursts of near-panic beginning to form against her senses.

Galhen didn't have his telepathy, obviously, but apparently the physical signs were indication enough for him to sense the same thing. "We're not going to hurt you," he said gently. "Can you tell me your name?"

"Oliven," came the whispered reply. The boy's eyes stayed determinedly on the ground.

"It's good to meet you, Oliven. You gave us a scare there, but your vitals are recovering now, and I believe you'll be all right."

He nodded at the boy's muttered thanks and continued. "Do you know where you are?"

If anything, Oliven's fear grew more pronounced. "You're the terrorists." The words were barely audible. "I'm on your ship, aren't I."

"You are on our ship, yes, but I assure you we are not terrorists, and we don't mean anyone harm."

Oliven nodded tightly, looking wholly unconvinced. Galhen gave him another of those serene smiles. "This is a lot to take in, and you still need a lot of rest. I've left you a comm on the bedside, and please don't hesitate to call me if you need anything. I'll be back to check on you in an hour or so."

He got up then, and Kerelle followed him out of the medbay with a smiling nod at Oliven. Kerelle held her question in until they were out of the hall.

"Is he *actually* going to be all right?"

Galhen let out a breath. "I'm not sure. His vitals are on the mend and all things staying the same, he should pull through."

"But?"

"But it will be some time before he's in any sort of health to risk removing the collar. And the longer he has it, obviously, the more chance that SysTech will kill him despite all our efforts."

"We've got bigger problems than *that*," Ilyen cut in. Kerelle started as he emerged from around the corner - apparently, he had no compunctions about eavesdropping when he felt like it.

Galhen raised his eyebrows pointedly at the interjection. If Ilyen noticed, he didn't care.

"As long as that collar is active, SysTech can use it to track us," the teleporter pointed out. "That's probably the only reason they *haven't* switched it to kill yet. They obviously don't give a shit about his value as an asset." He glanced around them, though there were no vidports on this part of the ship. "I mean, it'll take them awhile to get enough of a pinpoint to *find* us, since we're in the middle of pretty much nowhere, but it'll happen eventually. They're motivated."

Kerelle sighed. "We really do need to get it off quickly."

"Or just kill him." Ilyen shrugged. "He's just a C1, plus he's kind of a liability. We don't even know if he *wants* to be free or if he'll just go running back to SysTech. Though that would be pretty stupid," he added, "considering they're the ones that put a gunshot through him."

"I hope you're joking," Galhen replied icily. "I will certainly not allow the people in my care to come to harm."

"Doesn't seem like you're really in a position to do much about it," Ilyen countered bluntly. Galhen's whole body tensed.

"I am, though," Kerelle said firmly, stepping between them. "And Galhen is right. Oliven is our responsibility right now." She met the challenging glint in his eyes and held it. "Even if he wasn't, we don't hurt people who aren't a threat to us. We have to be better than SysTech is."

He looked away first, turning to roll his eyes. "Really, Evandra? I thought *you* at least would have some survival instincts." Ilyen shook his head. "Fine then, keep the time bomb. See if all that moral posturing gets you anywhere in a SysTech retraining cell." He lifted his eyes to hers again, jaw set. "When those dropships land, don't expect me to get captured with you. I'll space myself before I go back."

He vanished without another word.

"Dramatic, isn't he," Galhen said flatly. His hands were still clenched.

"Yes," she agreed, watching the empty space Ilyen had been standing in a moment before. "Dramatic and rather more ruthless than I'm comfortable with, but not entirely wrong." She glanced over at him. "We don't have a lot of time to wait."

Galhen's mouth compressed, and the wave of frustration that rolled off him was so intense she almost stepped backwards.

"I'm doing everything I can, which is very little," he answered bitterly. "This would be minutes' work if I were whole."

She rested her hand on his arm. He looked away.

SANDREL ASSURED everyone the repairs were going well, but an unspoken tension arose on the ship as one day became several. Kerelle tried not to think about how they were essentially trapped here until Sandrel finished restoring the hyperdrive. They could still take off if SysTech ships appeared, yes, but without hyper they wouldn't get far. She found herself thinking about what Ilyen had said, that he'd choose suicide over capture, and wondering which was worse. She hoped it never came up.

All the same, he wasn't wrong that SysTech would find them here eventually. It was impossible to say how long it would take to locate them in such a remote system, but everyone was aware the clock was ticking.

Oliven's condition continued to improve, though not quickly

enough. Initially he slept more often than not, his conscious interludes rendered foggy by painkillers. As the days passed, however, he was increasingly awake and, as Galhen steadily reduced his painkiller dosage, increasingly alert. Galhen confided privately to Kerelle that decrease was dictated as much by their rapidly dwindling supply as by medical need.

"We'll just have to hope no one else gets shot before we reach port," he'd commented tersely as he climbed into bed beside her. The ship felt crowded these days, and their little cabin was the only real privacy they had. "Sandrel's medbay is surprisingly, dare I say *suspiciously* well stocked, but it was never designed to function as a trauma center. It's a miracle Oliven survived the first night."

"He had an excellent medic to help him through it," she answered softly. He didn't say anything, and she let it go with an internal sigh. Instead she added, "And I would *hope* nobody would be getting shot before the next time we make port."

Galhen rolled over to give her the ghost of a smile. "With the way things have been going lately we can hardly make that assumption."

She grinned and kissed him lightly. "I prefer to stay optimistic."

He smiled back and stroked her hair, but melancholy lingered in his eyes. "We may all need a bit of optimism in our future."

"You're worried about the collar."

"We all are, aren't we? But removal simply isn't possible right now. Oliven has greatly recovered in that he can sit upright and hold a conversation. That's not *remotely* the same as being able to survive the stress of the removal procedure."

"We may not have a choice soon," she admittedly reluctantly. "We may need to attempt a removal before SysTech loses patience and activates it."

Galhen rolled onto his back and stared at the ceiling. Kerelle waited.

"He shouldn't even *be* here," Galhen said finally. He sounded angry. "We talked a bit, when he was doing better. He's *twenty-one*, Kerelle. This was his first assignment out of the Academy. I had to tell someone who's barely out of the schoolroom that he may never regain full mobility in his left leg, and soon I may need to tell him that we need to risk his very likely death in order to keep SysTech from finishing the job, and for what? Because the thugs they sent after us couldn't tell one psionic from another? Because he had the misfortune to actually accomplish his first assignment, and SysTech wanted to keep things quiet?"

Kerelle rested her head on his shoulder. She didn't have any answers.

"THEY CAN TAKE THEM OFF!" Nalea burst into the mess, nearly colliding with Ilyen. He blinked across the room in an instant, clutching his coffee protectively. Kerelle was seated at the table with Galhen, but put a steadying hand around her own mug just in case.

Nalea was practically vibrating with excitement, and didn't seem to even notice her near miss. "They can take them off," she repeated impatiently. "Not right out of the box, you need to rewire some of the mechanics, but they can take them off, just like that." She looked between them, clearly expecting more of a reaction.

"Can you back up a bit?" Kerelle asked carefully. Nalea gave a small huff of frustration.

"The psionic collars. I've been playing around with Ilyen's, and the control card that went with it, to see if I could find out more about how they work." The teleporter's eyebrows rose at the mention, but for once he said nothing.

Nalea went on. "I wanted to test a couple of hypotheses I had and, well, those didn't work out but it gave me another idea and - " She looked around at her audience and seemed to mentally edit. "I did some experiments, and then I did it. The control card was the key. Just a few small modifications to the hardware and *pop!*" She accompanied the *popping* noise with an exuberant arm motion. "Off it goes. No freaking out, no hopefully-temporary dying, just *pop* and you're done." She looked around, and seemed to notice the breakfast table for the first time. "Hey, is there any coffee left?"

They were all staring at her.

"You're certain of this?" Galhen asked urgently. "It's reproducible, it will work on collars besides Ilyen's?"

"Yes to the first, no data yet on the second," she answered. "You want me to try on the kid in the medbay, right?"

"Yes. If there's any chance we can get his collar off without risking his life it's imperative we not delay." He was already getting up. "Are there any physiological side effects that you could determine?"

"Only what I can conjecture on, since we don't have any data around using it with live humans yet. Based on my devices readings though, I don't expect anything nearly as traumatic as what we've *been* doing."

Galhen flashed her a quick smile and started toward the door. "Arguably there was nowhere to go but up on that. Meet you in the medbay."

Ilyen popped next to Nalea as she turned to go, and pressed a mug of steaming coffee into her hands. "Something tells me you're going to need this before it's all over."

THEY ALL STARED AT IT, sitting innocuously on the medbay counter as if it were a simple piece of jewelry. It was whole and undamaged. As was Oliven. The young C1 sat up silently in the bed, his gaze riveted to the now-dormant collar. The monitor's cheerfully regular chirps confirmed his vitals were undisturbed.

The control card, on the other hand, was a mass of connected wires that implied Nalea's definition of "a few small hardware modifications" was not remotely the same as Kerelle's. Nalea was reexamining it with a critical eye, making notations on her tablet of elements to consider later. Perhaps there were ways the method could be improved, but as far as Kerelle was concerned, it was enough that it worked at all.

"Nalea, this is incredible." She couldn't keep the wonder out of her voice. "I would never have thought this was possible."

Nalea shrugged nonchalantly and kept her attention on her notes, though a pleased smile crept over her lips. "The collars really aren't *that* much different than the devices I've worked with in my other research. The specifics are, sure, and definitely the *purpose*. I've done most of my work on prosthetics or enhancements or things that aren't about, you know, murdering people. But as far as how they integrate signals with the nervous system, I wasn't exactly starting from square one."

Kerelle suspected Nalea was being modest, but she didn't press. Instead her gaze slid back to Oliven staring at the symbol of his old life with an unreadable expression. She was determinedly staying out of his thoughts, but a bit of broadcast feeling snuck past her defenses anyway - enough to let her know their young patient was not at all sure how he felt about all this. She hoped all he needed was time.

Ilyen watched Oliven as well, half-hidden in the shadow of the corridor. He wasn't a telepath, she knew that for certain now, but he seemed to have picked up on the young C1's mixed feelings all the same. He met her gaze as she walked past him.

"He's not an active threat any more. He's still a liability."

The teleporter's voice was pitched low for her ears alone. Kerelle's lips compressed. She *wanted* to disagree.

"He might just need some time."

Ilyen gave her a skeptical glance. "Did you give him the same speech you gave me, about how getting the collar off meant a lifetime of people trying to kill him? Because he sure doesn't look like he signed the waiver."

Again she wished she could disagree. Instead all she said was, "We'll figure out what to do with him after we get the hyperdrive running again. With the collar off SysTech can't track us here. Worst case we drop him off at a port and go on our way. He doesn't know anything they could use to find us."

Ilyen just shrugged and blinked away.

TWELVE

DESPITE HER PROTESTATIONS that the improved collar removal was not so difficult, it was clear to everyone that Nalea had made a substantial achievement in uncovering it. It was soon equally clear that researching it had given her a distraction from the current situation. With the project over, the scientist's agitation seemed to increase hourly.

"Do we have any idea how much longer this little pit stop is going to take?" Nalea plunked herself down at the end of the mess table with her coffee, a somewhat disgruntled gaze flicking from Sandrel to Kerelle. She didn't look at Galhen. "It's been fun and all, but I've held up my end, and I'd really like to get off this ride and back to my real life."

Her eyes dropped to the table then. "Maybe I should *try* to get attacked by some crazy reptile. At least if I've got evidence of escaping from peril it might deflect some awkward questions when I get back to Olstenfel."

It was quiet a moment, and Kerelle suspected they all were thinking the same thing. It had been almost two months since their escape from Zharal V, with no real explanation for Nalea's whereabouts since. Regardless of what happened now, awkward questions would be a certainty. With a curl of guilt, Kerelle flashed back to their conversation after Kalnis. To everything Nalea had risked to offer them her help - and how little Kerelle could offer her in return for it.

Sandrel broke the silence. "I need another day on the engines, then they'll be as fixed as I can get them out here. We'll still need to take them into a shop for a few things I can't manage, but the ship will hold together long enough to get us there." He glanced over at Nalea. "You still planning to make out like you escaped Zharal and Kalnis, and call Olstenfel for a pickup?" She gave him a single nod. "Alright then. After the engines are ready it'll be another week in hyperspace before we put down in Xan Xaldanan. It's a decent-sized port, you should be able to plausibly call in from there."

Sandrel set down his drink and turned to her. "I know that's still longer than you'd like, but it's the best I can do. We're a million kilometers from anything out here, and there's no faster path back to civilization. If I could get you back sooner, Doc, I'd do it."

Nalea nodded tightly, her face unreadable. She drained the rest of her coffee and got up without another word.

Sandrel exchanged glances with Kerelle, who shrugged. She couldn't tell if Nalea was angry or just done talking. Either way, there was nothing they could really do except try to get home as soon as possible.

Sandrel downed his coffee as well and got up. He gave them a nod and a smile. "Alright lovebirds, I should probably get started to make sure we really do finish up today. Try to stay out of trouble while I'm working. The scenery's nice here, but I think we're all ready to see it in the rear sensors."

He left toward the engine room. Nalea was presumably locked back in her lab, Ilyen was off doing who knows what, and Oliven was well enough that he no longer needed Galhen's hovering presence to ensure his safety. For the first time since they landed, Kerelle and Galhen found themselves at loose ends.

"You haven't been outside the ship much since we got here, and the woods are actually quite lovely," Kerelle offered. "Do you want to go for a walk? We might even be able to find a few of those edible plants Sandrel mentioned, so the trip back isn't *all* instant noodles."

Galhen smiled back, open and relaxed, and with a pang she realized how little she'd seen him like this lately. Kerelle shooed away her thoughts then, determined not to dampen the positive here-and-now.

"That sounds delightful, darling," he told her, rising and offering a hand. "Will you give me the tour of the wildlands, then?"

THEY DID NOT TRY ESPECIALLY hard to look for plants. Kerelle kept an eye out here and there - it *would* be nice to have some fresh food on the journey back - but she was mostly content to just wander through the trees with Galhen's hand in hers. The succession of crises since the rescue had left them little time to simply *be* together. It was a far cry from brightly-blended cock-tails at a sun-soaked resort, but the freedom to meander together talking about nothing, with nowhere to be and no urgent hill to climb, was luxury enough.

It was a beautiful morning for a walk. The lush greenery spoke of frequent rainfall, but whether a luck of season or simply a quirk of local weather patterns, the temperate warmth and cloudless sky had held steady since their arrival. After several days and several trips through the woods without encountering danger, her initial fear of hostile reptiles had faded, and she could simply enjoy the soft-colored flowers and fresh moss-scented air for what they were. Beside her, Galhen's relaxed contentment hummed gently at her senses.

Inevitably, though, the conversation turned to their current situation, and that gentle feeling ebbed away. They both knew the moon's refuge was temporary.

"But we're out of Morafer now," she pointed out. "Hopefully that will dampen Dalanva's ability to reach us?"

Galhen grimaced. "Considering my powers are burned out and I look like a dock worker, she might not *want* me back."

The bitterness in his tone took her aback, and she paused to face him. He sighed and looked away. "In all seriousness - dampen, yes. Eliminate, no. I poured wine and stood quietly behind a lot of important people. Morafer is Dalanva's power base, but she's well-connected outside it."

Kerelle saw her opening then, in his words and in the peaceful, private quiet of the woods. Very carefully, she gathered both his hands in hers, the closest facsimile to the bond that had been taken from them.

Her question was soft. "Do you want to talk about any of it?"

He sighed heavily. "No. Yes. I don't know." His eyes fell on a gently-sloped patch of thick grass, sheltered beneath one of the larger trees. They sat.

For a long moment Galhen stared silently up into its branches, and Kerelle was beginning to think he had decided on "no." She kept his hands entwined with hers and rested her cheek on his shoulder, hoping her touch could provide some support and comfort.

Finally he spoke. "It's not what you might be thinking. She liked to flirt with me in front of her friends, but the furthest it ever went was one particularly unpleasant evening when she had far too much to drink, and slapped my ass when another tipsy socialite made a comment on the fit of my uniform. Hardly an experience I'd care to repeat, but more ridiculous than upsetting." His loud feelings told her otherwise; it had upset him a great deal. But she only squeezed his hands and said nothing. This was his story to tell.

"Even then, it wasn't about *me* at all - it was about having the shiniest bauble to make the other woman jealous. I was a status symbol to Dalanva, nothing more, like the galaxy's most expensive handbag. And 'handbag' was about the level of initiative and autonomy she wanted from me."

He went quiet again, and his roiling emotions pressed against her senses. He didn't want to talk about this, it was bringing the memories back. At the same time, he did - it felt like draining a wound.

"It was something silly," he said at last. His eyes were fastened on the horizon, but his fingers tightened around hers. "She set me a task, I suggested a more efficient solution. She didn't even say anything, just flicked it on and watched me scream. Told me that when I was ready to stop, I could ask my mistress's pardon for speaking out of turn. She was so *calm* about the whole thing, as if this were a perfectly rational way to treat another human being."

"The second time was even sillier than the first. She brought in a top-shelf designer to redo her staff uniforms, and she wanted a bespoke look for her new pet psionic. You know, just in case the fact that I was there at all didn't do enough to convey how rich she was." He didn't bother to disguise his anger. "Her designer suggested I cut my hair to finish the look. I should have known better than to say anything, but I was still in denial that I'd gone from managing planetwide medical operations to being dressed up for tea parties like child's toy. So I said I'd consider it, but I liked my hair the way it was, and then I spent the next several minutes on the floor of the solarium. That time she wouldn't turn it off until I apologized for my behavior and agreed it would be an honor to do as I was asked. The humiliation was almost worse than the pain."

"And the designer just *sat* there?"

"She was highly uncomfortable and felt slightly guilty for suggesting it in the first place, that much projected quite clearly. But yes, she just sat there. She didn't feel she could risk the sort of damage Dalanva could inflict on her career." He glanced over at her quickly. "I suppose that's what set everything in motion, actually. You must have seen the records shortly afterward."

Something in the way he said it made her uneasy. "Why do you say that?"

"Because you only saw two in my file."

Kerelle absorbed that as he lapsed into silence again. She held him and waited.

His voice was quiet. "The last time, we were at the winter estate. One of the cook's children was ice skating and fell into the frozen pond, and it took them too long to pull her out. I could have saved her. But Dalanva had guests arriving, and wanted me to attend her."

He leaned back his head and closed his eyes. Even without telepathy, she could see that this was a difficult story to tell. "I tried to go anyway. Surely she understood the stakes, how I couldn't simply abandon someone who desperately needed my help. Surely there was some drop of human empathy in her, *somewhere*." Galhen's voice had grown thick with emotion, and he took a few slow, deliberate breaths before continuing.

"I made it less than a meter out the door. She stepped over me and went to her luncheon. I lost my voice screaming. The girl died."

"That was the last time. After that I was careful not to give her a reason. Speak when spoken to, obey without question, always present myself so as to reflect well on her. I hated myself for being so easily broken."

Kerelle closed her eyes against the storm of feeling that churned in her guts, a mix of sick grief and burning fury. It was very good, she thought, that she had not heard any of this until now. If she had faced Dalanva at the manse with full knowledge of what Galhen had suffered at her hands, she suspected her resolution to avoid killing anyone would not have held.

"At first I thought SysTech might intervene. I knew the collar would generate reports, and I was a valuable asset with a sterling record. Later I realized what a foolish hope that was. SysTech had decided I was worth less than Dalanva's money when they signed the paperwork. And that was almost the worst part, wasn't it?"

He sat up again, and his voice was low with anger. "Everything I'd done, every team I'd led, every mission I'd salvaged, every life I'd saved, every *horror* I'd been obediently complicit in. None of it meant anything. I was a rich woman's doll now and that was the end of it."

Silence again, but Kerelle sensed he wasn't finished. She stroked his fingers as she waited. Finally he spoke again, but the anger had faded to a dull sorrow.

"It sounds so petty when I say it out loud. It could have been so much worse. It feels like I shouldn't be this affected, shouldn't be this angry, don't have the right to feel this...this violated. Especially..." he swallowed and turned his face away from hers. "Especially with everything you went through to rescue me. I will be eternally grateful you did, but what a poor reward you got. When I think of everything you sacrificed for me - "

No. "For *both* of us," she cut him off. "When they sold you, it made it clear we were never really safe, no matter how well we served. I was done with living in cages, no matter how well disguised." She swung herself over then to meet his eyes. "Dearest, there was no sacrifice. You were the only thing in my life that I couldn't bear to lose."

Galhen stared back at her, eyes bright, and a sudden drop rolled down his cheek. Gently, Kerelle turned his face to her shoulder and drew him closer. Her lover nestled into her embrace, and she held him in her arms as he cried himself out in the quiet of the woods.

"ENGINES ARE DONE," Sandrel announced without preamble. He strode into the mess - quickly becoming the ship's unofficial meeting space - and went straight for the tea. "As done as they're going to get out here, anyway. Water purifiers are done, and we've got enough supplies to get us through hyperspace to Xan Xaldanan. If anyone has any sentimental attachment to our current location, I suggest you make your peace quick. We're taking off first thing in the morning."

Nalea looked less happy than she might have expected to be - perhaps, Kerelle thought, because it meant this plan of hers was about to be put to the test. Ilyen simply nodded and reached for another helping of food. What this meant for him was less clear - it was, Kerelle realized, not entirely clear what it meant for her and Galhen either.

But she smiled then and met Galhen's eyes, only slightly red from earlier that day. He smiled softly back. Whatever Xan Xaldanan had in store, it was a new beginning for them both.

THIRTEEN

THE SOUND HURTLED Kerelle out of sleep. She blinked stupidly at the ceiling, trying to catch up with where she was and why the floor was shaking, and what was that *noise* -

Roar. It was a roar. And the shaking wasn't an earthquake.

She and Galhen locked glances.

"The reptiles," he breathed. They both broke into a run.

Alarms flashed as they sped down the corridor towards the cockpit. The ship shook more violently, and the roar changed tenor. Now it sounded angry.

They met Ilyen and Nalea at the cockpit, but while Nalea was pale and wide-eyed, Ilyen's face shone with excitement. It looked like he was going to get his fight after all.

A string of violent expletives burst forth from the pilot's chair. Sandrel was already here, and not happy with what he saw.

"Shields just took a major hit," he called back. "They're huge, there's more than one, they're trying to take a bite out of us. We need to get clear so I can take off." He spun around to face them. "Doc, lock down your lab and strap in, this is going to be a rough ride out. Fury, Knives, we need all the firepower we can get." He glanced at Galhen. "Do you have any weapons training?"

"Small arms yes, ship weapons no."

"Stay here then and monitor the shields for me." Sandrel spun back around to the controls. "Let's go people, I didn't spend a week fixing these voids-damned engines just to have holes punched in them by the wildlife."

Kerelle ran, grabbing Ilyen's arm as she passed. "Come on, we'll have the best view from the gunnery." He followed fast on her heels up the ladder, and they got their first full look at the enemy.

It stood upright on two massive legs, shorter upper limbs flailing as it lunged forward to bite at them. Something deep and primal quailed in her at the sight of those teeth, nearly half a meter long, embedded in jaws that could easily swallow her whole. The reptile was attempting to snap those jaws around the ship, the shields sparking against it as it slammed forward to try again.

The whole ship shook again under the force of it. A beady eye fixed on them, hungry and malevolent.

"Whatever it just did, we took a 15% hit to shields." Galhen's voice over the intercom was clipped. "I suggest we prevent it from doing so again." Even as he said the words, the ship shuddered again, this time from the other side. With a sick feeling, she recalled that Sandrel said there was more than one.

Time to get at it then.

She threw a wave of force at the one closest to the gunnery, hoping to dislodge it and gain some breathing room. It roared at her, but she'd underestimated its mass, and it held its ground. She set her teeth and gathered strength for another strike - preferably with a projectile this time.

Ilyen came to the same conclusion. "Less pushing, more stabbing, Evandra! We can keep score." He winked and was gone. Kerelle yelped in alarm as he reappeared outside the safety of the shielded ship - atop the head of the enormous reptile.

It whipped its head and threw him almost immediately. Ilyen flipped midair to slow his momentum and popped back to the broad crown of its skull. He drove one of his knives down into its flesh, seeking to create a handhold. It didn't seem to work terribly well, because in another instant he was tossed over again, and again reappeared at his favored perch.

Kerelle cast about for something to strike it with - there, a small-ish tree. She ripped the thin trunk mercilessly from the ground, its tangled roots spraying dirt all around. Another blow sundered the top branches, and she had a rather crude pike. She lined it up and tried to calculate the best angle to injure the beast without risking hitting Ilyen. *Stars* she wished he were a telepath.

The reptile convulsed suddenly, its roar more a shriek of pain. Ilyen leapt clear and reappeared beside her in the ship, breathing hard. One of his knives was still deep in a mess of gore that had been the beast's eye. It thrashed around in a frenzy and Kerelle saw her moment to strike. She drove the makeshift weapon forward like a ballista shot. The reptile shrieked again as it lodged in its side.

The ship shook violently, and another reptile thundered into view, attracted by the other's cries. It looked angry.

"Shields at 40%," Galhen cut in sharply. "Sandrel says he can get a clear takeoff if you deal with the other one, but it has to be soon."

Despite its injuries, the first reptile still struggled against Kerelle's tree trunk. The other simply roared its anger and charged towards them, the full force of its weight bearing down like a metro train.

Kerelle threw up a telekinetic wall to arrest its momentum. A smaller creature would've bounced back as if running up against a physical barrier, but the reptile's enormity was too much for her to stop completely. The force of its massive body striking her shield was like a physical blow, and only Ilyen's quick grip on her arm saved her from tumbling over. Kerelle's ears rang as she steadied herself. *Well* that *could have gone better.*

Still, the beast was slowed, growling with frustration as it struggled forward through the suddenly-resistant air. The engines leapt to life beneath them - Sandrel had his opening.

"We have to keep it at a distance," she panted to Ilyen. Already she could feel the last threads of her shield snapping. He gave her a quick nod and vanished again.

"Ilyen, shit, we're about to take *off!*" But he wasn't there to hear her, of course - because he was outside, scant meters from the raging reptile. He was, she realized with a jolt, trying to grab its attention. And succeeding.

It thrust forward and snapped its jaws at him. For a horrible second Kerelle thought he hadn't dodged in time. But no, there he was, running along its back. The ship started to move.

"Ilyen, get *back* here!" Kerelle pelted the reptile with anything she could grab outside - rocks, branches, woodland debris. It shook off the projectiles and snapped again over its shoulder. Ilyen danced out of reach, his gaze cutting to the ship. They were picking up speed.

A roar from the reptile. A roar from the engine. She was jerked backwards as Sandrel gunned it, unaware that only most of them were inside.

And then suddenly they were *all* inside, as Ilyen appeared in a graceless heap. At her expression, he gave a weak but triumphant grin.

"Evandra," he panted. "You worry too much."

"We almost *left* you! What were you *thinking?!*"

"That I could make it before you got out of range. And I did. Besides," He grinned again and lifted the knife in his hand, still thickly crusted in the reptile's blood. "I didn't want to leave my knives."

IT WAS some time later that they all gathered in the mess around a fresh pot of tea. They were, Sandrel announced, safely in hyperspace, and should make it to Xan Xaldanan on schedule and without complication.

"And yes," he added, "I realize I'm tempting fate by saying so. But unless SysTech pinned down our location *and* developed some way to track us through hyper - in which case we'd have *way* bigger problems - I think we're in the clear."

"As far as I know there's no hyperspace tracking," Ilyen answered, his tone unusually sober. He'd recovered quickly from his bout with the reptiles, with only a few bruises to indicate he'd been in a fight. "But they're not just going to slink away, either. They're trying to keep the whole thing quiet, obviously, but SysTech is freaking out. I mean, I don't blame them."

Ilyen continued as they all turned to look at him. "First there's the whole conference shitshow on Zharal V, then they have a top-ranked agent escape - who then turns around and busts out *another* high-level psionic on lease to a VIP client." He took another long sip of tea. "The best part is, you got away clean, Evandra. When they gave us the briefing, the record they pulled up still said KIA. So when that senator calls them up, says her pet escaped with a telekinetic, and then basically just describes *you*, they realize they've actually lost track of *two* agents, and nobody knew the whole time. Not a great look for management." He added that last bit rather gleefully.

Kerelle digested that with mixed feelings - it was bittersweet to know that the plan *had* worked. That they *weren't* going to look for her. And that now it was all shot to the void.

Galhen sipped his own tea. "How is the board taking it?"

Ilyen's grin was almost feral. "Yeah, not so good. The executive suite might be getting an all-new lineup. Especially," he added, "since I hear that Dalanva woman is threatening to sue for her money back plus damages."

That teased a faint smile out of Galhen. "May they bleed each other profusely in court." The smile faded quickly, though. "She does have the resources to keep dogging us, though, if she chooses to do so. Hopefully her efforts to recoup from SysTech will prove a distraction."

Kerelle sighed. "So we need to keep a low profile, basically forever. We knew that going in."

"About that," Sandrel interjected. "I've noticed that's not your strong suit." He said it with a teasing smile, but his eyes were serious. "Getting you off Zharal was a hell of a payout, Fury, but it won't last forever - especially with the kind of repair bills I've been racking up lately. I'm planning to pick up cargo on Xan Xaldanan and get back into business." He paused to sip his tea, and Kerelle exchanged a questioning glance with Galhen. He gave a tiny shrug; he wasn't sure where Sandrel was going with this either.

"Anyway you all can do what you like, but I'm going back to work and hoping all my contacts haven't dropped off while I was out of the game." He eyed her speculatively over his cup. "You ever thought about signing on with a freighter?"

"A freighter? Like...with you?" She winced inwardly. Hopefully her surprised tone hadn't sounded offensive.

"Yes, with me," he answered, sounding amused rather than offended. "It's been awhile since I had crew, and you're handy to have in a tough spot. Which is great," he added with a grin, "since it's been nothing *but* tough spots since I fell in with you crazy people."

Sandrel set down his teacup. "In all seriousness though - yes, if you're interested, I'll sign you on. *All* of you," he emphasized, meeting each of their eyes in turn. "It'll be the best security this ship's ever had, plus I won't have to patch *myself* up next time things go sideways. And flying under the radar is kind of my specialty."

Kerelle's eyes stung. She thought of Sandrel as a friend, all the more precious for being one of the few she'd managed to make on her own. And she'd seen the generous heart beneath his cool exterior, knew that the taciturn smuggler she'd met in Zharal V was at least partially a persona. Still, this was far more than she would have expected.

"Thank you. I..." she glanced at Galhen quickly, wishing for the thousandth time he still had his telepathy. "We'll have to discuss it, but...are you sure? I would have thought that... well...being involved with us is dangerous..."

"I'm already involved," Sandrel answered bluntly. "If SysTech ever gets wind of it I'm screwed, and now that they know you didn't die on Zharal I can't count on them not figuring it out. Knives is right, they're not going to just let the whole thing blow over, at least not in the near future." He shrugged. "And if SysTech comes knocking, I'd feel a lot safer standing next to you."

He stood up. "Think about it. We've got a week before we make port. You can let me know then what you decide."

———

A WEEK TURNED out to be wholly unnecessary; the decision was made before they'd finished the next pot of tea.

"I want to stay," Kerelle blurted. There'd been no time to think, *really* think, about what happened after they escaped. She'd had some vague idea about going into hiding someplace like Palhee, but now that it was actually becoming real she'd had the most unexpected revelation. Sometime over the last few months the ship had become home.

Her eyes quickly met Galhen's, and she realized belatedly

that he might not feel the same. His experiences on the ship had been a great deal more traumatic.

But he simply smiled softly back at her. "Then we stay."

"Are you certain? I wasn't sure you would want to, after…everything."

"Yes, well, I don't hold 'everything' against the ship. And besides, if I recall correctly, flying around space in a private ship was your childhood dream, was it not? I could hardly stand in the way of that."

"Definitely not, since you promised to be in my crew," she answered with a grin. "I'm surprised you *remember* that conversation."

"The time I somehow convinced the most beautiful girl in our year to come up to the rooftop and talk with me, when she hardly talked to *anyone*? I couldn't ever forget." His smile was warm, but the edges seemed tinged with sadness. Before she could say anything else, she was abruptly reminded they weren't alone.

"You two have been screwing since the Academy? Seriously?" Ilyen was glancing between them with interest.

Whatever Galhen had been thinking about, the moment vanished. Instead he turned to look at Ilyen with undisguised irritation. "I really don't see how that's any of your business."

Ilyen slurped his tea undeterred. "Burning stars, you totally *have*. How are you not bored yet?"

An unexpected flare of anxiety from Galhen, but his expression didn't change. Kerelle rather suspected Ilyen enjoyed getting a rise out of him, and leaned in to guide the conversation away.

"We're not bored because we *love* each other," she said firmly. "Have you ever been with anyone who was important to you?"

"Eh, that long-term shit sounds like a lot of work. I usually just sneak out before they wake up." He smirked. "Probably easier for me than you."

"It's never really come up," she replied drily. He snorted and got up.

"I guess I don't *have* to get it, so long as you take it back to your room. I don't like to watch unless I get to join in." He stretched. "Speaking of, guess I might as well ask Sandrel if there's a signup sheet for cabins."

"You're staying then?" Part of her was surprised. He'd struck her as the lone-wolf type.

Ilyen shrugged. "Not like I have anything better to do right now. I'll stick around until I figure out what I want to do next." *And it's kind of nice to be with people.* Kerelle blushed and upped her shields against the unexpected projection. Ilyen popped away without seeming to notice.

Galhen gave a barely audible sigh. Apparently he'd been hoping Ilyen would pursue other ventures.

Kerelle reached out a hand. "We'll want to check in with Sandrel as well, of course, but he *did* give us all week to decide. Plenty of time," she added with a wry smile, "to indulge in a bit of *boring* first."

He took her hand and rose with a smile of his own, and for a moment that aura of sadness was gone.

SANDREL ACCEPTED their decision with warm claps on the back, and a promise that they'd sort the details out when they got to Xan Xaldanan. He also agreed to Galhen's proposal to upgrade the medbay.

"We've got funds, and stars know the thing's been getting use lately. You're the ship doctor now, just tell me what you think we'll need."

Kerelle was not at all surprised when Galhen spent the rest of the afternoon cheerfully taking an inventory.

Later that night, she found herself lying in their darkened cabin, listening to his soft, steady breathing beside her. Whether it was the stress of the last few weeks finally catching up with her or anticipation of what lay ahead, she was wide awake, despite the clock's assurance that it was still very much the middle of the night. Finally she gave up; tossing and turning was getting her nowhere, and she didn't want to wake Galhen. She carefully got up and slipped out of their cabin.

Kerelle tried to keep her footfalls quiet as she made her way to the mess. There was still a stash of herbal tea in the cupboards; perhaps that would help lull her back to sleep. She rounded the corner to the mess, and stopped. It wasn't empty.

Oliven sat curled in one of the chairs, his own mug of tea clasped in both hands. He looked just as surprised to see her, and slightly alarmed. They stared at each other a moment as Kerelle cast about for something to say.

"Oliven...are you supposed to be up and about by yourself?" Wonderful, that hadn't sounded like a glorified hall monitor at *all*.

"Dr. Ambrel said I was well enough for short bursts of minor activity. And I thought...it's allowed, isn't it?" His tone took on a nervous edge, as though he thought she was going to march him back to infirmary at any moment.

"Of course it's allowed," she answered gently. "You're not a prisoner, Oliven."

He nodded tightly, eyes down. Even if she weren't a telepath, his anxiety would be palpable. And she didn't think it stemmed from unexpectedly meeting her in the mess.

She had a moment's guilty temptation then, to take her tea, wish him goodnight, and make this Galhen's problem. He was good with feelings, and he always seemed to know what to say to people. It would just be so much *easier* to walk away.

Or, she could be a responsible adult and try to help someone who obviously needed it right now. She gave a mental sigh and sat down beside him, summoning up all her limited experience coaching junior agents in the field.

"How are you doing?" She tried to keep her voice soft and nonthreatening. Oliven already looked like he might try to bolt as fast as his injuries would allow.

"I'm fine." Both his tone and his projections confirmed that he was the kind of "fine" where absolutely nothing was alright and everything was hopeless. She waited to see if he would say more. After a moment's quiet, he did.

"I just…don't really know what happens now, you know? I mean, leaving the PsiCorp was never something I even thought was possible."

"I didn't either, for most of my life," she answered. "I'm not sure it's quite sunk in yet that we did it."

"It's…" He stared down, his voice almost a whisper. "It's kind of scary, not knowing what comes next. Though I guess I didn't really have a lot to look forward to in the PsiCorp."

She gave him a questioning glance. He looked anywhere but at her.

"Even for a C1, I'm a weak telepath. I can receive alright, but my projection range is pathetic. I don't even know why SysTech bothered to conscript me. I guess when I was a kid they didn't realize how useless I was. I tried my hardest in the academy but there's only so much you can do without the talent, you know?" He added glumly, "It's not like *I* was ever going to see any of that glamorous PsiCorp lifestyle from the movies."

"What do you mean?" She asked him curiously.

"All the parties and the fancy private apartments and the payment cards that let you buy *anything*." Oliven sounded wistful. "The stipend on my card was okay. I guess I should be happy I *got* one. I had enough to buy some nice leather shoes right before I left, though I guess those are gone now. I wonder if they'll give my stuff to my flatmate or just throw it out?"

Kerelle hoped her expression was reassuring, because she had no idea what to say in response. Galhen's words came back to her suddenly, all those months ago on Elekar. *We are quite the favored children of the PsiCorp.* She was realizing now that she'd had no idea by how *much.* She had assumed - rather naively, she now recognized - that the perks of the PsiCorp were more or less the same for everyone. Apparently that was not the case.

A second uncomfortable realization followed on the heels of the first - the reason she had no idea how differently C1s were treated than C3s was probably because she really didn't *know* any C1s. She'd known some on Hasha of course, back in the primary grades when the PsiCorp children all learned and played together, but once they'd begun ability-specific training, she simply hadn't come into regular contact with anyone below a hard C2. All her schooling from then on, and her missions afterward, had been alongside other high-ranked PsiCorp.

Stars, she'd only even met *Galhen* because they'd been in the advanced program together for double-Class 3s.

But this wasn't about her, it was about Oliven. She forced down her whirling thoughts and returned her attention to the young telepath. She said the only thing she could think of.

"When we get to Xan Xaldanan, you can pick out another pair. Galhen and I will be happy to pay for them."

It didn't seem to cheer him up. "You don't have to do that, it's just..." He trailed off again. It was quiet a few minutes as he figured out what he wanted to say.

"I was actually really excited when I got the job to help look for the terro-" he flushed red. "Um, you. It was my one chance to prove myself, and *not* be useless to the company, and maybe escape getting leased out as a secretary to some jerk in a suit." He laughed a little, sounding dangerously like he might cry instead. "At least that's off the table now, I guess."

"I'm sorry for how this happened," Kerelle answered carefully. This conversation increasingly felt like a minefield, except that Oliven would be the one hurt if she stepped wrong. "The rest of us chose this, and you had that choice taken away from you. I'm sorry."

He gave a weary half-shrug. "Well, I'm happy to be alive, and I really appreciate that you saved me. I know it would have been a lot easier to toss me out the airlock. I know...I know that's what Ilyen wanted to do."

Oliven had good hearing.

"Well, Ilyen's an asshole sometimes," she told him firmly. "Don't listen to him. We would never have thrown you out the airlock."

He gave her a weak smile, and the next words slipped out before she could consider them.

"Oliven...if you *did* have the choice to leave, would you have taken it?"

He finally looked at her. "I don't know. Probably not - I think I would have been too scared to try. And I wouldn't...I mean, I know I *shouldn't* be happy you saved me. I feel like a traitor, after everything the company did for me, you know?"

Kerelle leaned back. She *did* know. When she was his age, she'd have felt the same. And when she'd felt that way, snapping at her that she was wrong wouldn't have helped.

"I certainly understand why you'd feel that way," she answered, hating how wishy-washy it sounded but wary of pushing too hard. "But if you *really* think about it, about *everything*, I think you'll find you did much more for them than they did for you."

He nodded, eyes far away. "I know I *should* go back, or at least, I should *want* to go back. But...I don't. I mean, being here is scary but...maybe things will be better than they were there?"

"I think they will be. And remember, Oliven, if you're planning to take Captain Marene up on his offer, then you're part of the crew. If you want midnight tea, you don't need to ask permission." She gave him a smile and a pat on the arm. "We're happy to have you here with us, as long as you choose to stay."

He blushed faintly, and gave her the first real smile she'd seen since they found him.

FOURTEEN

IT WAS early spring in Xan Xaldanan, a fragile accord between still-lurking chill and optimistically-budding trees. The city was more pleasant than Kerelle had been expecting from a port mainly chosen as a hiding spot. She had assumed they would be stepping into another Palhee, dark and winding and hopefully less dangerous than Kalnis. Instead, Xan Xaldanan was prosperous and gracefully architected, with wide avenues and an abundance of green.

The green, Kerelle decided, was her favorite part. Whether through good civic planning or simply force of local custom, little islands of shrubs and trees dotted the boulevards and ringed the alleys. There was a particularly lovely flowering tree overhanging the sidewalk cafe where she and Galhen were currently sipping coffee, its drifting blossoms lending the morning a festive air. The wide streets managed to let in enough sunlight to avoid the sense of overcrowding that had always bothered her about Tallimau, and overall she found it quite relaxing to simply sit there and soak in the environs.

Xan Xaldanan did, of course, have its seedier neighborhoods, one of which Sandrel had led them to shortly after arriving. It had been well worth the trip; Galhen had left with a convincing set of ID that said Garyth Dala Avlor, courtesy of the sizable stack of credits paid to Sandrel's "friend of a friend." It was also in one of those less-savory neighborhoods that Sandrel had engaged a shipyard to make the repairs to the ship he'd been unable to do himself. There were other repair shops in the nicer parts of town, but Kerelle guessed that when it came to *non-standard modifications*, Xan Xaldanan was not quite as open-minded as Palhee.

All in all they'd had a productive stay, now at the start of its fifth day. And yesterday, on a bright, crisp spring morning, the most important thing of all.

GALHEN HAD BEEN hesitant when she first raised the idea.

"It's not that I don't appreciate the sentiment, darling. Truly I do. But are you certain it's…wise?"

Kerelle stopped dead, her stomach giving an uncomfortable flip. Granted, it hadn't been the most *romantic* of proposals, more of a suggestion ventured over tea. But this was not at all the reaction she had been expecting.

She tried to keep her face and voice neutral. "Why do you think it would be *unwise?*"

"You know why." He wouldn't look at her. "We don't know the burnout is temporary. It is entirely possible - perhaps even *probable* - that I will be stripped of my powers for the rest of my life. The rest of *our* lives."

"I know," she replied quietly. It hurt to acknowledge it; she could only imagine what it cost him to say it. "And it doesn't change anything about how I feel about you. You *know* that."

"I know you're certainly still happy to take me to bed," he answered with the ghost of a smile. "But Kerelle, have you thought about this? *Really* thought about it?"

"I just said I have." She couldn't help feeling a bit stung. "Galhen, if you don't want to marry me, just *say* so. It's all right."

"It's not that. I mean, I *do*. It's just…" He gave a quiet huff of frustration and looked away from her again. Kerelle felt her own frustration beginning to build, but she tried to tamp it down. Something was agitating him, and his anxiety worried at her senses. There was a piece here she wasn't seeing.

"Kerelle, I know you feel responsible for what happened," he said finally. "But you weren't. You don't owe me anything. We both know you didn't sign on to spend your life bound to a mundane." He tried for a wry smile, though it didn't reach his eyes. "And once my looks go, I won't have much to offer you."

Kerelle couldn't help it; she stared back at him open-mouthed. "Is that really what you think of me? That I'm just staying with you out of…out of *pity*? Out of *lust?*"

"*No*. Ugh, darling, I'm sorry, this is coming out wrong. It's not *you* at all. But it doesn't change that I'm-" he turned his head to look away from her, and a burst of anguish made it past her shields. Her own heart twisted in response. Part of her wanted to stop this, to go to him and take him in her arms and soothe it all away. But the rest of her recognized that that would serve neither of them. Wherever this was coming from, it too was a wound that needed to drain.

He took a deep breath and turned to face her again. "That I'm not who I was when you fell in love with me, and I cannot stand beside you as I once did."

The missing piece dropped into place, and her burgeoning hurt fell away. This wasn't about *her* at all.

Carefully Kerelle reached out and took both his hands, and guided him to sit on the edge of the bed.

"I disagree," she said softly, trying to channel that comforting calm she'd seen Galhen himself use with patients. "I think you are exactly who I fell in love with, and you belong at my side as you always have. Why do you feel otherwise?"

"Kerelle, you *know* why," he groaned. "I've been worse than useless, to you and *everyone*. I *know* you've always been uncomfortable with telepathy, and I couldn't help you at the jump gate when you needed me. Oliven is only alive because my sister is the clever one in the family; when he was bleeding to death in our medbay, all I could do was try to stabilize him and *hope*. Last time we were under attack I had to leave you with *Ilyen* of all people."

Kerelle suspected that *Ilyen of all people* was a particular sore spot. Still, she couldn't help giving him a softly playful nudge. "Darling, even in full health I wouldn't expect you to help me fight off a giant reptile."

He gave a disgruntled shrug. "You know what I mean."

"I do," she answered carefully. "And I also know you're wrong. Oliven is alive because *you* got him through those first days when we almost lost him, more than once. Nalea got the collar off, but it wouldn't have been possible without you."

"But it wasn't enough," he answered quietly, his gaze fixed across the room. "What am I, if I can't even do that? What do I do if I can't do the only thing that ever made my life worth something?"

"Galhen. Look at me." She gently turned his face towards hers and met his eyes, shadowed with despair. "You are not your psionics. And you're worth more than just what you can do for other people. I didn't fight my way through the stars-damned *impossible* for Senior Agent Ambrel, C3 telepath, C3 regenerative. I did it for *my Galhen,* kind and witty and compassionate to a fault. You're still all those things. You're still *you*. And," she added fiercely, "you are still *very much* the man I want to spend the rest of my life with."

He gripped her hands back tightly, his touch more desperate than tender. "I want that too, more than I can put into words.

But not if…" His voice was barely more than a whisper. "It would break me, darling, if you came to regret. I could not bear it."

She leaned in and kissed him, slowly and deliberately. After a moment's hesitation he returned the kiss, and slipped his arms around her back. She opened her eyes and looked back at him.

"I have a lot of regrets," she said softly. "Most of my *life* is regrets. But Galhen, my dearest one. You will never be one of them."

AND SO THEY'D done it.

Appointments were scarce at Xan Xaldanan's office of civil records, but their datanet page noted that walk-ins would be accommodated first-come, first-serve. Thus the first rays of the rising sun had found them waiting for the office to open, greeting a startled magistrate who was clearly not excited to be faced with work this early. Nonetheless, he brought them into his office, plunked down some forms and promptly turned his attention to a sporting event on his tablet.

Which was just as well. If he'd been paying attention, he might have thought it odd that Kerelle had to sneak a peek at her ID to remind herself of Karia Vela Vendrys's date of birth. At least she and Karia were both thirty-two.

Not that the magistrate gave them more than a cursory examination to make sure all the fields were filled out; she probably could have written down anything she liked.

"Mm…all good…all right then, hands please." Kerelle's pulse quickened as she reached out both her hands to clasp Galhen's. This was it. It was actually happening. She met his eyes and saw her feelings reflected there - nervous excitement, wonder and joy. He gave her a half-smile and gently squeezed her hands.

The magistrate sighed quietly and reluctantly muted his sports game. He turned to her and started the traditional words with disinterested intonation.

"Do you vow today and each day after, in the sight of all peoples and in the light of the holy stars, to offer your love and your comfort, to give the best of your heart and your spirit, to turn your eyes from all others as long as you live, to take," he paused and checked the form, "Garyth Dala Avlor as your husband?"

Galhen Tarau Ambrel, her heart corrected. Aloud, she gave the customary response. "I do so vow, today and each day after."

The magistrate marked a box and repeated the ritual oath to Galhen. He held her eyes as he gave the response. Yesterday Kerelle would have said the words were so well-worn that they were rendered anodyne, but hearing them from Galhen's lips as his fingers enclosed hers sent a sizzle of excitement down her spine. She'd imagined this would be a dull formality, but there was power in this ritual, power in repeating the oaths to each other, even here in a conference chair under fluorescent lighting, with an officiant who clearly just wanted them out of his office.

She wished she could share the thought with Galhen. She would tell him afterward.

"Put the rings on each others' hands," the magistrate instructed. His eyes were on the score for the silent game.

The feeling was electric, as they slipped on the rings and their gazes met. Kerelle was suddenly very happy that the ceremony was short.

Their officiant rested a light two fingers over their joined hands, still watching the tablet. "I hereby declare this marriage to be valid and witnessed, by the holy stars and by the municipality of Xan Xaldanan. May your union be blessed with joy and abundance." He stood up as he said it, already moving to usher them out. Kerelle and Galhen exchanged amused smiles and took the hint.

It seemed surreal, as they stepped back outside, that everything should look the same. The street was the same it had been fifteen minutes before, a slow trickling of people starting their morning business as warm sunbeams slowly swept away the night's cold. It felt like there should be some sort of acknowledgement, that whole world had changed since she stepped through those doors. That she was holding hands with her *husband.*

But she was, and it meant so much more than she could have imagined. No more carefully worded letters, no more stolen glances, no more bittersweet dreams. No more hiding. It was her life now, her choice to make. She'd chosen to belong to Galhen, and he to her, and the rings they wore proclaimed it to the universe.

"Rather more heady than expected, isn't it?" he said softly.

"I was thinking the same thing," she answered warmly, and leaned in for a slow, tender kiss. Finally they broke apart, still close in each others' arms.

"Well my dear," she asked, "shall we find ourselves some coffee and waffles for a wedding banquet?"

"Mm," he answered, lips closer to her ear, "I was rather hoping the banquet could come after the consummation."

The laugh seemed to fill her whole lungs, and she gave him a giddy grin. "Race you back to the ship."

***

SITTING IDLY THE NEXT DAY, savoring the rather good coffee beneath the flowering tree and watching Xan Xaldanan swirl past around them, it still felt magical. Perhaps all the more so, Kerelle mused, for being unexpected. She'd never been one of those children who dreamed about weddings - PsiCorp didn't marry, so what was the point? And certainly nothing *material* had changed between them since two days before. Galhen had been her one and only for nearly half her life, and she knew she'd been his as well. The only real difference was a document now buried in the archives of a Xan Xaldanan clerk, and not even a document with their own names.

And yet she still felt that bright zing of delight when she saw the simple band on his finger.

They sat with hands loosely clasped on the table, Galhen's fingers absentmindedly caressing hers. Like her, he was content to bask in the morning sun and the gentle pleasure of having no pressing reason to be anywhere, and it was a comfortable silence between them.

She realized with a sudden grin that he was unconsciously tracing the slim band of her own ring. Galhen caught her expression and tilted his head in question, then realized what he'd been doing a moment later. He smiled back her, open and radiant.

The world seemed to slow around them then. Galhen leaned forward, and the early sun caught on the short golden hairs that dusted his head, lending him a bright halo in the morning light. Kerelle tilted her head in and brushed her lips to his, heedless of the street around them. If passerby wanted to stare, let them stare.

Finally she pulled back, though her eyes held his. Kerelle suddenly concluded she was very much finished with her coffee, and was about to suggest they return to their cabin straightaway, when another flash of gold caught on the corner of her vision.

Nalea didn't notice them as she walked back towards the ship. The scientist had kept to herself since they'd landed, though Kerelle knew she'd made contact with Olstenfel as planned. As far as Kerelle had heard, the call had gone well, and her transport from Olstenfel was due to arrive in the next day or so. Now, though, something was clearly troubling her.

Galhen followed her gaze, and his brow furrowed as Nalea

disappeared around the corner back towards where the ship was docked. "Do you suppose something's happened?"

"She certainly didn't look happy." Kerelle suppressed a sigh as she reluctantly closed the door on her budding plans to spend all day in bed with Galhen, and prepared to do the right thing.

"Let's see if she's willing to tell us what's wrong."

FIFTEEN

AS EXPECTED, they found Nalea alone in her cabin/lab. Not that there was much left of *her* in it - everything was neatly sorted and packed, as if she were planning to spring up and run for Olstenfel's transport the moment it touched down. Maybe she was.

If that were the case, however, the transport still had not yet made an appearance. Nalea sat tensely perched on the edge of the bed, reading her tablet with that same creased-brow expression that Galhen had worn outside. The one that meant worry.

"Nalea?" The scientist looked up quickly at the sound of Kerelle's voice, then dropped her eyes back to her tablet. Kerelle kept her voice soft. "Is everything all right?"

"Everything's fine," she answered too quickly. Nervous energy swirled at Kerelle's senses. "Did you two want something?"

Kerelle exchanged glances with Galhen. Whatever was wrong, Kerelle suspected Nalea would want as small of an audience as possible before she opened up about it. And since she still seemed uncomfortable around Galhen most of the time,

Kerelle was the one who should stay. This would be a great time for telepathy.

Fortunately, Galhen was rather good at social cues even without it.

"Darling, I need to finish my inventory of the first aid supplies," he said smoothly, as if he had not already done that at least twice. "I'll be in the medbay if you need me." Nalea gave him a vague nod as he left, her gaze still fastened on her tablet. Kerelle carefully took a seat beside her.

"Is there anything you need help with?" She asked it gently.

"I said everything's fine. Why do you keep bothering me about this?"

It probably wasn't a good sign that Nalea's porcupine defense had immediately engaged. Kerelle kept her voice neutral.

"Because you don't seem terribly happy for a woman who's about to get her ride home."

Nalea sighed irritably and looked away. She thrust the tablet into the Kerelle's hands. A message was open on the screen.

Dr. Ambrel,

I hope this finds you well, and that you are recovering from your ordeal. Please be assured that SysTech is taking this matter extremely seriously. I had a call just this morning with the head of client experience, and he expressed his deepest regrets for the incident and the difficult events that followed, and reiterated again our importance as a SysTech client. We are already in talks around compensation for damages and duress involved in breach of their service contract.

On that front, I have some good news for you. SysTech is quite eager to make amends, and as a show of good faith they've arranged for you to be transported home on an executive's daughter's yacht. Miss Phaera Velrin Beniwell should be arriving shortly; I've attached the information on the date and where to meet her. Do try the sparkling-wine fountain for me.

Best,

Dr. Salanza Emberia Beranime

Dean of Sciences, Olstenfel University

Kerelle read it twice, just in case she'd missed something the first time. But the words did not change, and she was left with a sinking feeling as she handed the tablet back. Phaera Beniwell was arriving tomorrow.

"You can't be planning to go along with this."

Nalea dispensed with pretense. "What choice do I have? If I say no, it'll just raise suspicions. Or worse," she added heavily, "confirm them."

Kerelle shook her head. "It's too dangerous. What if they *do* suspect you, and it's a trap? Write her back, and tell her you're more comfortable on a regular transport."

"What reason would I have to refuse, if everything happened the way I said it did? If I really did escape from Zharal V by the skin of my teeth, then get kidnapped and *also* escape from pirates, and definitely at no point get involved in any sort of insane psionic jailbreak scheme? Then I should be *thrilled* to put all that behind me and spend my whole ride home drinking sparkling wine out of a fountain on some sort of superyacht."

Nalea took a deep breath and let it out, as if trying to will herself to be calm. "All I can do," she said firmly, "is go, play it cool, and hope that either it's a coincidence and we're freaking out over nothing, or that their suspicions are satisfied when I show up and everything's normal."

She looked sadly at her tablet. "I can't bring my notes, though. There's too much risk they'll search my stuff while I'm busy." Nalea lifted her eyes to Kerelle's, and Kerelle was startled to see unshed tears. Nalea was more upset by all this than she was letting on. "Will you take care of them, if I leave them with you? I don't...I don't just want to destroy them."

"Of *course*," Kerelle answered. "I'll be happy to keep anything you want to leave. But Nalea," she added urgently, "why don't you leave *with* us, and keep your notes? Sandrel said repairs were done. We could fly out in a few hours and be safely in hyperspace before anyone knows we're gone. You know that Galhen and I are planning to stay on as crew with Sandrel, and Ilyen and Oliven are too. Sandrel would welcome you along if you wanted to join too, you *know* he would."

"You don't *understand*," Nalea asserted hotly, her voice laced with frustration. "If I just pull up stakes and disappear into the night, I'm walking away from any chance of getting my life back. Best case, Dr. Beranime thinks I'm unbalanced and fires me. Worst case, SysTech realizes I helped you escape and *hunts me down for the rest of my life.*"

Nalea rounded on her then. "I helped you. I didn't have to. In fact, if I'd said no in the beginning, I'd be safe at home right now, instead of sneaking around a seedy port hoping that my employer didn't just throw me to the wolves." She sighed heavily, shoulders slumping.

"All I want is to go *home*, Kerelle," she said with finality. "This is the only way that there's even a chance."

Kerelle gazed helplessly back at her. There was a brittle edge to her words, and Kerelle sank into a queasy realization that the giddy joy running through her veins that morning had been paid for, figuratively, with Nalea's life. Possibly *literally*, if things went badly. For all her prickles, for all her obvious discomfort with her brother, she had stepped into the firing line to save him. And unlike Kerelle, Nalea had realized the full extent of her risk. If all she wanted was to get her old life back, then holy burning stars, Kerelle owed her that.

Another realization struck her then, as she gave the other woman a reluctant nod. Nalea was *her* sister now too.

"I can't argue with that," she told Nalea quietly. "If this is what you want, then this is what needs to happen. Just let me go with you to the rendezvous." Nalea opened her mouth, and

Kerelle held up her hand to forestall objection. "I'll hang back. I won't be seen. But let me be there when you meet this Phaera. Just...just in case."

Nalea swallowed and gave her a small nod. "Just in case."

"SHE'S DOING *WHAT?*"

Galhen and Ilyen stared back at Kerelle with mirrored expressions, their usual antipathy buried beneath the unifying power of mutual outrage.

"I tried to convince her to stay with us instead, but this is what she wants. She wants her old life back and she says this is how to get it."

"No," Ilyen growled, "this is how to end up in a detention cell while an 'interrogation specialist' pulls out her fingernails. We're not letting her go."

"I understand why she's made this decision," Galhen said, his voice subdued. "But Ilyen is correct on the likely outcome. As much as I hope we're all being paranoid, Nalea doesn't truly understand what SysTech is capable of."

Ilyen gave him a sidelong glance. "And *you* do, regen?"

"I was brought in once to treat someone after interrogation," he said shortly. "I have an inkling."

Kerelle felt his spike of distress at the memory and slipped her hand in his. There was more to that story, years and years ago when he'd appeared pale and shaking at her door. The cold words he'd shared from his memory, before he'd been sick for half an hour and then wept helplessly in her arms, were seared into hers as well. *See that he doesn't die until we have our information.*

It wasn't her story to tell. But she felt his sharp fear for Nalea, radiating cold against her senses, and knew it was on both of their minds.

If Ilyen noticed, he didn't remark on it. "So we agree then."

His tone implied that the matter was settled. "We're not letting her do this."

"She's an adult, Ilyen," Kerelle reminded him. "We can't 'not let' her do anything." His brows drew together stubbornly.

"*But*," she went on before he could argue. "Nalea agreed to have me accompany her from a distance to her meeting with this Phaera Beniwell. If it goes wrong, I'll step in."

"*When* it goes wrong," Ilyen corrected irritably. "And I'm going with too."

Kerelle concealed her surprise. Enthusiasm for reptile fights aside, putting himself in danger for others hadn't seemed like Ilyen's tendency.

"Thank you. I appreciate your help."

He shrugged. "You might *need* my help. If SysTech really has connected her to us escaping, they might've sent an anti-psionic squad with this Beniwell girl. I know how to handle them."

The memory of the suppressant weapon, the way her psionics had simply gone out like a blown candle, sent an involuntary shiver down her spine. Kerelle only hoped they were being paranoid after all.

THE TIME CAME. Nalea managed to hug Galhen awkwardly goodbye, and Sandrel with much more enthusiasm. He murmured something in her ear that sounded encouraging, and for a moment it looked like Nalea was going to cry again. But she set her jaw and gave him a stoic nod, and turned decisively with her luggage. The two of them watched her go with grim concern.

They'd discussed as a group the night before. Sandrel, who had probably long since realized that arguing with Nalea just made her dig in her heels, had only nodded at her decision, and noted that she was welcome to come along with them if it didn't work out. Privately, however, he agreed with the psionics' assessment, and with their planned course of action.

Kerelle and Ilyen would discreetly accompany Nalea to her meeting, and be prepared to extract her if necessary. Sandrel and Galhen would stay with the ship, and keep the engines hot.

Kerelle watched carefully as Nalea headed down the street. When she reached the end of their block, a good ways away but still in sight, Kerelle started after her. She kept her senses wide open, but all she picked up was the normal activity of the city around them. She kept listening anyway.

Ilyen strolled casually beside her, posture relaxed but eyes alert. He was keeping a watch out, too.

Nalea had received a followup that morning, letting her know which dock Ms. Beniwell's yacht had arrived at. As she made her way to its location, they moved out of the bustling port streets, into the private docks where the wealthy parked their pleasurecraft away from prying commoner eyes. It fit, of course, with where a rich socialite would land her yacht, but it also meant far less foot traffic - and few potential witnesses. Kerelle's unease increased.

Apparently Ilyen felt the same. He leaned into her ear. "We're getting too visible. You stay on her from here, I'm going to follow from cover. I'll be close when you need me." He strolled nonchalantly behind a wall, and was gone.

When she needed him, Kerelle noticed. Not *if.*

There it was - Dock 18. It was easy to spot, because it was the one with all the guards. It wasn't unreasonable, of course, that a prominent family would use the private docks and travel with a significant security detail, but...

Projecting mundanity, Kerelle slipped behind a stack of equipment. She still had a clear line of sight on the ship, but hopefully the cover and her telepathic encouragement would be enough to keep them from noticing her.

A young woman's voice rang over the dock.

"Ah, Dr. Ambrel! Delighted to finally meet you." Nalea's hostess descended down the stairs from the yacht's entryway and into Kerelle's field of vision.

It was the girl from Dalanva's party.

SIXTEEN

SHIT SHIT SHIT.

Kerelle threw up mental shields around herself, Nalea, and Ilyen - she didn't know if this Phaera was a dual-gift, but they couldn't take the risk that she was a telekinetic/telepath like Kerelle.

Phaera was still smiling, engaged in some sort of conversation with Nalea that Kerelle was too far away to make out. Nalea's expression didn't indicate that anything was wrong, or any recognition, but -

Of course. She had no idea who Phaera was, she'd been on the ship prepping for the collar removal during the nightmarish struggle to escape Dalanva's estate. Ilyen hadn't been there either, and since he wasn't a telepath, Kerelle couldn't warn him. She'd located him by his thoughts, perched hidden in shadow on a nearby roof, but as far as communication was concerned he might as well be in another system.

Kerelle threw caution to the wind and dove into the nearest guard's mind. If there were other telepaths hidden in Phaera's entourage, there was a chance they might detect her, but it was a risk she'd have to take.

He was annoyed that this assignment had interfered with his intended time off, and impatient to be underway. *Doesn't look like she's going to be trouble though. Really not seeing why they needed a whole unit to arrest one scientist, terrorist or not. But whatever, once we get her on the ship she's Miss Beniwell's problem. The sooner we get out of here the sooner I can see if they still have rooms open at the Calaia - and if Darhen's still speaking to me after I practically stood him up. Besides, if Miss Beniwell is involved, then her father's involved, and I probably don't want to know what this is actually about.*

Shit.

Part of her had known from the very beginning that they were not being paranoid, that this was every bit as bad as it looked. But it would have been nice to be wrong.

She and Ilyen really should have agreed on some sort of hand signal. She looked up and tried to catch his eye, but despite knowing his general location she couldn't *actually* see him, and she had no idea if he saw or not. Even if he had, she wasn't sure how much her expression could be expected to convey. She might have to depend on him to follow her lead.

Phaera smiled and gestured up the ramp. Nalea started up the stairs. Kerelle couldn't let her get on that ship.

Time's up for subtlety, then. She grabbed Nalea as gently as she could, and yanked.

Nalea screamed as she suddenly shot backwards, the sound mingling with the guards' sudden shouts of alarm. Phaera's face darkened, and Nalea suddenly jerked to a stop in midair as Phaera tried to pull her back. Kerelle gave Phaera a sharp blow that sent her sprawling backwards, releasing her hold. Kerelle hurriedly landed Nalea behind her.

"I read the guards, it's a trap, stay close." That was all she had time for, before a dozen guns trained on them and she had to concentrate on shields.

The first round of fire bounced harmlessly of the shields, woven tightly around her and Nalea. There was a shout from

Phaera - something about shooting to disable, not to kill - that was almost immediately drowned out by a scream. One of the guards dropped in a spray of blood. Ilyen was right on cue.

Even as she deflected another round of fire, Kerelle felt a queasy pang, thinking of the guard who didn't even want to be here, and just wanted to finish his job and make it up to his date. "Try not to kill anyone," she shouted to Ilyen, though he had vanished again and she wasn't sure if he heard her. Or if he would care.

Burning stars, she wished he were a telepath.

The telekinetic blow came fast and hard. Focused as she was on the guns, Kerelle stumbled under the unexpected force. She'd forgotten how damn *strong* this girl was.

Kerelle pulled Nalea into her arms and threw a hard wave all around them, hoping Ilyen wasn't in the way - or that he could make a quick exit if he were. The guards around them were tossed backwards to the ground. Before they could rise, she made a snatch at the guns, hurling them away into the hallway.

Another telekinetic shove, but this time she was ready for it. Her shield absorbed the blow, and Kerelle spun around to see Phaera had regained her footing, glaring fiercely at her from the foot of the stairs. She threw another wave at the surrounding guards, weaker this time with her focus on Phaera, and readied a strike against the other woman.

Phaera gave a short shriek then as Ilyen appeared at her back, his hand snaking around to hold his knife at her throat.

"Call off your dogs," he growled, tightening his arm threateningly. Phaera's eyes narrowed.

Kerelle's warning died on her lips as his head snapped forward under the telekinetic blow and he dropped the knife, stunned. Phaera gave Kerelle a venomous look, and darted back up into her ship. The engine roared to life immediately.

Kerelle looked around desperately. Most of the guards were still down, some struggling to their feet and others ominously still. Ilyen steadied himself and met her eyes. She gestured forcefully to follow her. There was nothing to be gained by hanging around until the guards figured out what to do now that Phaera was gone.

She gave the guards a final downward shove - enough to bruise, not to seriously injure - and took off at a run with a deathgrip on Nalea's hand. Kerelle could hear the scientist's shaky breathing and sense her shock and fear and near-panic, but there was no time to deal with it now. They had to get back to the ship.

Ilyen appeared next to her and matched her pace, expression dark. He was silent as they hurried through the increasingly-busy streets, but Kerelle could sense he would have quite a bit to say once they'd reached the safety of the ship. This certainly wasn't the place to have any sort of sensitive conversation. Kerelle tried to project a shield of inattention around them, but their disheveled appearance and hasty pace would make it a tall order to go completely unnoticed. All the more reason to make an exit.

Inspiration struck and she sent her thoughts ahead, back, towards the ship.

Oliven? It's Kerelle.

Kerelle? Is everything okay? His response was more indistinct than she was used to; he hadn't been exaggerating his poor projection ability. At least he could receive just fine.

Not entirely. No one is hurt, but there was trouble, and we're on our way back with Nalea. Tell Sandrel we'd best leave in a hurry.

A moment's silence before she received his acknowledgement. At least the ship would be ready for them.

Sandrel met them at the door, all business. "I put in for takeoff clearance as soon as we got your message, and it just came through. Strap in, and we'll get out before there's any organized blowback."

"Organized?"

Grimly he handed her his tablet. "The bulletin went out a few minutes ago. Strap in."

Nalea Tarau Ambrel, wanted in connection with the Dalanva terrorists. Report any sightings to law enforcement immediately.

All the remaining color drained from Nalea's face. She spun and streaked down the corridor without a word, the slamming of her cabin's door the only sound.

KERELLE HELD her breath until they made it into hyperspace, but Sandrel's foresight paid off. If the Xan Xaldanan authorities made any effort to seal and search the ports, it was after they'd cleared atmosphere. They slipped into the anonymous safety of hyper with no pursuit.

Nalea's door was locked, and she made no answer when Kerelle knocked with a pot of tea. Worry for the other woman wormed in her gut, but if Nalea wanted to be alone right now, then she wanted to be alone.

Well, no sense in wasting a good pot of tea. Galhen was already there when she got to the mess, and Ilyen soon followed.

The teleporter wasted no time. "That girl was a stars-damned *psionic*! With no collar! She wasn't PsiCorp!" Outrage colored his voice.

Galhen started. "Was she - "

"Yes," Kerelle answered heavily. "It was the same girl."

"Wait, you *knew* about this?" Ilyen's voice went up a notch.

"She was attending the party at Dalanva's estate where we staged our escape. She attacked us as I was trying to get to the ship with Galhen. Trust me," Kerelle told Ilyen, "I was as shocked as you."

"How the hell is she waltzing around in a yacht doing secret shit while the rest of us were corporate property?

Fuck," he added as an afterthought, "I wonder if *she* gets paid."

"The note said she was an executive's daughter, and I picked up something from one of the guards about her father being someone important. If I had to guess," Kerelle answered drily, "I would guess she's in a yacht instead of a collar because her father's money and influence kept her out of the PsiCorp. Must be nice."

"It would still be in both their best interests to keep her abilities quiet," Galhen commented. "If she *does* get paid, it's probably as a consultant or an intelligence agent. That would be simpler all around, really - if anyone thinks her position seems odd, they're unlikely to look any deeper than nepotism."

"Either way," Kerelle sighed. "It's not good news for us. Especially now."

They were all quiet a moment.

"We had full clearance to take off, filed before the bulletin hit," Galhen said finally. "There's no record connecting Nalea with the ship, and as a commercial freighter we have a perfectly reasonable business purpose for departing when we did. If we're careful, there's not necessarily anything for them to track us on."

Kerelle hoped he was right.

GALHEN STOPPED in his tracks ahead of her, brow creased as he lifted a hand for her to listen. Kerelle paused, and then she heard it too. Muffled sobs, faintly audible, coming from the mess.

Kerelle hesitated. "Do you think she'd want us to…?"

"No," Galhen answered frankly. "But sometimes what we want isn't what we need." He turned his steps toward the mess. Kerelle followed.

Nalea was curled into one of the corners, a short glass on the table in front of her. She looked up at their approach and tried to blink away the tears washing down her face - then visibly gave up. Wordlessly they sat down next to her. Nalea leaned back, her eyes fixed on the ceiling. She spoke first.

"Do you know," she said shakily "how hard it was? Do you have any idea?" She took a gulp of her drink and continued before they could say anything. "All the way back in secondary school, I knew what I wanted. I wanted to be a researcher. I wanted to do experiments, and learn things, and *add to the body of human knowledge.*" Her voice took a derisive tone at those words, as if mocking the idealism of her younger self.

"But so did a lot of kids, you know? And my parents made good money, but not the kind that buys you a slot in a top-tier university program. I had to *earn* it. I outfought all the other middle-class kids who were vying for those same merit slots in the grad program. And then once I was there, I had to do it all over again, and you know what?"

She slammed her glass emphatically back on the table. "I *fucking did it.* I published more than anyone else in my year, and the top bioresearcher in the program chose *me* as a student. I put up with that pompous asshole for *three years,* treating me like her secretary, making me do all her classroom work, making me do her *stars-damned laundry,* and you know what? It was all worth it, because at the end of it all, my name on papers next to hers opened doors. I got a junior-faculty offer at Olstenfel the day I graduated. I worked my way up from there. The impossible dream for thousands of starry-eyed kids and I. Fucking. Did it."

She made an angrily dismissive gesture. "And so much for all that." Nalea downed the rest of her drink and slumped back in her seat. "So much for all that," she repeated in a whisper, fresh tears starting down her cheeks.

Kerelle had no idea what to say. How did you address this kind of enormity with words? Her own feelings stormed in her -

grief, cold and keening, for Nalea's loss; gratitude, intense and unflinching, for all that she had done; and guilt, guilt welling up like a bottomless sea. This was all because of her, and she could not make it right.

Galhen got up and retrieved the bottle Nalea had left on the counter, along with another pair of glasses.

"I'm sorry," he said softly as he refilled her glass. "This is a terrible loss."

Nalea seemed to notice him for the first time.

"This is all because of you," she said harshly. "Your girlfriend talked me into this whole thing, to help *you*. I didn't want to, because I was afraid *this* would happen, but she talked me into it anyway. Now here I am."

Her voice picked up intensity again. "And who even *are* you? Someone who sort of looks like a scared kid I saw disappear into a corporate car? *'This is a terrible loss,'*" she imitated, emphasizing the contrast between his crisp Tallimau vowels and her own flat Istel accent. "You don't even *sound* like my brother any more."

Kerelle felt his flare of hurt, but Galhen's expression didn't change, and he kept his voice gentle. "And you don't look like the sister whose hair I used to pull," he answered with a sad smile, "but I know she's still in there, and I've missed her a great deal. Neither of us are the children we were, but...I hope that perhaps we can find a way to be family again as adults."

He poured himself a glass. "But tonight? You're right, Nalea. You did something incredibly brave, for someone you barely knew." He met her eyes solemnly. "You bought my life and my freedom, and Kerelle's, at the cost of everything you had. We will never have thanks enough."

Nalea stared back at him, her brow creasing as tears welled up in her eyes again. Galhen scooted his chair closer and silently wrapped his arms around her as she started to sob. They sat there in tableau for some time, until Nalea began to subside into sniffles.

"You'll get through this," he murmured against the top of her head. "You're brilliant, and resilient, and it won't break you. But it's alright to admit it hurts. It's alright to mourn what you've lost."

Nalea nodded against his shoulder and lifted her head, blinking tears-laden eyelashes. She made eye contact with Kerelle and gave a helpless, hiccuping laugh. "He's better at this than you are."

"Yes," she agreed simply. On impulse, Kerelle put a hand on her arm. "You don't have to grieve alone, Nalea."

"Indeed, that's what we're here for. We can't restore what you've lost, but at least we can give it a proper wake." Galhen poured the third glass and handed it to Kerelle. He raised his own. "To more papers published than anyone else in your year."

Nalea sniffled, but clinked her glass to his with a hint of her usual spark. "To three years of Dr. Marilat's laundry paying off."

Three glasses became three more, became another bottle, became two. By the time Ilyen joined them, Kerelle had lost count. The teleporter grinned and pulled up a chair as he took in the scene before him - the deep flush on Nalea and Galhen's fair skin, Nalea's exuberant gesticulation as she acted out the story of an experiment that had not gone to plan, Kerelle's unsteady hand as she tried to pour him a drink. Nalea finished her story and they all raised another toast to science. It was at least the fourth one that night. Maybe the sixth.

Kerelle looked around at their little group as she downed her toast, a giddy warmth in her chest. *This was* the best *idea*.

SEVENTEEN

Kerelle groaned and shaded her eyes against the too-bright cabin lights, pain knifing through her head as she blinked into full consciousness. Her stomach twisted and lurched, as if to inform her head that in a competition for awfulness, it was playing to win.

Burning stars, I'm too old for this. I know better than to drink that much. And that much variety. The thought was not helpful.

Beside her Galhen stirred and groaned as well. She caught his projection as if he'd shouted it. *Blood and* flame, *I forgot what this was* like *without regeneratives to clean it all up.*

Kerelle stifled a moan of shared regret. If he had his psionics, he could fix *her* hangover too.

"Remind me," she rasped, "to never drink with you again."

"Since I'm never *drinking* again, that should work fine."

It was a slow morning.

Eventually they managed to put themselves together enough to stagger down toward the mess, eyes bloodshot and faces wan. As they got closer, they were rewarded with the heavenly smell of something frying. And coffee. Stars be praised, someone had made coffee.

"Someone," naturally, turned out to be Sandrel. He greeted them with an unabashedly entertained grin from his place at the stovetop as they painfully shambled in.

"And there's our sleepy instigators! Have a seat, next batch is almost finished." He gestured them towards the table. Ilyen and Nalea were both there already, blearily clutching their coffee. Oliven was at the table as well, carefully eating his breakfast and trying very hard not to look at anyone.

Come to think of it, as she levered herself into her chair, Nalea and Ilyen were sitting…very close together. Her eyes were suddenly drawn to the dark love bites visible against the light skin of Nalea's neck.

Oh.

She averted her eyes as heat flooded her cheeks. A wave of dismay radiated from Galhen as he noticed the same thing, though of course he said nothing. As he gulped his coffee, Kerelle caught a drifting thought about *terrible taste in men.*

Sandrel plunked down plates in front of them, and all thought fled. Kerelle inhaled for a moment, savoring the smell of the eggs and crisp-fried potatoes. It tasted as good as it looked.

"Sandrel," Galhen said between bites, "we don't deserve you."

"Nope," the smuggler agreed cheerfully. "Fortunately for you all, I'm the giving sort. Besides, when I saw how things were going last night, I figured we were going to need some morning fortification."

"Why didn't you join us?" Kerelle asked. That familiar guilt began to spin up again, that apparently they hadn't invited Sandrel to a party on his own ship.

"I did," he replied, dark eyes dancing. "You made me a drink, Fury. We gave a toast to *the body of human knowledge.*" He laughed at her look of dismay. "Eat your potatoes, you'll feel better." She did.

Sandrel settled down with his own plate, and for a moment they all ate in ravenous silence. The throbbing in her head receded somewhat before the food and coffee, though she still wouldn't describe herself as feeling "good" by any stretch. Still, when she finished her plate, she felt marginally functional again.

Sandrel set aside his own plate and cleared his throat.

"So," he started, suddenly serious. "That wasn't how any of us hoped that would go. Doc, I'm sorry things went down the way they did, but that means this next part concerns you too."

"While you all were emptying my liquor cabinet, I did a few short hops through hyper to lose any pursuit and put us on course for the job I picked up in Xan Xaldanan. We've got four days in space, then we'll be landing on Hallai for a few days to deliver and pick up. Everyone's at liberty until we get there, then I'll need some help on the unloading." He stood up, the amused smile playing again on his lips. "We'll discuss everyone's duties and cut of the profit when you can focus your eyes without wincing. Welcome aboard, new crew."

A WEEK BECAME TWO.

"Hold this, will you?" Nalea thrust the beaker into Kerelle's hand as she rummaged with her instruments. Kerelle gingerly gripped the glassware, its mystery liquid slightly fizzy. Nalea gave her an amused glance.

"It's harmless, Kerelle. I wouldn't ask you to hold a beaker of flesh-eating acid."

"Do you....have those?"

Nalea's eyes held a wicked glint. "That's for me to know and you to nervously wonder about when you're thinking about whether to interrupt me."

It was good to see her sister-in-law in high spirits, at least for the moment. Nalea had been understandably moody since the incident, but having lab work to occupy her mind was clearly doing her some good.

Nalea took the beaker back and took some sort of measurement from it, carefully noting down the results. Her expression didn't betray whether the exercise had been successful.

"So did it work?" Kerelle asked, gesturing at the beaker.

"Hm? Oh, this. There wasn't really anything to 'work,' exactly, it wasn't an experiment. I wanted to observe the reaction before trying anything more significant."

"Was the reaction…good?"

Nalea's lips curved in an enigmatic smile. "It was intriguing. Let's say that."

Kerelle peered into the mysterious beaker. "What's *in* here, anyway?"

"Several things you wouldn't be able to pronounce, and a dab of hemindrium."

"Hemindrium?" Kerelle drew back, surprised. "This is about the collars?"

"At this stage? It's not *about* anything, except learning more on the subject. I've read papers on work with hemindrium, but I haven't used it much myself." She shrugged. "Apparently I'm now officially the ship's Science Officer, whatever *that* means. I might as well research the hemindrium until somebody says otherwise."

"At the same time," she noted, carefully stoppering a vial with some of the solution inside, "we don't exactly have a huge supply, so I have to be judicious."

"I wasn't aware we had *any* supply."

"Mostly what I was able to get out of Ilyen's collar. Once that runs out I could crack open Oliven's, but since it's the only intact sample I have I'd like to keep it that way."

It was quiet for a moment as Kerelle's curiosity warred with her sense of propriety. Curiosity won.

"So…you and Ilyen…?"

Nalea leaned back against the counter, smirking slightly. "What, you jealous?"

Kerelle felt her cheeks flush crimson. Nalea's smirk widened.

"I was just…surprised. He doesn't really seem like your type." As she said it, Kerelle realized she actually had no idea what Nalea's *type* was. She'd never volunteered anything about her personal life, and Kerelle had never asked. From her expression, Nalea had the same thought.

"Out of curiosity, what did you assume my type is?"

Kerelle floundered a bit. "I…guess I just thought you'd be into people with similar background, like…other professors…"

"Well, that's *definitely* not Ilyen," she responded with a laugh, "though don't let him fool you, he's smarter than he pretends. But seriously, *other professors?* If they're not trying to steal your research, they're getting all clingy when you leave for a fellowship somewhere. Or pouting when you're working on a project and you don't have time to bother with them for a couple of months."

She shrugged, a small smile tugging at her lips. "Ilyen doesn't get in the way when I'm working, he's *amazing* in bed, and he doesn't think that now it all has to *mean something*. That's about as *my type* as it gets.

"If I'm stuck on this ship with you weirdos forever," she added with a wink, "I might as well have some fun."

TWO WEEKS BECAME A MONTH.

Voices caught Kerelle's ear as she approached the mess.

"So that's Eineka Ambrel Danakai, she's going to be eight

next year," Nalea was saying. "And this one's Tarasien Ambrel Danakai, he'll be five."

"Ah, he got the Tarau eyes." That was Galhen.

Nalea snorted. "Yes, yes he did. I think Mom's a little bitter that her only grandkids look way more like Dad. Well, that and they're Balheren's kids, so they're Danakais. She's been on me for years for some Ambrel granddaughters to carry on the family name. I keep telling her, nobody's got time for that."

Her nails clicked against her tablet. "Ah, there's a better picture, you can see Tari's hair is a little lighter than his sister's, he definitely got more from our side of the family. They both look way more like Celisce though." Nalea laughed. "Fortunately they take after her in personality too, they're both very sweet. Balheren's mellowed a little over the years but he's still kind of an ass sometimes." Her voice dropped somewhat conspiratorially. "To be honest, I always thought Celisce was way too good for him."

Galhen laughed a little as well. "You know, I remember him that way, but I was never sure if that was fair. I realize I could be a rather vexing younger sibling."

"A little of both, I think? Even when we were kids he was always pretty impressed with himself. I consider it my sisterly duty to take him down a few pegs." Nalea's tone sobered. "We got a lot closer, though, after…after what happened to you. A lot of things changed after that."

"Oh?" Galhen's careful syllable was heavily fraught.

Nalea sighed heavily, and Kerelle could pick up her aura of discomfort from out in the corridor. She might be becoming more comfortable with Galhen in general, but this subject was still difficult for her.

"I mean, I can only imagine what it was like for you, you *went* through it, but it was hard for us too, you know? We were a family of five and then you were just…gone. It was like you'd died. Mom and Dad were…well, they were busy dealing with it themselves, and they weren't really great at helping me and Balheren deal with it. I don't know if they thought we blamed them, or if they knew we were scared and there was nothing they could really say to comfort us except 'well you're too old, it won't happen to you,' which is a pretty shitty thing to say when you're all grieving. So they kinda ended up not saying anything.

"And we *were* scared. Like, I guess I was old enough that intellectually I knew parents weren't omnipotent, but deep down it still felt like Mom and Dad would protect us from the really bad stuff. And they couldn't protect you, and that was terrifying....anyway it was just easier to talk to Balheren for awhile."

Kerelle abruptly realized she was still hovering in the corridor. Her tea could wait - this wasn't a conversation she wanted to interrupt. It had also awakened, in the selfish part of her heart, that plaintive envy she'd felt as a teenager when Galhen told her about his life in Istel City. She immediately felt awful - she wouldn't wish it on anyone, what the Tarau-Ambrel family had gone through. But still...Galhen had been missed. Had been mourned. Had anyone mourned her?

She turned to go.

"Anything juicy?"

Kerelle jumped as Ilyen appeared at her elbow.

"Don't *do* that," she growled, and started down the corridor at a fast clip. He followed her, grinning.

"You realize, Evandra, that you can't bitch me out for eavesdropping any more."

"I wasn't eavesdropping," she shot back irritably, fully aware that she had *absolutely* been eavesdropping. "I was realizing they were in a conversation that I shouldn't disturb."

"Sorry, can't hear you over the sound of all these dropping eaves."

"Ilyen, what do you *want?*"

He shrugged, still grinning. "A snack, originally. But if the

Doctors Ambrel are having some kind of heartwarming family chat then I can wait. Might as well see what you're doing."

She leaned against the wall, irritability fading. She'd sort of deserved the playful reprimand. The other thoughts were still heavy on her mind, and she found herself asking the question before she even realized it.

"Do you remember your family at all?"

Ilyen glanced over at her, surprised. "No. Do you?"

She shook her head. "No. Flashes here and there, a vague idea of a dark haired woman who might be my mom, but that's it. I was barely five when SysTech picked me up. I don't even have a full name." That last part came out rather more bitterly than she'd intended.

"So?" Ilyen shrugged again. "What would change if you did? I've got one, but all that tells me is some guy named Kirana knocked up some woman named Vanadariel. I know jack and shit about who they were, or what I was to them. Maybe they were one of those perfect couples from the movies and they valiantly gave their lives trying to protect me from SysTech. Maybe they freaked out the first time I teleported and dropped me on the company's doorstep." He met her eyes. "Either way I ended up here."

"But don't you ever wonder? If your family is still out there? If anyone…if anyone cared?"

"No," he answered bluntly. "If they are, all we have connecting us is DNA. If they did, it didn't matter. If there's some alternate universe out there where I'm a nice boy who grew up in a nice family and doesn't know thirty-two ways to kill someone barehanded, then great. Doesn't change that in *this* universe I grew up in a shitty military program and made my first stealth kill at fifteen."

He cocked his head at her then. "Evandra, why do *you* care?"

"Well, I…" This was hard to put into words. "I guess I just wonder what it feels like, to have a family."

Ilyen gave her a look of disbelief. "First off there's that guy," he gestured back towards the mess and presumably Galhen, "who's totally into you and has that dumbass heroic streak where he'd probably take a literal bullet for you. Sure he's boring and kind of a pain in the ass, but hey, he's smoking hot and you seem pretty into him too. The captain likes you so much he's basically paying for us to live on his ship. Nalea's still talking to you after you blew up her life.

"You've *got* a family, Evandra. You've got *us*."

***

A MONTH BECAME TWO.

"How did *you* get started as mechanic, Captain Marene?" Oliven leaned forward eagerly, propping his elbows on the table as he cradled his tea. Sandrel sipped his own cup.

"It wasn't really something I ever decided to *start*. It's more like, my parents were freight haulers, and most of the year we lived on our ship. They were both good with engines because they had to be - we didn't make enough to support hiring a full-time ship's mechanic, and dropping your livelihood off at the shop every time it starts making a funny noise is a fast way to go out of business as a small shipper. Plus, if something happens when you're in deep space, you're on your own." He quirked a smile. "As soon as I was old enough to pass them the right tool, I got conscripted into helping with repairs."

If anything, this seemed to excite Oliven even more. "So you never went to school for it or anything? You just learned on the job?"

"School is *expensive*, Oliven. I learned everything I know from other people who taught me what *they* knew. Just like I'm teaching you now."

The young telepath beamed back at him and scooted his chair back from the table. "I'll try to get that transponder fixed up so you can look at it later today. I'll be in the engine room if you need me."

Kerelle watched him head off toward the engine room, a bounce in his step despite his limp. She met Sandrel's eyes with a quizzical glance.

"He's been in much better moods lately."

"Kid's really taking to the engine work." Sandrel smiled. "He's good at it, too. Learns quick."

"Galhen said the same thing," she commented. "Apparently he's been teaching Oliven a bit about first aid."

"I'm glad." Sandrel sipped his coffee thoughtfully. "He's a bright kid, I think he'll do well with whatever he wants to do. It's just a matter of building up his confidence a little." He glanced over at her. "He didn't go into a lot of detail, but it sounds like he spent most of his life with the PsiCorp telling him he was garbage."

"That's what I gathered too. I'm not terribly surprised. His telepathy is on the low end for even Class-1. All SysTech cares about is making money, and he'd never be able to bring in much."

"You and your man did, though." He sounded more curious than anything else.

"Stars, yes. Ask Galhen some time what SysTech charges people to be treated by a Class-3 regenerative."

"Oh, I'm aware," Sandrel answered, an odd note in his voice. He leaned back. "Why do I get the feeling, though, that he handed out *free samples* when he thought your bosses weren't looking?"

She grinned. "Because you've spent more than five minutes with him. Honestly, I suspect that's half the reason Galhen was transferred to field work after his mandatory residency period, instead of being kept on at the hospital. But back to Oliven, do you think he's got a future in mechanics?"

"If he wants to, sure. His psionics might be low-grade, but

most of us get through life just fine without any psionics at all. No reason he can't take up a trade and do well."

It was a few weeks later when Sandrel's voice crackled over the intercom.

"As a heads up, people, we're going to be dropping out of hyper for little bit. Don't freak out, nothing is wrong, we'll be back on our way to Zanaad pretty soon." The familiar sensation of coming back into realspace followed a few minutes later.

Curious, she made her way up toward the cockpit. Voices drifted out into the corridor.

"Captain Marene, are...are you sure this is safe?"

"Relax, kid. We're alone in the void out here, there's nothing you can crash into. Give it a shot."

"But what if I hit the wrong button and...and turn off the life support or something."

Sandrel chuckled. "Trust me, Oliven, there is no 'turn off life support' button on this console. Just keep your hands here - that's where you adjust course. Try taking us a little to the left."

The ship jerked abruptly. She heard Oliven's horrified gasp from down the hall.

"Calm down, it's fine, that's why we're doing this out here where you can't hit anything, remember? Just keep in mind that it's fairly sensitive, so you don't want to press too hard. Now this one controls acceleration and deceleration..."

The next half-hour was a bumpy one, but Oliven's exhilaration brushed her senses all the way on the other side of the ship.

TWO MONTHS BECAME THREE.

She would have expected it would get dull - carrying boxes, filling out forms, carefully tracking the accounts. It didn't get dull. Well, the box-carrying part did, but there were enough hands that it was never too onerous, and soon enough after they made port for a delivery she was free to explore. And exploring was glorious.

Objectively, perhaps the places they visited were not especially exciting. But to Kerelle they were windows into a world she had only ever seen from a distance, a world where people lived their lives and chased their dreams and suffered their setbacks without the watchful eye of the PsiCorp. Kerelle had traveled a great deal in her time in the PsiCorp, and she would have described herself as fairly cosmopolitan. But she was also beginning to realize how sheltered she had been within the confines of the PsiCorp, and how much of the galaxy she had missed inside its gilded cage.

She was determined now to make up for lost time.

One of her favorite parts of their travels was food. She and Galhen made a point of finding small local restaurants wherever they stopped, the ones tucked down the alleys and nestled in nondescript shopping parks. Sometimes they were good and sometimes they weren't, but they were always *different*. And different was delightful.

On the evening of an overnight stop in Kalsarrat, they found themselves leaving one of the not-so-good ones. It was a particular disappointment because she'd heard so much about Kalsarrat noodle dishes, and the menu descriptions had just sounded so *delicious*. She'd been expecting a lot, granted, but she was still feeling distinctly crestfallen as they made their way out. The worst part was they only had one night here; there wouldn't be an opportunity to try again. *Maybe if I explain that it's for noodles, Sandrel will keep an eye out for another job on Kalsarrat.*

Galhen chuckled. "You know, darling, he might. Our fearless captain does have an appreciation for cuisine."

Kerelle stopped dead and stared at him. He paused, looking at her quizzically.

"What is it?"

"Galhen, I didn't say anything."

He blinked at her. "What do you mean?"

"About the noodles. About wanting to ask Sandrel to come back. I thought that. I didn't say it."

His face went still and he stared at her, bright eyes full with that same painful hope that Kerelle knew must be reflected in her own. It had been three months since his injury, with no improvement. They'd never spoken of it, but Kerelle knew they had both quietly given up.

Part of her was afraid to look, afraid to *know* in case she'd imagined it and that fragile nascent hope was crushed again. She took a deep breath and took his hand, holding his eyes straight on.

Darling.

"I hear you," he whispered. "Clear as dawn."

They met in a wild embrace, his lips fierce and joyous against hers. *I love you*, she told him, *so very much.*

There, the faint, tentative pulse of affection in reply where their bond had been. Where their bond *was.*

They took their time walking home, savoring the feeling of being truly *together* in a way they thought would never be possible again. They discovered that Galhen was far from fully restored - he could hear Kerelle, but he could only project feelings back to her, rather than words. Still Kerelle could scarcely contain her joy. If he'd improved this much, he might still improve further.

"But it's so *strange*," Galhen marveled, not for the first time that evening. "After so long, to suddenly recover."

"I think you've *been* recovering," Kerelle said slowly, "and we just didn't see it. You knew Nalea was upset last week, though she didn't say a word about that article until you asked her what was wrong."

"Realizing my sister had a bee in her bonnet hardly required psionics," he answered with a smile.

"No but…you *knew*, and she'd barely walked in the room. I think you read it off her emotions. I think you've *been* doing that, and we weren't looking for it, so we didn't see it as the first sign."

He was quiet for a moment. "Maybe you're right. I…stopped looking for it, a while ago."

She squeezed his hand. "I did too. I'm glad we were wrong."

Another faint pulse of feeling, stronger this time.

Come on, love, she sent. *Let's share the good news.*

THREE MONTHS BECAME FIVE.

It was their last morning of a rather routine stop. Kerelle suspected their cargo hadn't been terribly legal - when Sandrel asked her to come along to meet clients, there was usually a reason - but they'd handed it off without incident. The clients had been perfectly professional, paid promptly and in full, and been on their way.

At one point she might have been concerned about what, exactly, they were trafficking in, but at this point she knew Sandrel better than that. There were a *lot* of things that weren't terribly legal in various parts of the galaxy, more for reasons related to the multigalactics' profitability and lobbying efforts than to any public good. Whatever was in their nondescript, neatly packed crates, Kerelle trusted that Sandrel wouldn't have taken the job if it were dangerous to the communities it ended up in.

Kerelle was finishing her tea and mulling a second cup when Galhen ducked into the mess and poured one for himself. He nonchalantly sat down next to her, pretending not to notice her stare.

He'd been steadily growing his hair back out after they'd shaved it at the jump gate, and when they'd gone to bed last night it was approaching being able to cover his ears. It was now several centimeters longer, the tips brushing his jawline again as it had on Elekar. Her eyes traveled down to his rolled-up sleeves. That large bruise he'd acquired loading cargo yesterday had mysteriously vanished as well.

He sipped his tea, continuing to ignore her look. She kept staring. Finally he glanced up to meet her eyes, lips quirked in a barely-hidden grin.

"Yes, darling?"

She looked pointedly at his hair, then down at his sleeve.

The grin widened. "Well, it has been some time since I've been able to access my regeneratives. I thought I might as well test them on something non-vital."

"Ah, of course," she remarked lightly. "That makes perfect sense." *You vain creature.*

He laughed aloud. *Permit me my vices, darling.* He'd been recovering steadily over the past few months, and his voice in her mind was strong and clear as it had ever been. *I'm not sure I'm quite at full strength - I certainly wouldn't try any surgery at the moment - but everything is there, and it seems to be intact.* There was a note of wonder in his voice. *Given my progress with telepathy, we have every reason to be hopeful for a full recovery.*

Joy and excitement and relief overlaid his thoughts, and the smile he gave her was radiant as the sun.

FIVE MONTHS BECAME SEVEN.

"Mm," the port inspector mused as he looked over the manifest. "Everything seems to be in order here." Kerelle held her breath and kept her touch light as a feather. *You don't need to inspect.* If that failed, of course, there was a secondary plan - lean on him to inspect the crate they'd carefully prepared with no contraband whatsoever.

The secondary plan wasn't necessary. The old man nodded at Sandrel and made his notations on the manifest, apparently with some difficulty. Galhen, Kerelle noticed, was watching the inspector's slow, stiff signature very closely.

Darling, this is going to sound vile, but I need you to trust me. When he turns to leave, can you trip him ever so slightly?

Why am I tripping a fragile old man, Galhen?

So that I have a good reason to grasp his arm to steady him. I believe it's arthritis that's bothering him, and if he could afford to treat it, he would have by now. It's simple enough for me to clear up, but I need a few moments of physical contact and there are precious few acceptable reasons to touch strangers.

I'll do what I can. Be ready.

Even knowing it was for a good cause, Kerelle still felt like the galaxy's biggest asshole as the inspector turned to go, and she gave him a tiny push to unbalance him. She spread a shield underneath to catch him, just in case he actually *did* fall.

He didn't. Galhen's hand shot out to grip his arm, helping him regain his balance. The old man flushed deeply and thanked him, his embarrassment evident. Galhen gave him a dazzling smile and said something about how it was no trouble, dialing up that radiant charm he did so well. A brief moment and he let go again, waving as the inspector made his way back down the dock. He was, Kerelle noted, shuffling rather less than on the way in.

There may have been some to deal with in the knees as well. Galhen's thought was infused with triumph.

I take it you were able to help?

Very much so. He should enjoy significantly more manual dexterity, and he'll walk more comfortably as well.

Abruptly Kerelle realized Sandrel and Ilyen were both watching them with narrowed eyes.

"So," Sandrel said. "I'm guessing we have something to discuss on the ship."

A short time later they were gathered around the mess table, Galhen having explained succinctly what he'd done and why. Sandrel's face was unreadable. Ilyen, on the other hand, was furious.

"So what's going to happen when he goes home and tells everyone about how he shook hands with a mysterious stranger and now he's all better, hm? What's going to happen when SysTech hears?"

"They won't," Galhen said firmly, though Kerelle picked up on the faint defensiveness threaded in his reply. "I can do more than just *heal*, Ilyen. I made sure he wouldn't connect it to us."

"You mean you *tried* to, and you *hope* he won't. Don't fuck with me, Ambrel, I know how telepathy works. You might be class 3, but your shit stops working once you get out of range, just like everybody else."

"If he's internalized the suggestion at that point, there's no *need* for it to keep working. Difficult as it may be to believe, you are not the only one on this ship with field experience."

"No, but I seem to be the only one who appreciates how *lucky* we've been so far." He slammed his hands on the table. "Remember how Nalea pretty much set her life on fire to help you? You going to just throw away everything she gave you so you can play hero?"

The blow landed. Galhen's eyes flashed as his body visibly tensed. Kerelle laid a gentle hand on his arm and sent calm through their bond.

"I am entirely cognizant of the price she paid for us," Galhen forced through clenched teeth. "And that using my regeneratives outside this ship is not without risk. There are ways to mitigate that risk, and I will employ them. But I have a very rare ability to provide help that many people desperately need, and it would be *immoral* to turn my back on them."

"Oh cut the *morality* shit," Ilyen growled. "This isn't about *helping people*. This is about making yourself feel better for all the shit you did at SysTech."

The room went silent.

"You have no idea what I did at SysTech." Galhen's voice was quiet and dangerous.

"I can guess. There's a lot of skeletons in the corporate closet. You might not've put them there but you helped whoever did."

"Ilyen - " Kerelle started. He cut her off.

"Save it, Evandra, your record's as red as as mine. We *all* did shit at SysTech. You can't fix any of it now."

"And you don't feel any need to try?" She asked softly. "Now that your choices are yours to make, you don't want to do *better*?"

Ilyen looked away, some of the belligerence going out of his stance. "The past is over. Throwing our lives away now won't change anything we did then."

"I don't intend to throw them away." Galhen had calmed down somewhat, though Kerelle could still sense the remnants of his anger, like embers smoldering through the bond. "I'm serious, Ilyen, we'll *be* cautious. More cautious," he acknowledged reluctantly, "than I was today. But we have a real opportunity to save lives. And," he added with a glance at Sandrel, who was after all the owner of the ship, "I'd like to start doing it regularly, and offer clinic services when we make stops in areas like this one."

Sandrel had spent the entire exchange staring into his tea, his dark eyes far away. Finally he looked up at the three of them, all waiting for his answer.

"Ilyen isn't wrong," he said quietly. "This does increase our risk of exposure, which endangers everyone on this ship. I can't allow that lightly." He swirled his mug, sending the tea leaves whirling amidst the now-cold water. He didn't seem finished.

"So." Sandrel gave a heaving sigh, and continued, his voice

unusually subdued. "So when I was twenty-two, my dad got sick. At first we thought it was just a station bug, nothing serious, but the cough just kept getting worse. My mom and I finally scraped together enough money for a doctor, who told us it was Taskal."

Galhen's arm twitched beneath Kerelle's hand. *Lung condition,* he told her silently. *The cause is unknown, but it's extremely treatable. If you can afford the treatments.*

Kerelle got a horrible feeling about where this story was going.

"Apparently there's pills that can clear it right up, but that little bottle of pills cost more than we made all year. That's actually how I got started in *this business,*" he added, his emphasis clear that *this business* meant smuggling. "I was hoping to make enough in time. I didn't."

Something clicked into place in Kerelle's memory.

"Is that when your mother sold their ship?" She asked softly.

He confirmed her suspicion with a nod. "My parents were proud to be honest shippers. My mom didn't approve of me being otherwise, no matter the cause. She said she'd rather see the ship scrapped than used for smuggling. We haven't talked much since."

He set the tea down again. "If we'd docked next to a runaway regenerative doing charity work, my dad would still be alive." He looked up then to meet Galhen's eyes. "Ilyen *isn't* wrong. But there's millions and millions of small-time freighter families out there like mine. And station brats. And slumrats. If you're really willing to help them, Galhen, I can't tell you no."

"Thank you, Sandrel," Galhen answered sincerely. The smuggler nodded, his expression still distant. Ilyen grumbled something under his breath, but acquiesced. Their clinic was in business.

SEVEN MONTHS BECAME A YEAR.

"Breathe in for me again?" The young man in miner's coveralls obediently drew a deep breath while Galhen listened. "Ah, there it is."

Her husband gave what Kerelle had come to think of as his professional smile.

"You have a minor lung infection, but you should recover just fine." He rifled around briefly in the portable cabinet and withdrew a small vial of green liquid, pressing it into his patient's hand. "Get plenty of rest and fluids, and take 30 milliliters twice a day until you've had the whole vial."

Not so minor then, if he was dispensing the colored water they used as a placebo to cover for using his psionics. That had been Nalea's idea.

"Thanks." His patient gingerly took the vial. "But then do I owe you...?"

"There's no charge," Galhen responded warmly. "Just get better, and remember to wear your oxygen filter mask in the deep tunnels so it doesn't come back again."

The young miner was the last of the visitors for the day, and she helped Galhen take down their little clinic tent after they'd waved goodbye.

How bad was it actually? The miner hadn't seemed that sick.

Not too bad yet, but it could've gotten serious without treatment, especially if he kept on with skirting the safety protocols. I understand the filters are awkward and uncomfortable, but this is precisely why we have them.

He packed the last of the tent into its little bag and straightened. *In any case, I removed most of the infection and boosted his immune system. He's young and otherwise healthy, he should fight it off without difficulty now. And hopefully be scared straight on protective equipment.*

Hopefully. She paused and looked back at him, a smile curling over her lips. *And now that we're finished up…do you remember what day it is?*

"How could I forget," he murmured as he took her hand and they started back toward the ship, "that today marks a year since I married the bravest, most beautiful woman in the galaxy?"

Kerelle grinned back. "I made us a reservation at that place with the whiskey tastings, if you want to try it."

"How could I refuse?" He kissed her, relaxed and happy as they made their way home. The sun was beginning to sink below the skyline, and as they strolled through the orange-lit streets Kerelle reflected warmly on the year behind them and all its adventures, the strange little family their ship had become, and many more adventures she hoped were ahead.

She was, she realized with a soft smile, the happiest she'd ever been in her life.

EIGHTEEN

THE MAN'S frantic cries for help reached them before he appeared, dashing at full speed through the heavy flap that served as the clinic's door.

"You have to come," he panted. "It's my daughter, she can't breathe. Please!"

The man's distress was palpable, even through Kerelle's shields. Galhen was on his feet before he'd finished speaking.

"Kerelle, can you close up here for a bit? I'll be back as soon as I'm able." He hurriedly snatched one of the colored vials from their place in the cabinet, and followed the man out the door at a brisk pace.

Kerelle put out the sign that indicated they weren't currently open for patients, and busied herself with packing up the clinic as she waited for Galhen to return. Fortunately it was already near the end of the day, so they didn't have a line out the door of locals hoping for treatment. Sandrel had been prescient about the clinic's demand; at each stop, once word got out that they were offering free care, they received a steady stream of people in need of it. Not all of them needed psionic healing, and in fact the majority did not. Galhen's share of profits from the smuggling business now went mostly to conventional medical supplies - easy to procure, easy to use, but still out of reach for the frequently impoverished people who came to them for help.

For the minority who *did* need his psionics, well, that was what the colored vials were for.

With the clinic taken care of and no sign of Galhen, Kerelle started back towards the ship. She was just beginning to wonder how things were going when Galhen's stab of alarm struck her through their bond like a psychic blow.

She stopped dead, desperately reaching back to him. *Darling, what's wrong? Where are you?*

Before he could respond, his consciousness cut off abruptly from the bond. In her mind, there echoed only silence.

Panic surged through her.

Breathe. Breathe. He's not dead, you would have felt *it if he was dead, you have to breathe.* The worst may not have happened, but this was bad.

She had to get back to the ship.

Sandrel was waiting grim-faced at the ramp.

"Sandrel, something's happened -"

"I know." He handed her a crumpled piece of paper. "Street kid brought it just a minute ago. Said he was paid to give a message to 'the dark-haired woman' on this ship. I told him I'd pass it on."

She practically tore it out of his hands. The grimy sheet of paper had been inscribed in a firm hand.

You owe us big for the stunt on Kalnis, and the Ash and Bones are here to collect. Word is the pretty blond doctor is your lover. Be here at 22:00 tonight if you want him to stay pretty. Come alone. An address was written below.

The paper shook in her hand. She lifted her eyes to meet Sandrel's. He sighed heavily.

"Come in. We've only got a couple of hours to prepare."

"THIS IS EXACTLY what I *said would happen*. I said this do-gooding shit was going to get us discovered, and *here we are*." Ilyen paced the mess like a caged lion, his agitation scraping at Kerelle's senses. Agitation, and anxiety. Despite his posturing, Ilyen was worried too.

"Knives." Sandrel's voice was firm. "You're not helping." Ilyen scowled, but he didn't say anything as he angrily dropped himself into the chair next to Nalea's.

Nalea herself was white as bone, drawn up in a ball on her chair as if trying to make herself as small as possible. She'd been wide-eyed and silent since hearing that the Ash and Bones were once again on their trail.

"Okay." Sandrel took a deep breath and let it out. "Let's start with what we know. Kerelle, you said you were both at the clinic when someone came in."

"Yes," she responded mechanically. It felt like all this was happening from far away, to someone else. The rational part of her mind recognized she was probably in shock, but that observation did not seem terribly useful. "A man came in, said his daughter couldn't breathe and needed help. He didn't seem…his panic seemed real."

"It probably was," Sandrel answered bluntly. "If this is the setup it looks like, then his kid probably *was* in danger for her life - from the Ash and Bones, if he didn't succeed in luring your man away."

"How the hell does a C3 telepath walk into an ambush, anyway?" Ilyen's grumble sounded almost more curious than accusatory.

"Galhen shields heavily around his patients," she answered numbly. "He says it's too overwhelming to concentrate otherwise. He wouldn't have picked up anything beneath the man's surface fear."

Sandrel picked up the thread again. "So we're guessing Galhen follows this guy home, or somewhere anyway, and the Ash and Bones are waiting. They ambush him, send the charming note, wait for you to take the bait." He looked at her. "The *first* time we dealt with these assholes, you were able to find the Doc with telepathy so we could swoop in and get her." Nalea blanched a bit further. This entirely incident was clearly bringing back memories she'd rather forget.

Sandrel gave her a sympathetic nod and continued. "Can you do that again to find Galhen? I know they gave us a time and place, but this is the kind of party I'd rather get to before they're done setting up."

Kerelle shook her head. "I sense minds, not bodies. I found Nalea by following her thoughts. Wherever they have Galhen, I think he's unconscious." *Or dead,* a horrible part of her mind supplied. *Maybe you* did *feel it. That sudden silence might have* been *it.* She shoved the thought down viciously. A growing flame of anger was kindling inside her, and the numb, disconnected feeling began to melt before it.

The table was silent for a moment, as the same thought clearly occurred to the others.

"Evandra..." Ilyen's tone was unusually quiet. "Are you sure...?"

"Yes," she growled, as much to herself as to them. "He's alive. I would have *felt* it."

"Then we may have to show up for the ambush tonight," Sandrel conceded reluctantly, "and figure out how to come out on top."

The angry flame was a furnace now. "I'll come out on top. They don't understand what they're dealing with."

"They sort of *do*, though," he pointed out gently. "You left their base in pretty bad shape back on Kalnis, they've *seen* what you can do. If they're going after you like this, they must think they have a way to account for it."

She almost snapped that there was no way for the pirates to account for what she could do to them, but reason reasserted itself in time. Kerelle closed her eyes and forced herself to breathe deeply, and disengage her emotions. Treat it like a mission. Succeed first, feel later.

She'd thought she was done with that.

"I'll keep that in mind," she answered calmly. "Sandrel, please be ready to leave when we return. Oliven and Nalea, stay with the ship and be ready as well. Ilyen." She met his eyes, not entirely sure of what she was going to see there. "Are you willing to help me with this?"

"Of *course*." He looked mildly offended she'd had to ask.

"What if it's another trap." Nalea's voice was only a whisper. "What if now they're luring *you* away, and then they come to the ship again, and this time they don't just throw us in the brig." Her eyes darted up to Kerelle's, wide with fear, and her voice held a trace of hysteria. "What if this time they cut us up and put us on their wall." A tear rolled down her cheek and Kerelle had to up her shields against Nalea's burst of fear, for herself and the nightmare she thought was behind her, and for *stars don't think about it, what could they already have done to Galhen -*

To Kerelle's surprise Ilyen's face softened and he drew Nalea into an embrace, resting his forehead against hers. "It's alright, babe. We're not going to let them hurt you. Evandra and me are going to get your brother back, and we'll fuck up those pirates for taking him. And if they show up at the ship, I can be back here before they can fire their guns."

Nalea said nothing, but she held to him tightly, and Kerelle felt her terror slightly ease.

"Ilyen's right, Nalea," she added, trying to sound encouraging. "We won't let you be captured again. And we are going to *fuck them up.*"

She meant every word of that.

TO NO ONE'S real surprise, the note's address turned out to be an abandoned warehouse in a dark and derelict industrial district. Between the ransom note and the locale, the Ash and Bones were proving unimaginative in their kidnappings.

True to instructions, she approached it alone. Ilyen was somewhere close by; she could sense his thoughts in near proximity, but she trusted him to stay hidden. For all his quirks otherwise, Ilyen was all business on the battlefield, and very good at his job.

She paused before her destination, senses wide. Now that she was closer, she picked out over a dozen pirates, including a pair hidden on either side of the entrance. No surprise there. She'd expected it to be an ambush. That it was a classic "hide behind the door" ambush just added to the lack of flair.

Well, she'd known from their base on Kalnis that subtlety was not an Ash and Bones characteristic.

The warehouse's rusted metal doors were thrown haphazardly open. She strode forward through them.

As expected, they clanged shut behind her before she'd taken more than a few steps inside. The two waiting pirates surged forward, guns flashing. Their projectiles clattered harmlessly off her shields.

How stupid did they think she *was*?

There was a mighty clang as she slammed them both against the wall, suspended several centimeters high so that their feet dangled beneath them. She took a threatening step towards the closer one.

"Ah ah," an unseen voice cautioned. "You probably don't want to do that."

The lights suddenly switched on, the sudden brightness blinding her - though her open senses let her track the pirates' movements anyway. None of them moved from their semicircle further in, though she wasn't sure who the *speaker* had been...

Her vision cleared. Standing in front her was a richly-dressed, *heavily-armed* man who looked like the leader - presumably the mysterious *boss* they'd invoked on Kalnis. Troublingly, he was also wearing a rather nice psiblocker. That was the extent of the detail she had time to notice, however, before her attention was torn away to Galhen.

He was slumped over bound in a chair beside the pirate boss, eyes closed and apparently insensible to the pirate who held a knife against his throat. He groaned and shifted slightly at the sudden bright light; his guard hurriedly jabbed him with a syringe and he subsided again.

"Why don't you let them down slow and easy," the boss was saying, "then step over here so we can talk. It'd be shame if there were any..." he glanced at Galhen and smirked. "Misunderstandings."

Kerelle dropped the two pirates, more gently than she would have under other circumstances. Shields tight, she started toward the pirate lord.

"That's close enough," he said lazily. "I have to say, after the mess you left for us on Kalnis, I was expecting a little more. Instead this one comes along as trusting as my sweet old granny, and you come along right after him. I'm almost disappointed."

Oh, give her time.

"What is it you want?" she asked coolly. She forced herself to make eye contact with him, instead of watching Galhen.

He smirked again. "It was the funniest thing. I'm home on Kalnis, cleaning up after *you* and minding my own affairs." The other pirates snickered and his smirk widened, clearly enjoying himself. Burning stars, he was so voids-damned *theatrical*. "One day, I get a call about that scientist we tried to ransom to Olstenfel, though if I'd known SysTech was interested in her I'd have skipped the university and gone straight for the big fish."

He began to pace leisurely back and forth. "Of course I didn't *have* the scientist any more, thanks to you, but it turned into a very interesting conversation about the experience. Which turned into an even *more* interesting conversation about how SysTech lost two PsiCorp agents, and the extremely generous bounty for anybody who brings them in alive."

He stopped pacing and made eye contact, a current of anger seeping up through his genial facade. "And whaddya know. One of them is a dark-haired woman who can blow things up with her mind. Sure rung a bell. File photo *sure* looked familiar.

"And well, I'm a man of opportunity." The false joviality was back in place, and the pacing resumed. "Our new business part- ners even threw in some toys." He gestured upwards, the psiblocker glinting in the harsh warehouse lighting. The surrounding pirates snickered again, and several hefted their guns. She had to assume they were anti-psionic weapons, cour- tesy of SysTech.

"So we start asking around about this ship you stole from us, found out its medic would treat the street trash for free. Found out he was *awfully* good at it. And what do you know." He stopped again and swept his hands dramatically. "Here we are."

"Now there's good money for either of you alive, but there's *best* money for both. Number of eyes, teeth and fingers, however, weren't specified." The pirate boss leaned forward, his face lit with sadistic glee. "Now be a good girl and put your hands behind you, before anyone suffers an unfortunate slip of the hand."

That was the other pirate's cue; he let his knife drift upwards towards Galhen's eyes.

Kerelle held the boss's gaze unblinking, a cold fury coursing through her. She'd held back, on Kalnis. Tried not to use lethal force, when she *could* have left them a pile of corpses in the ruins of their base. And then these people had stalked them like prey, out of pride and greed. They tried to turn Galhen's compassion into a weakness they could exploit. They were threatening now to mutilate him, simply to frighten her. She could practically *smell* it rolling off the pirate boss - an almost sexual anticipation of seeing her fear. She'd held back, and this is how they repaid her mercy.

They wanted the PsiCorp? Then she would give them the *voids-damned PsiCorp.*

She snapped the neck of the one holding Galhen without so much as a twitch. The other pirates began to shout, raising the anti-psionic weapons that had made them overconfident. None of them made it. The shockwave she threw outwards slammed them against the warehouse walls with enough force to *hear* their snapping bones.

Kerelle ignored them and slowly advanced towards their leader, her eyes never breaking contact. The pirate boss's eyes had widened, his struggle to process the speed of the changed situation plain on his face. Muffled screams and groans sounded from around the warehouse; Ilyen was cleaning up the surviving pirates.

The boss made a grab for Galhen, still unconscious and bound. Kerelle flicked her wrist and whisked her husband safely behind her, chair and all. The pirate lord's face began to take on a shade of panic, and he clutched a hand to his psiblocker as if it were a holy talisman to ward her off. From his expression, he realized it wouldn't be enough.

"On Kalnis, I tried to avoid killing," she told him softly. "I thought enough blood had already been shed. I see that I was wrong."

She snapped a jagged chunk of rebar from one of the rusted supports, and floated it up behind her. "Perhaps now," she said, holding his eyes, "it will be enough."

NALEA QUICKLY DETERMINED that the pirates had just given Galhen a sedative, and that it should wear off within a few hours with no lasting effect. Relief flooded Kerelle at the pronouncement.

But that also meant she now had nothing to distract her from her thoughts.

She'd made it through the awful confrontation and its aftermath, because she had a decade's practice compartmentalizing. She'd been solely focused on Galhen's health and safety, and she could deal with the rest later.

Well, it was later, and after two rounds of vomiting she still felt sick.

She'd left the body of the pirate boss pinned to the floor of the warehouse with his own crews' knives, like some sort of grotesque science exhibit. And before that, the other pirates, sliding motionless down the walls like broken toys. She had just killed over a dozen people, in cold blood, without a whisper of remorse. It wasn't the first time she'd killed, of course, wasn't even the first time since leaving the PsiCorp, but it was the first time she hadn't even tried not to.

More than that, she'd enjoyed it. That terrible fury had fueled her, and it had been viscerally satisfying to snuff them out. Like insects.

She barely made it to the lavatory in time before round three.

Stars. The thought pounded through her mind afterward, as she knelt shaking on the cold floor of the lavatory and tried to steady her breath. *Stars and holy flame. I really* am *a monster.*

She couldn't blame SysTech for this one. Just how well she still fit the role they'd molded her to.

Even Ilyen had seemed taken aback. He'd been quiet on the way back to the ship, stealing sidelong glances at her when he thought she didn't see. She'd left it to him to tell Nalea later that the Ash and Bones were no longer a concern.

She hoped he left out the details.

All the same, she avoided the mess. Let Ilyen tell Nalea, and probably Sandrel, whatever he wanted to include; she didn't want to discuss it. Perhaps it was childish to lie here curled up in a ball in their cabin instead of facing what she'd done. At the moment, it was all she felt capable of.

A slight twinge from Galhen got her attention. He still lay unmoving beside her, but she could sense his mind drifting back towards awareness again.

He deserved comfort from someone better than her, someone more like himself who made the universe better instead of worse. With a cold pit in her stomach, she wondered if he'd even *want* her any more, knowing what she was? Maybe she should leave, should get Sandrel or someone else. But in this too, she was consummately selfish; if he ultimately sent her away, then she wanted these last moments at his side.

And so she took his hand and kissed his brow, and answered his mind's groggy flickers of pain and anxiety with soothing reassurance that he was safe and loved. Finally his eyes blinked open again, regarding her with confusion.

"Kerelle?" His usually smooth voice was more of a croak. "What-?"

She stroked his hair. "Shh. It's all right, darling. Nalea says they gave you a sedative, and that it should wear off soon."

He blinked at her a few more times, absorbing what she said. "Sedative," he repeated, furrowing his brow. He closed his eyes for several long moments; when he opened them again they were clear.

"Ugh. Now that *that's* out of my system," Galhen levered himself upright with no apparent difficulty. "Darling, what *happened*, exactly? The last thing I remember is being on a house call, and then I think I was struck from behind. Clearly the situation has progressed from then."

She filled him in on what had transpired - the kidnapping, the ransom attempt, the pirates' alliance with SysTech. Coward that she was, she gave only vague detail on the actual confrontation and rescue.

Galhen didn't seem to notice. His face had taken on a distinctly embarrassed flush as the story went on.

"That's twice now you've had to carry me insensate back to the ship," he admitted ruefully. "This is becoming a rather humiliating trend." He gave her a sideways glance. "Ilyen's going to be *insufferable* about this, isn't he."

She tried to smile. "He is."

He paused and looked at her closely. "Kerelle, is everything all right?"

No, it definitely wasn't.

She stared back at him helplessly, her silence answering the question. His concerned gaze sharpened.

Darling, what's happened?

Her eyes shied away from his, and instead found themselves resting on his wedding band, gleaming faintly in the dim cabin light. She had to tell him. And then...and then, if he wanted, she would release him from their vows.

Even thinking about it closed up her throat so as to make speech impossible. Instead she just leaned forward to rest her forehead against his, and pulled him into the memory.

It was even worse to relive it all again, this time with an audience. But she forced herself not to hold anything back - not her violence against the pirates, and not how she'd felt about it.

Finally she drew back and steeled herself for his reaction.

He looked back at her, troubled. But the rejection she'd expected didn't materialize; instead he drew her down to lie in his arms. It was silent for some time, as he sorted through his own thoughts. Kerelle said nothing, at war between the terrible hope in her breast that he was still willing to touch her, and the sick knowledge that she didn't deserve this. She should just leave the ship altogether. Maybe there was a cave somewhere she could live, away from anyone she could pose a danger to.

Finally he spoke. "You aren't a monster."

She could only whisper the words. "Galhen, you *saw*. I killed all those people, and I *liked* doing it."

"Yes," he acknowledged. "But you aren't liking it now. If you were a monster, you wouldn't feel bad about it afterward, might even look forward to doing it again. You definitely wouldn't be thinking ridiculous thoughts about becoming some sort of hermit so that you never hurt anyone ever again. And apologies, dearest, but your projections are nearly deafening at the moment."

He gave her shoulders a gentle squeeze. "I understand why you feel that way. I'll be honest with you, it was rather disturbing to watch. But you didn't kill those people because you like killing. You did it to protect us. And those pirates weren't soldiers on the other side, just trying to do a job. They chose to devote themselves to harming others." He rolled over and met her eyes. "You probably saved innocent lives by ending them."

"I just...I don't..." He waited while she struggled to find the words. "SysTech raised me to be a weapon," she managed finally. "And they did an excellent job. I thought I left that with the PsiCorp. I guess I didn't."

She lifted her eyes back to his. "You can find some...some sort of balance. For everything we did in the PsiCorp. You can help people, now, and try to...to make things more right than wrong. All I'm good for is spilling blood. There's no balance for me."

"You are good for *far* more than spilling blood. But I understand what you're trying to say." He paused for a moment, as if unsure to continue.

Darling, you are *a powerful weapon, when you choose to be. And sometimes weapons are necessary. They can defend as well as destroy.*

She lay awake pondering that, long after his breathing had taken on the even cadence of sleep.

NINETEEN

KERELLE WAS nervous facing the rest of the crew the next morning; she wasn't sure quite what Ilyen had told everyone, or if they would be as understanding as Galhen. When Sandrel asked to speak to her privately, her stomach lurched. Perhaps she'd be leaving the ship to find that hermit cave after all.

"So I had a chat with Knives after you all got in last night," he started without preamble. "You doing alright?"

She blinked back at him, the apology speech she'd been mentally rehearsing halting in mid-syllable. "Me?"

"You. After last night. From what he said things got kind of intense."

"What…did he say, exactly?"

"And I quote, 'Evandra got pissed and laid them out like it was nothing, and now I think she's kinda freaked about it.' Oh, and that I should tell you you're alright because, and I quote again, 'Ambrel will probably tell her she's alright, but she might think he's just saying it because he's fucking her.'" He gave her a half smile. "Nobody will ever accuse Knives of being the eloquent one on the ship, but his heart's in the right place more often than you'd expect."

Sandrel's face grew serious again, and he leaned in. "So, Fury," he asked softly, "*are* you alright?"

Kerelle sighed. "I don't know. I mean, yes, I think. Galhen *did* try to help last night. I just...I've never struck in anger before. Not like that. And not of my own choosing."

"I get being freaked out about the striking-in-anger thing. Honestly, knowing you were able to do this sort of thing is what scared the shit out of me when I first found out you were a psionic. And it probably would have scared the shit out of me if I'd actually watched you do it. But given that I've never even seen you lose your temper, I wouldn't say you have a *problem* with anger. I'd say you were provoked and you snapped."

"But I have to control myself better than that," she whispered. "If I don't, people can die."

"And did, this time," he agreed. "And now you know you need to be careful not to lose control when you're angry. But these weren't exactly innocent bystanders who got caught up in it all. They came here - they *hunted us down* - with the intention to do us harm. After they sold you back to SysTech, they probably intended to kill me and Nalea. And not quickly."

"I still-"

"Remember the wall," Sandrel told her bluntly. "You've seen with your own eyes what they did to people, people who were most likely *actually* innocent bystanders. Shipper families like mine live in terror of people like them. You did the galaxy a favor."

She nodded silently. Galhen had said much the same thing, but it did little to lessen the guilt that weighed down on her.

"I know you feel bad. Actually, it would probably be a bad sign if you *didn't* feel bad. But you'll get through it, and we're here for you." Sandrel smiled again and offered her a hug. She returned it, oddly touched.

"There you go then," he told her simply. "Now are you ready to come in for some tea?"

THE REST of the crew were already gathered in the mess when they got there. By unspoken agreement, everyone seemed to understand that they needed to discuss what happened now.

Sandrel took his seat at the head of the table and poured himself some tea while Kerelle quietly slipped into the seat next to Galhen. Ilyen shot her a quick glance, as if to assess her current level of "kinda freaked," but said nothing.

The others were tight-faced as well, though Nalea seemed to have regained some of her equilibrium - no doubt because Ilyen had filled her in that there would be no third act in their drama with the Ash and Bones. Oliven, for his part, seemed tense but calm. A year ago she might have expected him to be cringing like a kicked puppy, but their little C1's confidence and self-possession had grown steadily alongside his skill in the engine room and the pilot's chair.

Which was good, because whatever came next wasn't going to be easy.

"So." Sandrel set down his cup with an air of finality. "First off, it's good to have you back in one piece." He inclined his head towards Galhen, who blushed slightly but only nodded. "I've also been reliably informed that the Ash and Bones pirate gang will not be causing further problems. For us or for *anyone*."

Nalea met Kerelle's eyes for a moment, and she was surprised to see fierce approval. Apparently she had even fewer qualms about Kerelle's handling of the pirates than Sandrel did.

"But it seems the Ash and Bones were only part of the problem." Sandrel looked to Kerelle as if to indicate that she should take over. Well, she *had* been the one to actually talk to the pirate boss.

"It was SysTech that put them on our trail," she explained. "From what their leader said, the Ash and Bones were enthusiastic about tracking us down for revenge, but it's not clear if they would have actually come after us themselves without prompting." She filled them in on the rest of the details - how SysTech had found the Ash and Bones by following the lead of their attempt to ransom Nalea, how they'd provided information and anti-psionic weaponry, how the Ash and Bones had combined their knowledge of Sandrel's ship with SysTech's additional info about Galhen to track them down. The room was quiet after.

It was Ilyen who finally said what they all were thinking. "This won't be the end of it. SysTech doesn't do charity, and those pirates had some expensive tech. Whatever info those assholes used to find us, we have to assume SysTech has it now too."

He set his mug down with more force than strictly necessary. "Shit, they probably didn't even expect them to bring us in - the Ash and Bones were probably just convenient. And oh hey, now SysTech knows their information's good. The next time it won't be this amateur-hour shit. They'll send the black ops. And they'll send a lot of them."

He leveled a frank gaze around the table. "Evandra's good. I'm *really* good. But they only need us to fuck up once."

"You're always the optimist at this table, aren't you." Sandrel's tone held more weariness than rancor. "All right then, what do we *do* about it?"

"I don't know," Kerelle admitted softly. "We can't take them head-on, not with only two of us. Ilyen is right; neither of us is omnipotent, and we only have to make one mistake. What's more, we can knock down everything they throw at us and they can just keep sending more, waiting for us to *make* that mistake."

It was quiet again, everyone lost in their own thoughts.

"What if," Nalea whispered into the quiet, "there were more than two of you?"

Five heads swung around to look at her. Ilyen cocked his head for a moment, then his eyes widened.

"Babe, you think the thing you've been working on - ?"

She nodded quickly. "I got the prototype working this morning."

They stared at each other for a moment before Sandrel cleared his throat.

"Are you going to share with the rest of us?"

Nalea flushed slightly. "Since we managed to pop Oliven's collar off without damaging it, I've been able to use it for some research. It took a lot of manual rewiring when I reconfigured Ilyen's control card to work for removal, plus some makeshift hardware modding when we needed it to work for Oliven. I've spent the last year working on a device to repurpose the collar circuit, with no pliers or thermal glue required." She blushed deeper under a table of stares. "You know. Seemed prudent."

"And you never mentioned it?" Galhen sounded rather disappointed not to have been included.

"I wasn't sure I could get it to work. I didn't want to say anything before then, in case I couldn't."

Except to Ilyen, apparently, Galhen sent with some disgruntlement. Kerelle gave him a mental shrug, and he sent back shades of resignation. They'd both noticed that while Ilyen and Nalea's relationship may have started out as a strictly casual sexual liaison, it seemed to be evolving into something else. It wasn't yet entirely clear what that something else *was*.

"But you *did* get it working?" Kerelle prompted her. Nalea nodded slowly.

"I want to run some more tests before we take it out to the field but...yes. Right now I have every reason to believe it will function as intended."

"You say it can repurpose the circuit." Galhen leaned in. "How quickly?"

"Less than a minute."

Dead silence fell. Kerelle was finally the one to break it.

"With this...we could free anyone in the PsiCorp." Her heart rate picked up as possibilities ran through her mind. "We could free *everyone* in the PsiCorp."

"It only works one at a time," Nalea cautioned. "But...yes. We could grow our little group. Or at least give SysTech someone to chase besides us."

"A bigger group would be harder to hide," Sandrel noted. "Even with just a handful of you, that's twice they've found us."

"Twice because we were *dumb* about it," Ilyen cut in. "Sorry babe," he added with a glance at Nalea. "But we left them a trail to follow, first with the University and then by drawing attention. But yeah, more people *is* more opportunity to fuck up and get discovered." He leaned back then, his expression turning thoughtful. "Unless hiding's not the goal any more."

"You mean we turn it around," Kerelle said softly. "We go after *them*, instead of them coming after us."

Ilyen's eyes gleamed. "We're not the only ones in the PsiCorp who'd want in on that. And if they're going to find us eventually, we might as well see how many people we can bust out and how much hell we can raise before they do."

"And maybe... maybe we free enough of our people that they *can't* catch us all." It seemed impossible even as she said it - but Nalea's device made it tantalizingly real.

Sandrel raised his hands. "Let's calm down for a minute here. You're talking about something way bigger than any of us signed on for. This isn't even a jailbreak. You pull this off, you're talking about a *revolution*."

He looked at each of them in turn. "Taking on SysTech directly is suicidal enough as it is. But even if you pull it off... people are used to collared psionics, safely under corporate control. As long as any of us remember, that's how it's been. And there are plenty of people across the galaxy who'd want to keep it like that, because otherwise the thought of people who can smash things with their minds is pretty damn scary."

Kerelle remembered their first tense discussion when he'd learned her secret, and his fear that she might use her telepathy to control his mind. "Not to mention that popular media has given people an outsized idea of what we're capable of."

"That's probably by design," Galhen commented softly. Her husband's brows were pulled in thought, his expression otherwise unreadable. "Feeding fear of us reinforces the status quo."

"But what if this is our chance to change it?" Kerelle offered. "To really, *actually* change it? What other group of psionics have ever had this chance?" Even as she said it, she glanced involuntarily at Ilyen and shivered, remembering her thought at the jump gate that the existence of anti-psionic commandos might indicate they weren't the first to escape. Perhaps they were just the first to survive this long.

Ilyen gave her a half-shrug - apparently he'd followed her line of thinking. "You're the first rogues I was assigned to hunt. Doesn't mean there weren't others before you, but if there were it's top secret somewhere. The only information I ever got was need-to-know. Or," he added with a hint of a smirk, "whatever I could pick up otherwise." Ilyen's propensity for eavesdropping suddenly clicked into place - not that that helped them now.

"This is...a lot to think about," Sandrel said finally. "And thinking is what we all need to do, me included. This isn't the kind of path you get to walk back up again once you start down it." He looked around the table again, at each of them in turn. "This would be the end of life as we've known it. And everyone at this table needs to look long and hard at whether that's something they really want."

KERELLE BUZZED with nervous energy as she shut the door to their cabin behind her. Part of her was screaming that all this was *utterly insane*. But the other part couldn't stop thinking of the possibilities. It would be hard, certainly. Harder than anything else in her life. But it was a chance to *mean something*. To make things better for other psionics, across the galaxy. To defend instead of destroy.

Galhen was still quiet as he sat down on the edge of the bed, his lips set slightly down. A thread of worry wove through her mind; he didn't seem to share her budding enthusiasm.

She sat down next to him. "I want to do it."

He looked up. "I know."

She searched his face. "But you don't."

"It's not that I...*don't*, exactly. It's more that I have concerns."

"About how dangerous it will be? I'm scared too, honestly, but...we're *already* in danger. We'll *always* be in danger, as long as SysTech is hunting us. And that's forever, unless we do something now."

"It's not the danger to *us*, exactly." He sighed deeply and turned to her. "Kerelle, what Sandrel said, about the mundane population fearing what we would do if we were free. Those fears are not entirely groundless. Think back to some of the people we knew in the PsiCorp, the ones who cared only for their own pleasure and never gave a second thought what their orders were. Those are not people who would hold back from using their powers to harm mundanes, either to get something they wanted or simply to amuse themselves."

"SysTech tried to raise *all* of us like that. It didn't always work."

"It didn't always work...and sometimes it worked quite well." He sighed again. "Even the PsiCorp themselves, Kerelle. Some will want this, yes. But some will not."

"What do you mean? Why wouldn't they - "

He cut her off with a frank look, and drew the memory from her mind.

The club's bass thumps relentlessly, its driving force dominating the space. Kerelle sways in motion with it. The ambrosia is taking effect, and she feels as if the world around her brightens, intensifying the sensations that sweep across her. She is light and air and shimmer, and the pulsing beat stamps its rhythms into her blood and bones. All around them the dark room swims with undulating partygoers, caught up in the ecstasies of alcohol and ambrosia and sound.

She is twenty years old, as of last week. Her corporate payment card still sparkles with newness, and the mere sight of it parted the doors to the VIP lounge like a magic spell. They both have them, tangible proof that they are now officially agents of the PsiCorp.

She slides up against Galhen as they dance, delighting in his lean, hard-muscled body as she presses it to her own. He leans forward with clear intent; she takes advantage of the kiss to stroke his tongue with hers, sending him a mental pulse of affection and desire. He answers her immediately, not that she needs him to. His body tells her clearly how ready he is.

Giggling she tugs his hand and they slip through the crowd to the lifts. Galhen's glassy eyes glitter in the lift's sparkling lights, his pupils nearly swallowing the bright green irises. Their mouths lock again and she thinks of straddling him against the side of the lift, but they reach their floor and so instead they make it down the hall to tumble into their suite.

Neither of them can wait to make it to the bed, and as the door slides shut Kerelle is against the wall, legs locked around his back as he holds her up with effortless strength. Afterwards they each take another hit of ambrosia, and this time they do make it to the bed, slowly savoring each soft caress. Their minds are linked fully, and she feels Galhen's every shiver of pleasure as clear as her own. They climax together and he collapses to lie atop her, his breathless ecstasy fluttering against her senses. The euphoria of the ambrosia is receding to a soft contentment, and they float together through a soft landscape of satisfaction. The opulence of the penthouse surrounds them like a warm embrace, and

Kerelle reflects fervently on how very lucky they are. To have their gifts, to have their ranks, to have each other. Her last thought as she drifts into sleep is that she would not trade her life for anything.

Kerelle came back to herself, cheeks burning. She wasn't especially proud of that period in her life - brief as it had been. She'd soon found such entertainments more exhausting than fun.

Galhen held her gaze as the images faded. "Would we have wanted to be free, then? What was freedom, compared to the luxury we had at our fingertips?" he asked softly. "We were new to the life, and we had over a decade of indoctrination to reassure us that it was all we could ever want. We had only seen the privileges of the PsiCorp, with none of the cruelty or the cost."

"You're right," she conceded. "We *wouldn't* have wanted it. We wouldn't have understood. But," she lifted her chin, "if we do nothing, the cycle will continue, with the psionic children that come after us, and after them. They'll be raised to be self-absorbed corporate toys just like we were, and by the time they realize the truth it will be too late for them. Like it should have been too late for us, except for good luck and your sister's courage.

"This is our chance to *break* the cycle, Galhen." Her voice was barely more than a whisper, and she didn't trust it to stay steady. *This is my chance, to help instead of harm. To use the tools SysTech gave me to make the world a better place, instead of worse.*

He closed his eyes and took her hands, leaning her against him. His thoughts were overlaid with acquiescence. *It is our chance to break the cycle, and who if not us. In this and all things, darling, you will always have my support. But we must keep ourselves mindful that this will not be as simple as just opening PsiCorp collars.*

He opened his eyes then and regarded her, his smiled tinged with sadness. "Well then. Let's go set the world on fire."

TWENTY

THEY WERE SAFELY IN HYPER, and the ship guided itself along
the designated route with no need for human intervention until
they drew close to the drop point. Kerelle had a suspicion,
however, that she'd find Sandrel in the cockpit anyway. She was
right.

The smuggler leaned against the pilot's chair with an empty
coffee mug, staring unreadably out the vid port at the shapeless
blur of hyperspace. He didn't look up as she joined him. They
gazed out together in silence.

Finally he spoke. "You're going to do it." It wasn't a
question.

"Yes," she answered simply. "I have to. But...you don't. This
isn't your fight, Sandrel. You've already done so much for us,
none of us expect you to do this." She meant every word, but
the thought of leaving him and the ship that had become home
left a dull ache in her chest. Ilyen's words suddenly rose in her
mind. *You've got a family, Evandra. You've got us.* At some point over
the last year or so, Sandrel *had* become family.

His eyes stayed straight ahead. "I know. I also know that it's
crazy and most likely to end with everyone dead."

"Yes," she whispered. It was only the truth. "When I really *think* about it, it terrifies me. But if we just hide again, and keep hiding, then nothing will change. This is a chance to *mean* something."

"Yeah," he agreed with a violent sigh. "It is."

Sandrel finally turned to face her. "This terrifies me too, and I'll be honest, I thought long and hard about dropping you all off at the next port and wishing you well. And then I could go back to what I've always done, and that would be that."

He sighed deeply and ran a hand through his hair. "And then one day I'd take the wrong job or cross the wrong person, and I'd die the way I always figured I would, and none of it would ever have mattered. I always thought I was fine with that. Now I'm not sure I am."

He gave her a sidelong glance. "I'd say some of your man's sense of duty is wearing off on me, but that might be a bit ironic, since he didn't seem real enthused about the idea last night."

"He's worried not all the PsiCorp can be trusted to act responsibly with freedom," she conceded. "And he isn't wrong. But the alternative is to just do nothing, and...I can't. We can't. We'll just have to figure that part out."

"I'm glad you're aware of that, at least," Sandrel told her. He was back to staring out the window again. "And if it looks like you're about to forget, I'll remind you."

She gave him a sharp glance. "You'll - "

"Be around to do it? Yes." He gave her one of those half-smiles, though she could see the worry lingering in his eyes. "I guess this is my chance to mean something too. Besides, I've gotten pretty used to having you lot around. It'd be awfully quiet around the ship without you."

IN THE END, they all chose to stay.

Nalea had simply shrugged; if SysTech was already making her out to be a dangerous terrorist, she might as well keep on with it. Ilyen's wolfish enthusiasm was undimmed, and Kerelle didn't miss the way his fingers curled towards Nalea's when she announced she would stay. Even Oliven, who had the best chance of escaping into quiet obscurity, opted to help in whatever way he could.

Now they just had to decide on the actual way forward.

"We should probably start small," Kerelle mused aloud. "And we'll need to be particular about who we recruit, at least in the beginning." *Assuming, of course, that anyone in the PsiCorp wants in on this at all.* But she couldn't believe otherwise; Galhen was right, some would choose their current lives of comfortable bondage, but there were others dissatisfied with the status quo. There had to be.

"I actually had a thought on that," Galhen interjected unexpectedly. They all turned to look at him.

"My last assignment before Elekar, the outbreak on Baleal Ring, I was partnered with another C3 telepath - Lilika Anhei Charyth. We worked quite closely together for nearly three months, and in addition to being very skilled, I found her to be rather more...responsible than some of our other PsiCorp brethren. Not to mention," he added with a small smile, "that she had a background in espionage and nerves of steel. She would be quite an asset, if she were willing to join us."

"I'm assuming that since you brought it up, you think she might be."

"Indeed. We had a conversation one night near the end of the mission, after perhaps more wine than either of us should have been drinking, that ventured into rather seditious territory." He gave a half shrug. "Of course, there's a large difference between whispering discontent in the shadows and actually signing on for a lifetime of conflict and uncertainty. But I think she would at least be intrigued."

"And you trust her?" Ilyen sounded skeptical. "If she's a spy, she might not have been straight with you."

"It's a risk," Galhen agreed. "But the entire venture is nothing *but* risk. If we made contact with her, I don't believe she would immediately report it to SysTech. I believe she'd want to hear what we had to say. But we'll certainly want to keep the engines hot."

LOCATING Lilika proved easier than expected. Galhen remembered that she'd been based out of Cildazya, and they made landing in the city under their commercial freighter guise, hoping she was in residence.

Fortune was with them. She was.

Galhen was familiar enough with Lilika after their time working together that he could reach her telepathically from the ship. Kerelle paced nervously during what seemed like an extremely long conversation, though she knew only a few moments had passed.

Part of her was screaming. This was *real* now, they were actually here at the edge of the lion's den. In all their time running freight with Sandrel, they'd steadfastly avoided the SysTech strongholds, no matter how good the money might have been. Now they were within a few kilometers of the Cildazya PsiCorp base. She kept tight shields over the thoughts of the crew, as much to make herself feel better than because of actual danger.

That same part of her insistently pointed out that it was not too late, that they could still turn tail and run and forget this whole insane idea. It was harder to ignore than she would have liked.

She wasn't the only one feeling high-strung. Ilyen had been

outwardly calm throughout, but to Kerelle's senses he radiated a restless, nervous energy that reminded her of a bee trapped in a jar. He would never admit to anything like fear, naturally, but the magnitude of what they were about to do was not lost on him. He would *certainly* never admit to contemplating that it still wasn't too late to back out - but Kerelle was willing to wager the thought had crossed his mind as well.

Galhen opened his eyes. "I've spoken with Lilika," he stated unnecessarily. "She's quite wary, naturally, and rather surprised to hear from me, but I think she's interested. She's agreed to meet us in person to discuss further, though she'll commit to nothing beyond that. Given the circumstances I think that's the most we could reasonably expect."

"Which could totally be a trap," Ilyen asserted.

To Kerelle's surprise, Galhen didn't argue.

"It *absolutely* could be a trap," he agreed instead. "Which is why I may have forgotten to share most of the details. I only mentioned myself and Kerelle, and that it's a matter related to what she and I discussed on Baleal. She's agreed to meet the two of us in a neutral location for more information. I said nothing at all about you, or that we've devised a way to remove the collars. SysTech may know or have guessed as much, but if not, it seemed prudent to keep something up our sleeve."

Ilyen cocked his head, looking slightly mollified. "I'm kind of surprised you thought of that."

"As I've said before, Ilyen, you are not the only one on this ship with field experience." He sounded more resigned than irate. "And recent events have rather reinforced the need for caution."

Galhen paused for a moment, and Kerelle got the sense he was wrestling with something. Finally her husband stood and turned towards the teleporter.

"Ilyen, I don't think either of us would argue that we've never gotten on particularly well. But now more than ever, we're on the same side, and we're going to have to work together. And we're going to have to *trust* each other." He offered Ilyen his hand. "I do respect your abilities and experience, and I promise to take your concerns seriously when you have them. Do you think you can do the same?"

Ilyen hesitated a moment, then took his hand and shook it. "You try to be less of a dumbass, I'll try to be less of an asshole?"

Galhen gave him that half-smile. "Something like that."

TWENTY-ONE

LILIKA HAD CHOSEN the venue - an upscale spa, the kind of place a senior PsiCorp agent might take a private room without raising any eyebrows. If Cildazya was anything like Tallimau, the local businesses were probably accustomed to the PsiCorp - and the good money to be made in catering to them.

The spa itself was several blocks from the base. It was close enough to be within the radius of normal for an agent to venture - the far end of walking distance from the base, and not so far that it might beg the question of why she was passing up establishments closer to home. At the same time, it was near the edge of that radius; while they were still far closer to the PsiCorp base than Kerelle was comfortable with, they weren't right on top of it. Lilika truly did seem to have chosen the closest thing she could to neutral ground. Kerelle hoped that was a positive sign.

Kerelle's hands shook as she buttoned her jacket. She and Galhen were dressed strategically for the meeting - their clothing was professional and high-quality enough to blend in with the neighborhood, but still as nondescript as they could manage. Hopefully no one would even look at them twice.

Kerelle's role in the PsiCorp hadn't created much need for businesswear; she could hardly scrabble through combat operations in a blazer and tailored slacks. On the rare occasions such attire was called for, she'd never quite lost that feeling that she was a child playing dress-up. The impression seemed particularly apt now, as she donned what she could only think of as a costume - or protective camouflage. Her dark suit jacket felt almost like armor.

Galhen, naturally, looked impeccable. His golden hair was slicked back, managing to both disguise its length and lend unusual prominence to his cheekbones. The suit was off-the-rack, of course, but fit him like it had been custom-made, accentuating his lean form in all the right places. The overall effect was one that could have walked out of the boardroom at any bank in the city. *He* certainly didn't look like a child in his father's shirt.

Despite the gravity of the situation, she couldn't resist sending him a burst of playful disgruntlement.

Darling, why are you always so obnoxiously *polished?*

She felt his mental grin, with its faint emotional overlay. He knew he looked good, but he still liked to hear that she thought so too.

"Practice, dearest," he answered aloud. "And the suit does half the work." He gave the sleeve another critical examination. "It's not bad for department store, I must say. Not quite up to the ones I had made on Tallimau, but then it *is* about a tenth of the price."

He looked up at her then with a faint smile, and offered her his arm. "Shall we make our date with destiny?"

THE WALK to the spa was utterly surreal. All around them Cildazya bustled about its business, no one giving a second glance to another pair of professionals on their way to a meeting. It felt like it shouldn't be so *ordinary*, not when what they were doing was so momentous. But ordinary it was, to everyone but them.

All the same, it was a relief to have Galhen managing the *actual* shields, adding subtle psychic reinforcement to the impression that they were no one to take note of. Kerelle kept her senses open as they made their unhurried way to the spa, but no passerby questioned the prosperous anonymity he cloaked them in.

The closest they came to discovery was a sudden terrible moment when a group of PsiCorp crossed the street toward them, intent on a nearby wine bar. Kerelle tensed and she felt Galhen's shields tighten.

Steady, he urged firmly. *Don't give them a reason to look.*

She focused all her energy on maintaining her equilibrium, carefully smothering her racing heart in calm. She and Galhen were just another pair of mundanes, doing whatever dull things mundanes did to fill their time. The PsiCorp wouldn't look. They wouldn't care. Unless she gave them a reason.

They passed the group, eyes straight ahead. The PsiCorp didn't even look up.

She kept her sigh of relief mental, and Galhen gave her the mental equivalent of a squeeze on the hand. He'd been worried too.

Thank the stars there were no PsiCorp based out of Cildazya who knew them by sight.

They slowed down as they reached the block where their destination was located, and Kerelle cast her senses upward. Ah - there was Ilyen, somewhere on a roof. As usual he was well hidden from the naked eye, but this time he'd gone the extra length to hide from psychic view as well.

"It's some kind of clear-your-mind meditation shit," he'd

told her. "Makes you think quieter, or something. Closest thing us non-telepaths can do for shields."

She'd been skeptical. "Have you ever actually used it against a real telepath? Are you sure it actually works?"

Ilyen had given her one of his looks. "Ask me about that time the division head thought I wasn't trying hard enough, so they stopped feeding me unless I could sneak past telepath guards. It fucking works."

She had to hand it to him, it did. Kerelle had been able to find him, because she knew him well and also knew he was there. Lilika or other nearby telepaths *might* be able to pick him up, if they were strong enough and searched intensively, but Kerelle wasn't sure she would have noticed him on her own. Hopefully it was enough.

Ilyen's in position, she conveyed to Galhen, and discreetly tapped her comm. A second later it buzzed back - acknowledgement from Ilyen. They were going inside, and he'd be ready.

The inside of the spa was about what she'd expected, all lush plants and polished marble. The receptionist looked up to greet them, then seemed to lose her train of thought. Her brow furrowed in confusion.

"Thank you for answering our question," Galhen said smoothly as he guided Kerelle past the desk at a brisk pace. "We'll call later for an appointment."

"You're welcome," the girl answered reflexively. She still looked confused as they ducked around the corner.

Will she remember us? Kerelle asked.

Unlikely. She might vaguely recall a couple came in, but I doubt she'd be able to describe much more than a general idea of what we're wearing.

Now we just find Lilika?

In the Summer Petal Room, yes.

They found it without much difficulty - it was the largest suite on the floor, exactly what Kerelle would expect a high-ranking PsiCorp agent to book. She and Galhen exchanged glances.

Well, this is it. Hopefully we get out as quietly as we came in. She didn't have to tell him she had her shields dialed all the way up, around mind and body both. He could sense it through their bond well enough.

Indeed. For the first time she felt a brush of his misgivings - he'd recommended Lilika, and he believed she *would* join them, but after the pirate incident he didn't trust his own judgement quite as much as he once had. A flash of determination then, and another mental hand-squeeze. *We've taken precautions if events take an unpleasant turn.*

She returned the feeling, and reached out to open the door.

The first word that her mind produced to describe Lilika was *elegant*. The other woman gazed back at them with the sort of sculpted beauty that inspired artists, her smooth, dark skin and close-cropped curls accentuated by the soft pale silk of her artfully-draped blouse. Even seated as she was, at a small table in the center of the room, Kerelle could tell she was tall and graceful, and carried herself with a sort of effortless style that reminded Kerelle of Galhen. No wonder they'd gotten along.

Another thing that reminded her of Galhen - the serene, utterly unreadable mask she regarded them with. However Lilika felt about this meeting, she was giving nothing away.

Galhen greeted her with one of his warm, professional smiles. His mask, Kerelle noted, was also firmly in place.

"Lilika. It's good to see you again."

She gave him a cordial smile in return. "Galhen." Her eyes lingered for a moment on his bare throat, but she said nothing, and Kerelle detected no surprise. Whether or not Galhen had told her, she'd known.

Lilika turned her gaze to Kerelle. "And this must be…?"

"Lilika, this is my wife, Kerelle Evandra, lately of the

Tallimau PsiCorp. Kerelle, this is Lilika Anhei Charyth, C3 telepath, senior agent of the Cildazya PsiCorp."

Kerelle didn't miss that he'd skipped listing her designations, and she doubted Lilika had either, though she said nothing. Lilika's eyebrows *had* raised a fraction at the word *wife,* but she only gave Kerelle a polite nod and gestured for them to sit down.

Kerelle could read nothing at all from her - the other woman's mind was locked down hard, and despite sharing the C3 designation there was no question she was a stronger telepath than either Kerelle or Galhen. Pure-gift telepaths often were, possibly due to simply the concentration that it afforded.

What that lockdown portended, Kerelle couldn't say. It could mean this was a trap, and she was maintaining her facade until it was sprung. It could mean that she didn't trust *them,* or that she was afraid of being monitored in some sort of hidden trap herself. It could simply mean that she was nervous and didn't want it to show.

It could mean all of those things, or none of them. Only one way to find out. They took their seats.

"Thank you for agreeing to meet us," Galhen started. Kerelle fully intended to let him do the talking on this part. She kept her senses stretched wide, listening for anything that seemed out of place. She wouldn't be able to detect any assailants if they were wearing psiblockers - and it went without saying that they would be - but she might pick up a hint from the rest of the staff. Her hand rested lightly on her comm, ready to signal Ilyen at any indication of trouble. Her telekinetic shields stayed up.

"I imagine you may have heard some of this story already," he continued. They were tightly linked through their bond, and she felt him watch carefully for a reaction.

"I've *heard* very little," Lilika replied a tad archly, "But I've discerned some, yes." Her gaze flicked back to where his collar had rested. "Why don't you share with me what *actually* happened, and why you are here?"

The version he gave her was a carefully edited recounting of the last eighteen months. He went through being sold to Dalanva, and subsequently rescued by Kerelle; he made no mention of Ilyen or Oliven, and though he referenced assistance from Nalea and Sandrel he did not name them. Lilika listened impassively throughout. As Galhen wrapped up the story, she nodded with no reaction.

"I see," she said finally. She lifted her gaze to meet his, and asked in that cordial tone: "Why are you telling me this?"

They exchanged mental glances. Time to put their cards on the table.

"Kerelle and I were freed of our collars by a difficult process that carried considerable personal risk. Our allies have since developed a method to safely remove a PsiCorp collar in seconds."

Lilika's eyes widened slightly, the first hairline crack in her serene mask. They had her attention.

"Conscripting psionic children may be legal, but ultimately the multigalactics have treated us like chattel because the collars allowed it. Without the collars, our *mandatory contract agreements* won't be worth the data used to generate them." He leaned in. "Come with us. We can *do something*, Lilika. We have a chance to make a difference like no other psionics before us."

Lilika said nothing, though her brows drew together in thought.

"We very much understand it's not a choice to be made lightly," he followed softly. "And we appreciate you've already taken a risk simply by meeting with us. If you decide you want no part in this, we'll walk away and never contact you again."

She lifted her gaze. "Until we meet on the battlefield, you mean." Her tone was frank. "SysTech will not simply capitulate. What you're talking about is a direct assault on a major source of their power, and they *will* come for blood. You say you are giving me a choice, but all of our people will be pulled into this conflict regardless. There will be no 'choice' about that."

Kerelle spoke for the first time. "They can choose what side to be on. That's more of a choice than any of us have ever had. And if we succeed, the psionics that come after us will have more choice still."

The other woman nodded wearily. "They will. If any of us survive the cost to give it to them."

Lilika sighed deeply and looked between them. "I would like very much to see psionic bondage ended, and I would like very much to have a hand in ending it. But as you say, this is not a choice to be made lightly. What is your deadline for my decision?"

"Three days," Kerelle told her. They'd agreed on it with Sandrel beforehand. "Cildazya is too dangerous for us to stay much longer than that."

"Three days then. You'll have my answer by the end of it. Regardless of what I decide," she said firmly, "this conversation will not leave this room." She gave them both a cordial smile, and rose. They followed suit, and Lilika's voice echoed through both their minds.

I don't believe I was followed, she said. *Or that anyone suspects anything. But if I should be wrong - when I give you my decision, I'll give the name of the wine we drank on the last night on Baleal. If I do not, assume I've been compromised.*

Galhen gave her a slight nod. She turned to go, and paused with a faint smile, the first real expression Kerelle had seen on her face. *By the way, your man outside is quite good. If I hadn't been watching quite so carefully for tails I don't know that I would have noticed him at all. If this is the calibre of talent you're attracting, we may have a chance yet.*

A slight nod back to them, and she was gone.

THEY LINGERED a bit longer in the room, counting several minutes to give Lilika time to leave. Kerelle was not quite sure what to make of the elegant telepath.

Did that go well?

Quite, he answered with an overlay of satisfaction. *Lilika isn't one for outward displays, but unquestionably we had her interest.*

Do you trust her, then?

Well, no one has leapt forth yet to murder us, which must be a good sign, though it's certainly possible SysTech would prefer to arrange a later meeting where they could swoop in for us all at once. But she also told us she could sense Ilyen. If she were planning to betray us it would be rather more strategic to keep that bit to herself. He paused for a moment, thinking carefully. *Regardless of whether she decides to join us, I don't believe she would betray us to SysTech. Her distaste for the PsiCorp is as genuine as ours.*

Kerelle hoped he was right.

The walk back was as mundane as the walk in, but still managed to be more harrowing, now with a greater possibility that they were being followed. Kerelle swept around them as they went, seeking any thoughts that seemed out of place, but nothing materialized, and after a few roundabout detours they made it back to the ship without incident.

Ilyen appeared in the corridor the moment the hatch shut.

"Well?"

"She'll give us her answer in three days," Kerelle told him, "but Galhen doesn't think she'll betray us, no matter what she decides."

Ilyen opened his mouth to respond and closed it again. Kerelle caught a quick thought about *try to be less of an asshole.*

Galhen seemed well aware of what Ilyen had been *going* to say. "Yes, I could be wrong and it could still very much be a trap.

And we'll be ready, if that should be the case. But I don't believe it is."

"So three days then?" Sandrel ducked into the corridor, Nalea and Oliven hot on his heels. He didn't sound enthused about the delay - but neither did he sound surprised.

"Three days," she confirmed. "In the meantime I guess we wait."

IT WAS QUITE POSSIBLY the longest three days of her life. With the PsiCorp base practically on their doorstep, she and Galhen kept shields over the entire crew at all times, and it was impossible to relax. Kerelle found herself jumping at every noise, her nerves instantly coated in dread that SysTech had found them. Sandrel tried to find tasks to keep them all occupied with something besides worrying - himself chief among them - but there was only so much they could do without leaving the ship, and the hours passed agonizingly slowly.

Halfway through the third day, Galhen nearly dropped the tea he'd been idly sipping, his gaze shooting up to meet Kerelle's.

"It's Lilika," he told her, and hurriedly linked with her so that she could hear too. Kerelle's heart rate spiked, and the butterflies in her stomach seemed to multiply.

On our last night in Baleal, we went through several bottles of a red blend from Melia Vineyards on Hasha. You liked it, I thought the cherry undertones were too heavy. Lilika's tone was measured and calm, as if they were actually discussing wine. *I've thought it over, and the cause is worth the risk. I'm in. As are a dozen of my students.*

TWENTY-TWO

KERELLE AND GALHEN blinked at each other.

Students?

Yes, she answered somewhat drily. *I haven't been stationed at home for the last year to simply sit on my hands. I'm currently tasked with providing advanced training to some of the Academy's brightest. There are about a dozen of them under my care, all C3 or hard C2, ages between fifteen and nineteen. I will not leave them.*

Galhen hesitated. *Is it…prudent to bring children into this?*

I don't think you entirely understand what this is likely to set off. It would be far more irresponsible to leave them.

Kerelle caught a flickering thought, of black-clad fighters in psiblockers kicking in a dormitory door at night.

You think SysTech would harm your students? Their own trainees?

Trained by a defector, and thus suspect. She paused. *I was interviewed by internal affairs at length about my association with you, Galhen, following the Dalanva incident. I wasn't told why, of course. There was never any sort of announcement about what had happened or that you were involved, except for the news reports that Dalanva had been attacked by terrorists. But it didn't take a great deal of sleuthing to piece together why they were so interested in what I knew about you and if we were still in touch. And, I believe, if I had any seditious leanings myself.*

I'm so sorry, Lilika.

If Lilika were sitting with them, Kerelle got the impression she would have flicked her hand dismissively. *It wasn't too much trouble. I said I'd respected your skill as a regenerative, but we hadn't had reason to stay in touch after the mission. I also insinuated that we'd slept together and it was rather disappointing, and that I'd lost interest in you afterward.*

Galhen made a choking noise beside her, his face flushing deep crimson. *You…what?*

It was the sort of PsiCorp answer they'd expect, and it deflected suspicion. We don't all *have convenient long-lost siblings to save us, my dear Agent Ambrel. I used the tools at hand.*

Apparently Lilika had "pieced together" Nalea's involvement as well.

But my point, she continued firmly, *is that there were already suspicions that this went further than just yourselves, and we are about to confirm them. I doubt I was the only one of your associates to be examined before. Now they'll wonder how many others may be concealing involvement.*

Kerelle's gut twisted with worry as she thought of Mila. Sunny, well-meaning Mila, who could be fierce as a tiger in battle but didn't have a duplicitous bone in her body. Had she been interviewed by internal affairs as well? Had they read something more sinister into her kind-hearted attempts to help Kerelle?

Would she be in danger, in the days to come?

We are starting a war with this, Lilika stated bluntly. *Don't fool yourselves into thinking otherwise.*

They exchanged glances again. *Then we'll plan for your students as well,* Galhen answered. *It will be a tight fit in the ship but we'll manage. If we're adding a dozen teenagers, however, we'll need to reexamine how we plan to escape.*

Oh, that won't be an issue. I've already started arrangements.

ANOTHER VENTURE out into the city, another costume. This time it was a low-cut, form-fitting ensemble, all black with sparkling bangles to add interest. It was years since Kerelle had been to a nightclub, not counting that awkward outing with Mila, and she felt almost as ridiculous as she had with the business suit. At least *this* disguise offered excellent freedom of movement, and if she ditched the ridiculous bangles it would provide decent cover for blending into shadows.

That was something, at least.

Galhen looked as well put together as always, and showed none of the nervousness she sensed twitching through their bond. He *did* show a tendency to rest his hand protectively atop his zippered pocket, as if to assure himself its precious cargo was still there. Nalea's device was still a bit bulky, and Kerelle's critical eye could discern its shape interrupting the sleek lines of his silhouette, but fortunately it was still small enough to be carried on his person. Carrying a separate bag invited complications.

Nalea herself hovered anxiously as they prepared, her emotions loud. She warred between confidence that her device would work, and worry that an unforeseen variable might prevent it from doing so.

"It performed beautifully in a lab setting," she said for the third time, "but remember we've never tried it in the field. I'll prep for the old-fashioned way just in case but...hopefully it works."

"I'm sure it will, Nalea, and thank you." Galhen smiled at her, and his attempt to project calm reassurance echoed through the bond. "You've given us an amazing gift."

"Hopefully," the scientist answered under her breath. She

looked up again at them. "But if it *does* work…you can thank me by bringing back as many inert collars as you can. Preferably intact. Until I get more hemindrium to work with, that *amazing gift* is going to be one of a kind…and I won't be able to make any upgrades without more test hardware."

"We'll do our best," Kerelle reassured her. Hopefully that would be an easy promise to keep, and they'd return with armloads of inert collars, a group of free psionics, and no pursuit.

Hopefully. Their plans tended to fall apart on that last bit.

Ilyen watched them with a scowl from beside the hatch. There had been a fierce argument over who would attempt the rescue, and who would stay with the ship. Over his vociferous objections, Ilyen had been assigned to the latter. Kerelle's position had been straightforward: she was better at crowd control, Galhen could provide medical aid if things went south, and Ilyen was best equipped to handle any threats that materialized at the ship while they were gone. Sandrel had agreed with her reasoning and Ilyen had finally conceded, but he made no effort to hide his disgruntlement.

Nalea gave him an annoyed glance. "Oh, stop sulking, Ilyen. You'll have plenty more chances to stab people before all this is over." He gave her a withering look back, though Kerelle detected a hint of affectionate amusement beneath it.

Kerelle increasingly suspected that their assassin had fallen rather hard for her sister-in-law. She wondered if Nalea's interest in *him* had evolved past his skill in bed and willingness to stay out of her way.

Sandrel and Oliven joined them. The smuggler's cool professional mask was back in place, concealing his radiating worry. Oliven, on the other hand, looked like he was going to be sick. By virtue of being the only telepath left on the ship, he'd been drafted as their communications liaison. All the hard-won confidence he'd built over the previous year had melted like hot ice as soon as they'd asked him to use his psionics.

Kerelle felt guilty for asking, but they didn't have a lot of options. While they had the comms, telepathy was safer.

Galhen gave Oliven a smile and gripped his arm. "Thank you for agreeing to help us with this, Oliven. You're going to do fine."

"I sure hope so," he agreed shakily. "I've never been very good at this."

"All we need you to do is receive," Galhen reassured him. "You've never had trouble with that. If anything happens, we'll reach out and you can tell Sandrel. Kerelle and I will do all the work of projecting."

The young C1 nodded jerkily, not looking entirely convinced, but Kerelle sensed determination under his fear. He wanted to help, any way he could.

Sandrel clasped her arm. "The usual drill. You get what we're here for and get out, I'll have the engines hot when you run back with half the city on your tail."

"The vote of confidence is appreciated," she answered drily, and returned his grip. He gave them each a nod and stepped back. Kerelle and Galhen gave each other a final once-over, and headed out the hatch.

IT WAS EARLY ENOUGH that the nightclub didn't have a line, and Kerelle and Galhen were waved in with only a slight lean of mental suggestion on the bouncers. Inside it looked much the same as any other club, dark except for the neon lights and too loud to carry on a conversation in, though its patrons were largely ignoring the pounding beats in favor of clustering at the bar. The first tentative swirls of a dance floor were beginning to form at the crowd's edges; probably within an hour the place would be packed.

Kerelle reached out to Galhen through the bond as he did the same, forming a tight link between them. The familiar susurrus of his thoughts and emotions settled in the back of her mind, distinct but still a part of her. Lilika would be able to speak to both of them at once.

We're in. No trouble on the way here.

Good, Lilika replied. *None on our end as well. Officially, I'm treating the class to an outing to celebrate their success in a training exercise. This is a popular venue with the PsiCorp and nobody batted an eye when I booked the VIP room for tonight. Up the stairs behind the bar.*

The upstairs room was more opulent than the main club below, softer lights illuminating plush seating and copious buckets of chilled sparkling wine. As promised, it was also full of teenagers.

Kerelle had to hand it to them - the kids were giving a convincing impression that they were actually there to party. Most of them had full glasses of sparkling, and a small group danced to the pulsing electronic music. Here and there a couple had ducked into a corner to sample each others' lips. If she weren't a telepath, able to sense the nervous anticipation rising from their thoughts like hot steam, she would never have guessed the scene was anything more than it seemed.

Lilika was chatting serenely with a girl in a sparkly dress, a wine flute in her own hand. She met their eyes over the girl's head and gave them a slight nod. Kerelle felt a spike of anxiety from the girl as she darted a glance over as well, but she gave no outward sign she noticed them, instead drifting away to join another group.

Your students are good at this, Kerelle noted.

They are. Most of them were intended for the industrial espionage group; I've been teaching them the finer points for the better part of a year. They also know the escape plan if things go poorly, and they'll be able to make it out with or without me.

Is everything ready, then?

Yes. Grab a wine flute, wait six minutes, then follow me. She turned and walked away, nodding at the kids as she passed, and carefully let herself through a door near the back of the room.

Six minutes later, they joined her.

The door deposited them in a small alcove-like room that seemed to be used for storage. Lilika glanced between the two of them.

So this is it.

It is, Galhen answered, and withdrew the small device from his pocket. Lilika stared at the unassuming little cube, expression blank. *My sister's lab testing indicated it would work quickly, and there should be no side effects, but I'm on hand for anything unexpected.*

Well then. Let's give your sister her first field data. He gave her a nod, and fitted the little device against her collar.

Kerelle had expected it to struggle with the unfamiliar hardware, or perhaps to spend several long moments processing new data. It did neither of those things. Instead, scarcely thirty seconds later, Lilika's collar gave a soft *pop* and slid off into Galhen's hand.

The three of them stared at it. Lilika's hand went slowly to her throat, and for a moment her mask cracked to reveal a mix of shock and wonder. Just as quickly, she visibly clamped down on her emotions. Kerelle did the same. The job wasn't finished yet.

Stay here, she told them. *I'll start bringing in the students.*

They came in sets of two or three, some shy and frightened, others bright-eyed and buzzing with excitement. The device worked beautifully, releasing collar after collar. Kerelle was careful to gather up the discarded hardware, commandeering a bag from their storage alcove for transport. The least they could do was secure Nalea her requested additional materials.

There were only a handful of kids left when Kerelle's open senses suddenly twanged. She froze and locked eyes with Galhen. He'd picked it up too.

SysTech security. A *lot* of SysTech security. Rapidly converging on their location.

Lilika -

I sense them. The other woman's face stayed utterly calm as she quickly gathered her charges. "Trouble is incoming and we have to go. Helia, Khoren, Siuris." She briskly named off the kids still in their collars. "Stay close to Evandra and Ambrel. We'll have to do you on the way out. The rest of you, do as we discussed. Stay safe."

At the unspoken signal, the students scattered towards the exits in a sudden flurry of urgency. Lilika beckoned sharply and they followed her down the fire escape, the three teenagers close behind.

Kerelle reached out to Oliven as they skidded down the slick metal steps. *Complications. Tell Sandrel to be ready for another quick exit - and also for a dozen kids to show up in small groups. We're on our way back now.*

Affirmative, came the faint response. *Captain Marene says we'll do our part, you just get back in one piece.*

That's the plan.

They leapt down the remaining steps and followed Lilika down the alley at a run. She clearly knew where she was going.

We're keeping to the back roads. If we get separated, the fastest way back to your ship from here is along Pala Street. A map appeared in their minds, overlaid with the route. Kerelle sent back her acknowledgement and hoped it would be unnecessary.

She could sense the SysTech forces, closer but still at bay. The streets around them were a warren of curves and alleys, and their pursuers would be forced to fan out to follow them once they discovered the club room was empty. That should buy them some time.

Except, she remembered abruptly, that they could track the collars of the students following behind them.

Lilika was clearly thinking the same. After another minute of solid running, she pulled their group into another alley. *Let's get the collars off here, before they have any more time to follow us.*

The seconds it took to disengage the first collar seemed like an eternity, and again as they moved on to the next. Kerelle could feel SysTech getting closer to their location - and that was only the foes she could sense. The possibility that there were pursuers in psiblockers tied knots of tension down her spine.

As the second collar popped off in Galhen's hand, the last girl collapsed with an ear-piercing scream.

Shit.

The other two kids stared in openmouthed horror; they'd probably never seen a collar go active before. Meanwhile their pursuers drew ever closer. They couldn't afford to wait here.

Take the others and run, Kerelle sent at Lilika. *It will be easier for me to fight them off with fewer people to protect. We'll meet you back at the ship. Don't leave without us.*

Lilika hesitated a split second, then gave her a firm nod and barked an order at the other two teens. They visibly pulled together and followed her at a run.

Behind her, Galhen swore quietly. He knelt beside the thrashing girl, the cube flashing uselessly as he held it against her collar.

It doesn't seem to work once the collar is active. We'll have to take her back to the ship and hope Nalea can do something.

Galhen set his jaw, and she sensed him steel himself through the bond before her muted it on his side. He gathered the girl in his arms and picked her up with a pained grunt. Her screams subsided to a soft whimper.

"Are you *shielding* her?" She hadn't realized he could *do* that.

"I'm absorbing some of the effect," he answered through gritted teeth. A bead of sweat was already appearing on his brow. "We need to keep this short."

As if on cue, a group of grey-clad SysTech soldiers appeared at the mouth of the alley, guns trained on them.

Kerelle threw up her shields, deflecting the first volley of shots. She shoved back hard enough to send the lot of them flying. They hit the pavement hard, one crashing against a wall, but she could already sense reinforcements close behind. She tugged on Galhen's hand and started to run.

Kerelle strained to keep Lilika's map in her mind as she plunged forward. The dark, twisting streets before her looked very different from the map's aerial view, and they couldn't exactly stop to puzzle out street signs. From what she could sense, the SysTech forces were converging on them.

The detached part of her observed that SysTech probably had the girl's collar active to slow them down; they wouldn't switch it to kill as long as they needed to follow it. It wasn't a terribly comforting thought.

Behind her Galhen's pace was slowing, the strain of carrying their charge while shielding her from the collar's full force beginning to take its toll. He met her eyes and she read the same thought in his face - they weren't going to make it like this.

"Hold her, I'll hold you," she whispered fiercely. Without waiting for an answer, Kerelle swept them both up with her power. Floating them close, she started to run again. To an outside observer, they must have looked ridiculous, but she succeeded in picking up their speed.

The enemy was getting close, though the mazelike nature of the streets made it hard to judge *how* close. Up the street, through an alley, down a side street -

The side street curved left, instead of right like she was expecting, and straight into a group of SysTech troops.

The walls lit with gunfire. Kerelle threw up a shield in front of them, barely deflecting in time. She sent a wave of force crashing against the group, scattering most of them like sport pins. The handful that dodged fired back again and flung something that registered as grenades just before they detonated, rocking her shield hard enough to nearly throw her off her feet. The effort of holding it took all her concentration, and Galhen's hissed intake of breath echoed in her ears as she accidentally dropped him to the ground. He drew himself up to his feet with difficulty.

More shapes appeared in the alley. Another SysTech squad had arrived.

She sent a hard push forward, but it was more to buy time than anything else. There were simply too many of them - they wouldn't be able to escape this way.

A scuff caught her attention and on instinct she wrapped the shield around their backs. The ones who'd been chasing them earlier caught up, fanning out to block the way they'd came. They were surrounded.

The enemy hung back and circled, watching her warily. They weren't moving to engage, but they *were* cutting off her escape. Very much as if, she realized with a burst of anxiety, they were mostly trying to hold her until a better-equipped force arrived.

SysTech likely didn't have antipsionic troops stationed around the galaxy as a matter of course. If Kerelle didn't think of something, she and Galhen were probably about to find out how quickly the antipsionics could deploy when needed.

All the more reason not to stick around.

Forward was out. Back was out. She glanced up. They were in an older neighborhood, somewhere between "quaint" and "rundown," and the buildings here weren't as tall as they'd been near the base. One of the closest ones had a sloping wooden overhang covering a porch that was lower still. She'd never tried this before, but it couldn't be *that* much different than when she'd leapt those stairs on Kalnis. Hopefully Galhen didn't have some well-concealed fear of heights.

Kerelle took a step backwards and looped her arm through his, worming her way past the shivering girl he held. The bond heightened with physical contact, as it always did, and even muted she could feel exhaustion beginning to set in for him and his charge alike. Even with some protection against the collar, the girl was still suffering - and whatever Galhen was doing to help her, it was draining him quickly. She shoved down the thought that this was even *more* stupidly dangerous with Galhen's dexterity compromised. She'd carry them both again if she had to.

Besides, staying here was the most stupidly dangerous of all. *Trust me and hold on*, she sent, and threw out a hard shockwave in a circle around them. As the SysTech squad stumbled, she leapt.

This time she sent the wave of telekinesis *beneath* them, lifting them up over the lip of the overhang's gutters to drop on its sloping roof. It creaked ominously as they landed rather harder than she'd intended. Her stomach dropped as she realized the overhang might not be as solid as it looked - and that her initial shockwave might have hastened its decline.

It only had to last long enough to get them up to the roof proper. That, at least, was brick, and hopefully more hardy.

Shouts came from below as the squad charged where they'd been, and she was forced to shift concentration to warding off gunfire. She caught some hurried thoughts about application of force to the porch - shit, they'd caught on to the overhang's instability as well.

Kerelle threw another energy wave down towards them, but between maintaining shields and preparing for the next jump, it was more of a distraction than an actual hindrance. The overhang shifted with another concerning groan. The brick roof was higher up, she'd need to make sure she had enough force for this next part -

A grenade landed between her and Galhen, as if it had been guided with a homing beacon. Time slowed as she heard his sharp intake of breath and the faint hiss of its internal mechanism counting down.

No time. She leapt over it to nearly tackle him, flinging them both up in a reckless wave. The overhang splintered and buckled under the impact, and as she watched from above the grenade rolled down through the cracked beam, a half-second before the entire porch was shredded in a violent blast.

Kerelle instinctively pulled a shield around them in a tight ball as wooden shrapnel was flung into the air. But she could only hold it for a few seconds - they were still flying upward on the momentum of her last wave, but soon that momentum would falter, and in her haste to escape the grenade she hadn't plotted their trajectory. They weren't close enough to land on the other roof.

One of those headaches was beginning to form behind her eyes, the kind that meant she was approaching exhaustion herself. As usual, she was going to have to ignore it.

Okay. Concentrate. You did this on Kalnis. And like on Kalnis, if she got this wrong, none of them would survive to deconstruct the mistake.

She pushed toward herself, against the shield that enclosed them. It reluctantly corrected its course to a few degrees right. Stars, this was like trying to run in two different directions at once.

Another push, harder this time to add some momentum. They were over the brick roof now - and in danger of sailing past it. Praying she didn't crush them by accident, Kerelle simultaneously tightened the shield around them and pushed it down to hit the brick roof.

The impact sent them all sprawling, but the shield had held, and they were all in one piece. Kerelle forced herself upright, that headache abruptly sharpening. Galhen wasn't the only one running out of juice.

As they stood, she caught sight of a bronze sign overhanging the street below the building's other side. Pala Street. They were almost there.

She grabbed Galhen's hand and started to run along the roof. They were above the SysTech squad's reach for now, but she had no doubt the soldiers would soon catch up to them again. After all, they had a beacon to follow.

She was aware, as they ran, that this meant she was also leading SysTech back to the ship. But there was nothing to be done for it, except hope Sandrel could get them away in time.

They were able to skirt across several adjacent roofs, but finally they hit a street break. They were close now, she could sense the rest of the crew at the edge of her awareness. They just had to make it across this street and down the rest of the block.

Kerelle set her jaw, resolutely tamped down on the pain in her head, and backed them up to get a running start.

She felt like a human sportball as she sealed them again in a tight shield sphere and threw it across to the nearest roof on the other side. But they made it again in once piece. This was proving quite the useful trick - she really ought to practice it sometime when they weren't running for their lives.

Galhen groaned from beside her, and struggled to rise off his knees. The girl's whimpers had crescendoed back to a keening wail.

"Come on, darling," Kerelle whispered as she tried to help him up. "Just a little bit further." She reached out to Oliven as she did - *we're coming in hot, with injuries. Tell Nalea to be ready with the old fashioned way, and Sandrel to be ready to take off.*

To her surprise it was Lilika who answered her. *They're both aware. Everyone else has made it back, we're just waiting for you. How far?*

Kerelle tried to send her an approximation of their location, overlaid with an image of her current sights. Lilika gave her the telepathic equivalent of a curt nod.

Help is coming.

Less than a minute later, Ilyen appeared a few meters away.

"Who gets to stay with the ship *next* time, Evandra?" He muttered darkly as he offered Galhen a supportive arm. Galhen shifted the girl over his shoulder and leaned on him gratefully, albeit a bit awkwardly given his taller frame. Ilyen's lips thinned slightly as he took in the girl's collar, but he only gave Kerelle a quick nod as they started off.

It was faster with the extra help, and they grew closer and closer to the end of the block. Kerelle could see the shipyard from here, safety so close and so far all at once.

"Ilyen, can you teleport with another person?" Stars, she hated how strained her voice sounded.

"Nope. Small objects only, nothing else with a pulse. You think we'd still be out here if I could port us back?"

"I don't know, maybe you're enjoying the excitement."

"Ambrel's heavy and scenery on this roof is crap."

"All the more reason to get off it."

The shipyard was growing closer, a bright haven of lights in the darkened streets. She just had to float them down, then it was a straight shot in.

Boots echoed on the concrete, and a grey-clad troop skidded between them and their objective. Even as they ducked beneath the roof's facade, Kerelle knew it wouldn't do much good. They couldn't *really* hide as long as the collar was giving away their location.

Ilyen popped a glance from behind their weak cover. "Guess it's time to get to work. Evandra, I hope you're good to get back down from here by yourself."

"I can float us down, yes. Are you - "

But he was already gone. The street below them erupted in gunfire. She risked a look.

It was easy to forget, seeing Ilyen sprawled on a chair in the mess or talking with his mouth full, just how stars-damned *graceful* he was. He flitted between their opponents like a knife-wielding ghost, striking and vanishing again, a dance of death that was almost beautiful. Two of them were down already, the others panicked and firing. A flash, a bullet reflected, here and gone again. He dropped two more in seconds, and the rest began to run.

Their distraction lent her an opening. She got a good grip on Galhen and their charge, and took a leap.

"Controlled fall" was a better term than float, but she softened their impact with a shield and they stayed on their feet. One of their fleeing opponents paused to try to get a shot off on her. She smacked him back against a wall without second thought. They ran.

Ilyen popped next to her a few minutes later, easily matching pace. Up ahead she could hear the ship's engines whirring - it hovered a few centimeters above the ground.

There's more of them coming. Hurry! That was Lilika again, and Kerelle could make out her silhouette through the open hatch. Shouts and running steps grew in volume behind her.

"Get in the ship," she hissed at Ilyen. Then quickly to Galhen - *apologies darling, this may be a bit rough.* Before he could respond, she flung him and their young charge the remaining meters to the ship. Now she just had to get there herself.

The footsteps were closing in. She ran with all her might, struggling to keep a shield up as she did. There, *there -*

She leapt into the open hatch as blasts sounded behind her.

Breathing heavily, Kerelle looked down to see that the SysTech troops had been thrown back against the fence of the shipyard, some struggling to their feet and others apparently unconscious. Beside her, one of Lilika's students stared down at the scene with wide eyes. Kerelle knew that look. She was shaking and wanted nothing more than to pass out, but she knew that look.

She clasped the young telekinetic's arm as Lilika rapidly keyed the sequence to close the hatch. "It's always hard the first time, to use your power against other people. You did well. Thank you for helping me."

He gave her a small nod, his eyes darting quickly to Lilika. She gave him a smile back. "You did very well, Peralen. I think the others are gathered in the mess - go and join them."

The boy nodded again and vanished down the corridor. Kerelle felt a pang of regret as he went, that Lilika's young students were getting pulled into this at all. He was even younger than she'd been, when she'd seen her first live combat. It made it hard to feel they were doing the right thing.

Her thoughts must have shown in her face.

"They'll have to fight sooner or later," Lilika told her quietly. "For SysTech or against it. None of us will have the luxury to simply observe." Lilika met her gaze, and a fierceness burned in her dark eyes that belied her calm expression. "If we succeed, they will be the last children raised for war."

The ship rocketed upwards then, throwing them both back against the corridor's wall. The proximity alarm broke out a moment after. Sandrel's voice crackled over the intercom.

"Anyone who's not strapped in, do it now. I can outrun what they're throwing at us but it's not going to be smooth."

As they began to struggle down the corridor towards the safety seats, Lilika's voice echoed into her mind.

And so it begins.

TWENTY-THREE

"WELL, at least now we know it's consistent." Nalea glared into her cup as she poured tea, her voice a mix of resignation and that acerbic edge she tended to acquire when stressed. She set the tea kettle down harder than necessary.

Kerelle glanced quickly around them but the kids paid them no mind. Safe now in hyperspace, they were huddled around the mess in pairs and small groups, their earlier excitement faded as the significance of it all sunk in. Wedged in the far corner on the floor, one of the younger boys was crying softly, as two of the older students tried to comfort him.

Again she felt that twist of guilt, at dragging a group of teenagers into this, but she knew Lilika was right. They were *already* dragged into it. SysTech had seen to that.

Which sent her mind back to the source of Nalea's dark mood. They'd left the girl Helia sobbing in the medbay as Galhen tried to soothe her, softly reassuring her that it had happened to him too, that he had recovered in time, that there was hope the loss of her psionics was temporary.

"You did the best you could," Kerelle offered. "She's alive, and there's every reason to believe she'll recover like Galhen did."

"There isn't, actually. Galhen is the only other data point we have on forcible removal while the collar is active. We don't know if he got lucky in regaining his powers, or unlucky in how long it took to recover, or really anything at all about what a normal prognosis is. We're flying blind and hoping for another good outcome." She plunked her mug down, frustration plain on her face. "The only way to study this and learn from it is to get more data, and I can't exactly do that intentionally."

"And I certainly hope we *don't* get more data points any time soon," Kerelle agreed. Her heart ached for the girl in the medbay.

Nalea sighed. "It's good to know the removal device doesn't work on active collars, though. I'll try to figure that one out, hopefully before we need to use it again." She picked up her mug and stood. "I need some quiet. Let me know when the next crisis hits." She headed toward her lab without another word, avoiding looking at any of the newcomers.

Kerelle was tempted to do the same. She could barely carry on a conversation with unfamiliar adults; teenagers were completely off the map. Still, it felt wrong.

She was saved from having to make a decision when Lilika appeared at the door of the mess.

"Kerelle, may I speak with you?"

She nodded and rose to follow her, trying to quash the feeling that speaking alone with Lilika was only marginally less intimidating than trying to chat with the students in the mess.

Lilika closed the door behind them. "I've learned the source of our visitors from SysTech security," she announced without preamble. "And I owe you an apology for allowing it."

"Allowing it?" Kerelle asked warily.

Lilika's lips pursed. "Yes. If you do a headcount on the class I brought with me, you'll find we have only eleven. One of my younger telepaths, apparently, decided she would rather take her chances with SysTech. The only positive is that this was a last-minute decision, and so SysTech did not have time to summon their more dangerous operatives. If there had been an antipsionic force ready for us, we would not have escaped without casualties."

"You know about the antipsionics? From what Ilyen said I thought they were top secret."

Lilika gave her a wintry smile. "Much of my career at SysTech was devoted to ferreting out secrets. And most of the senior managers are not nearly as subtle as they believe. But back to the point at hand." She made an irritated gesture. "The fault is mine, for not monitoring her more closely. She was the newest of the group, and had the least cause to trust me with her life."

"How did you find out it was her?" A thought struck Kerelle with alarm. "It's not just because she's missing, is it? What if she was captured - "

"It was her," Lilika answered grimly. "She had some involvement with one of the boys near her age, and tried to convince him to leave with her. He didn't, but also didn't tell us she had gone. I got the whole story out of him shortly after we took off."

"Ah." The boy in the corner downstairs.

"Still." She met Kerelle's eyes. "This is a taste of things to come. A rather pesky part of offering people free choices is that sometimes they make the choice we don't want."

"Galhen said something similar, when we first started to consider this."

"And we would do well to keep it in mind."

Lilika rose then with a sigh. "I'll deal with the issue, but I wanted you to know." She paused and looked Kerelle up and down. "And it's a pleasure to finally meet you, by the way. I heard a great deal about you on Baleal."

"ARE you sure you're going to be alright? Especially with all the kids?" True, Lilika's students were clearly skilled, and some of them were close to the end of their training anyway, but they were still quite young. And there was a world of difference between the Academy and the real world. Kerelle's misgivings were still very much in place.

Lilika gave an elegant half-shrug. "We'll be as safe there as anywhere. Palhee is a good place to disappear, and we know how to avoid notice. We certainly can't all stay on this ship." She nodded at Sandrel. "As fine a ship as it is."

That was simple truth. The ship was already uncomfortably full with an additional dozen people. Even their unofficial war table in the mess was beginning to feel cramped with Kerelle, Galhen, Sandrel, Nalea, Ilyen, Oliven and Lilika all gathered around it.

"Besides," she added, "SysTech will be looking for all of us. We'll be safer in separate locations."

"So that's the plan then?" Sandrel asked. "We drop you off at Palhee, you get yourself settled, we figure out our next move from there?"

"Indeed," she confirmed. "As we've discussed, the most important thing at this stage is recruiting. I have contacts that may prove helpful in plotting our course forward."

Ilyen looked somewhat skeptical. "So what then, we just sit around doing nothing?"

"Think of it as avoiding unprofitable danger. There is no point to engaging SysTech without more resources and more of a fighting force. We are still stretched thin on that point, formidable as Kerelle and yourself may be."

Ilyen still frowned, but he subsided somewhat at that - after all, it was essentially what he'd said himself when they first discussed the subject.

She nodded around the table. "We all agree that my trainees should be kept out of danger, to the extent such a thing is possible, and I myself can provide little assistance in direct combat."

Her lips quirked then, in a wolfish smile that reminded Kerelle rather unexpectedly of the teleporter sitting beside her. "Indirect combat, however, is an entirely different affair. I look forward to the engagement."

IT WAS NOT that Palhee had changed since their last visit, Kerelle finally determined as she munched her *ranla* on the edge of the market. It was that she had.

Looking out over the colorful stalls and boisterous crowds, Palhee held that same sense as before, of being alive with secrets and hopes and potential. But instead of filling her with excitement, this time she felt the familiar pang of regret that had accompanied new sights in her PsiCorp days. That there was a whole wide world out there, but it wasn't for her.

Then it had been true because of contract to SysTech, the lack of power she had over her own life. Now, it was because she was part of something bigger than herself, something that didn't include exploring new cities for fun. She'd chosen it, this time, and she didn't regret the choice. But she still felt the loss of that open door, and knew in her heart that it was unlikely to open again. She wished she'd done more with it.

But it wasn't all melancholy. For all that she missed that exhilarating feeling of freedom from her first visit, there'd been an empty void then that dampened the joy. She'd done what she did for a reason, and one of those reasons was sitting beside her.

You weren't exaggerating, darling. These are delightful. Galhen was finishing up his own *ranla* with enthusiasm. She smiled and let her gaze linger on him, taking a moment to simply appreciate that he was there.

Galhen noticed her look and tipped his head quizzically. She leaned in to brush a spot of sugar off his nose, and reached out with her mind to share the memory of her last visit. How she had regretted his absence and resolved to return with him at her side, to take in the sights and eat *ranla* together. The smile he gave her back was radiant.

He drew her closer and knotted their fingers together. *And here we are, love, doing just that. You did it.*

She sent back a pulse of affection. *I suppose I did after all. Though I fear what comes ahead will make this part look like a picnic.*

Entirely probable. But whatever comes, this time we'll face it together.

Lilika emerged from the crowd and made her way towards them unhurried. The other telepath was transformed from when they had met her - her clothes were now plain and worn, and she held herself with the slouching posture of someone who spent all day bent over her work. She was still quite lovely, but her face had taken on more of a world-weary air, with none of the regal elegance Kerelle associated with her.

She looked, in other words, like she belonged on Palhee.

Espionage background, darling. Galhen reminded her with a shade of amusement. *One gets much further in that field by blending in.*

Lilika took a seat nearby and unwrapped some sort of filled bread that Kerelle presumed had come from one of the street vendors. She leaned back and watched the crowd as she ate, ignoring them.

We've found accommodations, she sent them both. *Not exactly a luxury flat, and certainly not in an excellent neighborhood, but it's large enough to fit the lot of us. Besides, this is Palhee. "Excellent" is not a word I would apply to any neighborhoods.*

What will you do now?

Settle in, then see about putting together a network. As I said, I have a few contacts in the PsiCorp who may be of great help, and we'll need agents outside of it as well. I'll keep you apprised.

Kerelle's comm beeped.

"We're all supplied and ready to roll," Sandrel's voice crackled over the device. "Just waiting on you two. Head on back when you're ready and we'll be on our way."

They stood, with a last sweeping glance around the market.

I guess we're off for now, Kerelle sent. *Good luck, Lilika.*

And yourselves. We'll be in touch.

A final mental nod, and they turned to head back. Kerelle slipped her hand in Galhen's as they started down the boulevard toward the spaceport, and an unknown future. Anxiety still snaked down her spine, at the thought of the enormity ahead of them, but Galhen had spoken the truth.

Come what may, they would face it together.

I'm glad you came along with Kerelle as she tried figure out life outside the PsiCorp, and even finally got a break from constant crises (at least for a little while!). Things are certainly heating up now, though...

Read on for a sneak peek at what comes next, and if you liked this book, **please consider leaving a review on Amazon or Goodreads**. It really does help indie books find the people who want to read them!

THE STORY CONCLUDES IN THE
STARS ABLAZE

Kerelle and her allies are done running.

After their close escape from SysTech's pursuers, one thing is clear: the multigalactic will never stop hunting them...and the only way forward is to take the fight to SysTech instead. With the help of a powerful new ally, Kerelle's group begins working to free other PsiCorp members from corporate control - and the Psionic Rebellion is born.

If the rebels succeed, it could mean freedom for psionics across the galaxy, and an end to the future conscription to the PsiCorp. But SysTech will stop at nothing to see them crushed, and soon Kerelle and her new allies are locked in a desperate struggle for survival. As the stakes rise and difficult choices are made, only one thing is certain: come victory or death, the time for hiding is over.

Keep reading for a preview of **The Stars Ablaze** (Gift of the Stars, Book 3), available now!

THE STARS ABLAZE: CHAPTER 1

Kerelle kept her shields locked tight, and tried to look nonchalant. All around her the port buzzed with activity, and she did her best to blend in with the bustle as she projected disinterest to the mundanes passing by. She was just another dock employee, and there was no reason to take note of her.

If anyone knew who she was, of course, there would be *every* reason to take note of her. The humming port around her was the largest on Eisra XI, the center of the booming hypernium gas trade, and SysTech's regional headquarters in the Eis Orlata system. It was, really, one of the *last* places an escaped PsiCorp agent and budding psionic revolutionary ought to be.

She tried to keep her face turned down, and occupied herself making notations as though she truly were here doing some sort of work. Hoping she looked suitably legitimate, she cast her eyes about for the reason she was here.

Lilika had given her a mental image of a man in late middle age with medium-toned skin and a receding hairline. Now that she was here waiting for him, she was realizing just how many men around the port fit the general description of their latest field agent. Few, she hoped, fit his circumstances.

"Lost a child to the PsiCorp around fifteen years ago, wife committed suicide a few years after," Lilika had summarized. "He made some noise on the datanet about the injustice of it all and got on a SysTech watchlist, which of course means he's been barred from all but menial employment since. It didn't take much convincing to recruit him to our cause."

"Are there a lot of people like him? That might help us?" Kerelle had wondered aloud. Lilika had just shrugged.

"If you mean families of PsiCorp specifically, it's hard to say. There's a certain stigma attached to producing a psionic child, and some families are perfectly happy to hand them over. The ones that aren't still don't usually talk about it. But," she'd added with a frosty smile, "if you mean people disgruntled with the multigalactics in general, well. That's a resource with *considerable* potential."

Looking around the bustling port at the sea of SysTech logos on shirts and bags and jumpsuits, she wondered if there were others in the busy crowd who would strike out against the multigalactics if they could. Everyone certainly *looked* content enough.

Someone brushed against her sleeve, and her eyes darted up to meet Ilyen's.

He too was dressed like he worked here, his coveralls providing both a disguise and, knowing Ilyen, convenient concealment for any number of knives. There had been a security station with a weapons scanner at the entrance to the port concourse, but Kerelle suspected Ilyen had simply ported past it.

She'd gone through; her weapons weren't the sort that showed up on a scanner.

Ilyen leaned toward her ear, making a gesture at her nonsense notes as if discussing their contents.

"Bet you didn't think we were signing up to be the post service," he muttered to her. "Any sign of our guy?"

"Not yet," she murmured back. "He's a few minutes late."

"'Late' better just mean 'the elevator was slow,' not 'got rolled and sold us out, *already.*'"

"Here's hoping."

A bloc of grey in the crowd caught her eye, heading in their direction.

SysTech security.

For a moment her heart caught in her throat, but Kerelle forced herself to breathe regularly and remain calm. This was a large SysTech port; there were a million reasons for a security team to be here that *didn't* involve them.

Cautiously she reached out and skimmed the thoughts of the closest guard. *I wish Customs & Inspection would take care of this shit themselves. There's no reason they actually* need *a security unit to write someone up for undeclared assets.*

A quick hop to a second guard. *I hope they're just calling us in so C&I can get their bribes paid. I do* not *want to deal with the paperwork if they actually found contraband. Maybe I can get Inspector Wenra to do the forms, in exchange for not mentioning to anyone that she's taking a cut. Wouldn't kill her to buy me a beer, too.*

She kept her sigh of relief mental. These guards were simply going about their routine after all.

Beside her Ilyen tensed. He'd seen them too.

"Steady," she said softly. "They're not here for us, and they won't notice us unless we give them a reason." His stance relaxed, though she could sense he remained at high alert.

Kerelle held her breath and tried to look natural as the group passed by them, projecting that there was nothing interesting about them, nothing worth looking twice at. It worked as they walked past, caught up in their own thoughts without any reason to take note of the two dock workers -

Except one, who slowed her pace, eyes suddenly focused on Ilyen.

Kerelle's stomach lurched as she instinctively reached for her telekinetics. This was a bad place to fight, for them and for the hundreds of civilians surrounding them. She dove into the woman's mind, hoping for a way to convince her she hadn't seen anything after all…

That ass, damn. *Nice jawline, too, looks like he walked off a fashion feature. He must be new, I would've remembered if I'd seen him before. Wonder when he's off work, I should get his contact….*

Oh for stars' sake.

The guard was lagging behind the rest of her group now, angling towards where they were standing. Kerelle did the only thing she could think of. *Stars and* blood, *I wish you were a telepath.*

She laid a hand on his arm and squeezed tightly, then leaned in to kiss his cheek. "I'll see you at home, sweetheart," she said loudly. "Tell your mom thanks for me, I really appreciate her watching the baby today." She gave his arm another sharp squeeze, hoping he could understand what she was trying to tell him.

"Of course babe, I'll let her know." His eyes promised merciless teasing about this later, but he gave her an acknowledging squeeze back and turned away, heading back toward the bays where they'd left the ship. Kerelle didn't turn her head to look at the guard, but disappointment radiated against her senses. The feeling receded as the other woman moved on to catch up with the other guards.

Thank goodness Ilyen was quick on the uptake, telepath or no.

Kerelle wandered a bit in the crowd, staying near the designated meeting spot. If their agent didn't appear soon, she was going to have to call it a loss. She wasn't looking forward to telling Lilika that the only outcome of the trip was Ilyen narrowly avoiding a date with a SysTech port guard.

As if summoned, an older man matching Lilika's description materialized out of the crowd, dressed in the dusty uniform of a dock laborer. He made his way unhurried over to a nearby bench, and sat down heavily as if to rest his feet.

Kerelle waited a moment, and drifted over to the bench as well.

"Long shifts for a busy week?" She offered the signal phrase quietly.

"Every week is a busy week," he replied in low voice, confirming the code. He surreptitiously slipped something small onto the bench beside her. "My regards to our mutual friend."

He got up and walked away, melting back into the crowd without a backward glance. Kerelle palmed the small data stick he'd left behind and counted to sixty, pretending to be absorbed in her tablet. Finally she got up too, and started the circuitous route back to the ship.

Time to find out if this field trip was yielding anything more than wasted time.

Lilika's eyes glinted as the device's contents flashed up on the screen. "Oh, he did brilliantly. This is exactly what I was looking for."

They were all gathered around her computing station, watching the data begin its download. It was the first time Kerelle had been inside the Palhee safehouse; it was larger than she'd been expecting, certainly larger than the mess on Sandrel's ship, but still felt full with all of them packed in. Several of Lilika's students hovered curiously at the edge of the group, adding to the sense of crowding.

"That's good to hear," Kerelle answered. "So what is it?"

"Transport records, for every time a PsiCorp agent passed through the main Eisra port in the last six months."

Ilyen glanced from her to the monitor, still scrolling data. "And this helps us...how?"

"It helps by giving us the locations of a number of potential allies," she answered matter-of-factly. She kept her eyes on the flow of data, and suddenly darted out a hand to pause the download. The device was mid-transfer on a single name's records: *Riyel Ceilas Valessa, C3 TLP C1 TLK.* Lilika broke into a genuine grin.

Galhen leaned forward a bit, and Kerelle caught his words to Lilika through their bond. *That's* your *Riyel, isn't it.*

Yes, Lilika replied simply. Her answer was overlaid with affection and hope, though her outward expression had already returned to its usual impassivity. *He passed through to the Jamanar colonies less than four months ago, no record of return passage. He could be in Jamanar still.*

We'll find him, Lilika.

Kerelle hadn't meant to eavesdrop, but now that she had, she couldn't help asking Galhen. *Who is Riyel?*

He's a PsiCorp telepath, formerly based out of Cildazya before being transferred. He and Lilika have a similar relationship to ours, except that they never had the dreaming to keep them close. They've been out of contact since he was transferred away, and Lilika has missed him a great deal.

She told you all that? Kerelle suppressed a surprised glance at the other telepath. *That seems…unusually forthcoming, for her.*

Well, we had those weeks locked in a bunker together during the riots on Baleal. It rather helps you get to know a person.

Wait, what? Riots? This time she *did* give him a startled glance. *I thought you said the Baleal mission went* well.

It ended *well. I may have glossed over some of the details in between.*

"So 'a number of potential allies' sounds promising," Sandrel noted. "Any idea where to start?"

"Yes," Lilika answered with a ghost of a smile. "I need you to take me to Jamanar."

"Thirty minutes til we drop out of hyper," Sandrel's voice announced over the intercom. "We're coming out far enough from the colony cluster that I don't anticipate trouble, but everyone be on alert anyway."

That struck Kerelle as odd. Usually their little freighter was nondescript enough to escape notice - initially, anyway. "Trouble?" She echoed, as much to herself as to the group assembled around the mess table. "Does Jamanar not get much shipping traffic?"

"Yes and no," Lilika answered. "The colonies are not secret, obviously, but it's *also* no secret that they were established to give SysTech a near-monopoly on celsum. You can imagine that ConEn sabotage is a concern. Touching down in one of the colony ports will require rather more security clearance than simply requesting a space to land."

Ilyen shrugged. "Won't be the first time Sandrel's made us up a legit-sounding excuse to be someplace. He's good at that."

"We may not need to enter the colonies at all," Lilika noted. "Most of Jamanar is still unsettled, and there should be ample space to slip in unnoticed." She took an unhurried sip of tea. "I should be able to reach Riyel as we approach orbit. Whatever I hear from him may inform our choice of landing spot."

A little under a half-hour later, they gathered in nav as the ship dropped back into realspace. The Jamanar gas giants loomed distant in the vidports, bright orbs of orange and blue against the endless dark.

"I brought us in a few hours of realspace travel away from the colonies," Sandrel told the group. "There's five of them, clustered across the temperate zones on two of the bigger moons." He glanced over at Lilika. "As far as I know, anyway."

She gave a slight nod. "There's five. No secret outposts to worry about tripping over."

"Good, that's one less complication when I bring us down. All the same," his fingers flew over the control keys in a complex pattern, "let's not tempt fate." The stealth field hummed to life around them.

Lilika raised her eyebrows, and her lips curved in a subtle smile. "Why Captain Marene, I knew I liked you."

He gave her a small smirk in response and turned his attention back to the vidports. "Four hours until we get visual on the colonies. You'll be able to get us more information then?"

"Yes. I assure you my range is excellent, but even *I* can't make contact from this far out."

Galhen's eyes cut up to meet Kerelle's.

We need to tell her about the dreaming.

She blinked. *The dreaming? Why?*

Because it gave us exponentially greater range than we could have otherwise achieved. It didn't occur to me, before, that it might be something others could learn to do as well. But if they can, it could be an invaluable tool for communications. He paused a moment. *And it will give Lilika and Riyel what we had, if extracting him proves rather more complicated than we hope.*

Kerelle turned that over in her mind. That awful selfish part of her offered a stab of irrational resentment, at sharing something she'd always thought of as their private escape. But he was right; if it was something they could teach others, it would be a powerful - and safer - way to communicate. And how could she deny Lilika the chance she herself had had, to keep close to her partner when SysTech tried to keep them apart?

Besides, she woke up every morning with her husband curled beside her. They no longer had need of a private escape.

All right, she answered. *Let's see what we can do.*

Lilika listened carefully throughout, her expression thoughtful.

"That's remarkable," she said finally. "How did you discover it?"

"It was right after the Academy," Kerelle recalled. "I was sent out on my first mission as a full PsiCorp agent, and Galhen stayed behind on Tallimau for his hospital residency. It was the first time we'd been apart for any length of time since we'd met, really. The dreams started then.

"At first I thought they were *only* dreams," she explained. "It wasn't anything we were doing consciously. I thought....I thought I was having repeated dreams about talking to Galhen because I missed him so much, or because I was lonely without anyone I *could* talk to. It wasn't until the project was over and I went home to Tallimau that we realized they hadn't just been dreams after all."

"Because of course, I'd had them too," Galhen added. "At first I made the same assumption Kerelle did, that it was simply an invention of my subconscious to address how lonely I was without her. I was also quite hurt that she hadn't written me at all, and I thought that might have been part of it. But when she returned home, we discovered I already knew from the dream everything that had happened in her time away."

"I take it you'd been warned *off* of writing?" Lilika asked. Kerelle gave a short nod.

"I'd been given a talking-to by one of our mentors on the flight out, about how the Academy was a very special time in our lives, but now that it was over I needed to focus on myself and my own career. It was the usual thing, of course, a lot about how much promise and potential I had and what a shame it would be to underachieve, but she also got rather direct about her concerns that I might prioritize personal relationships over work. She explained very kindly that I had to understand that Galhen was a very handsome and talented boy, and would certainly have no shortage of lovers, and that she would be so disappointed to watch me waste my own potential because I was preoccupied with a one-sided infatuation."

"The usual thing indeed," Lilika responded drily. Kerelle

rolled her eyes in agreement.

"Yes. I was quite anxious about it the whole time, particularly since I was afraid to reach out in case I was being watched, which just made me *more* worried that he would think I'd lost interest and move on while I was gone."

"Which was probably the goal," Galhen observed. "Of course, rather the opposite happened. When Kerelle returned and we realized the dreams were something *more* than dreams, we explored the ability and learned how to control it. It's kept us close our whole lives since."

"But I still don't know *why* it came naturally to us, and not to other people," Kerelle confessed. "We're not....other people who care about each other are separated too," she finished lamely. She wasn't sure if she was supposed to know about Lilika and Riyel; it also felt a bit callous, to be talking about the gift they've been given when Lilika was a stronger telepath than either of them, and yet *she'd* been forced to rely on easily-monitored messages and limited psionic range.

Lilika seemed rather more intrigued than offended, however. "We may never know for *certain*," she commented. "But you are both powerful telepaths, and you formed a very strong emotional bond when you were both quite young. The minds of children are often more elastic than adults. Perhaps this ability unlocked for you because you didn't yet realize it couldn't be done. And who knows?" She gave them a small shrug. "You said yourselves that you've never told anyone else of this. Perhaps it's more common than we know."

"Since we don't quite know how it happened, we don't know if it's something we can teach others," Galhen commented, "But we're certainly willing to try."

Lilika gave them another of her rare, genuine smiles. "Shall we find out, then?"

The Stars Ablaze is available now!

ABOUT THE AUTHOR

Lena Alison Knight grew up reading space opera and high fantasy, and started writing her own as soon as she could hold a crayon steady. She lives with her husband in the San Francisco Bay Area, and when not writing she can be found taking brisk walks, haunting local coffee shops, or sprawled on the couch playing video games.

Lena's Gift of the Stars trilogy is now available on Amazon. You can find her online at lenaalisonknight.com, and join her newsletter to get a free Gift of the Stars novelette, and keep up with what's coming next.